Destiny's Freedom

Captain Jane Thorn Series: Book Two

Pamela Grimm

Published in Australia in 2019 by SisterShip Press Pty Ltd

Part of SisterShip Magazine, NSW, Australia
www.sistershippress.com

Printed and bound in Australia by SisterShip Press Pty Ltd

National Library of Australia data:

SisterShip Press Pty Ltd, 2019, Destiny's Freedom

ISBN: 978-0-6484283-6-7

Also available as an ebook, ISBN: 978-0-6484283-7-4

In collaboration with SisterShip Magazine

www.sistershippress.com
www.sistershipmagazine.com

For my grandmother,
who believed you could not know
who you were if you did not know whence you came.

CONTENTS

MARYLAND

Back River

Baltimore

Tracy's Landing

Delaware Bay

New York

Chesapeake Bay

Bloodsworth Is.

Tangier Is.

VIRGINIA

Tappahannock

Fishermans Is.

Norfolk

Chesapeake Bay entrance to New York, 267 nm

I
Making Ready

Port of New York
April 17, 1821

"Watch yer head, Captain, ma'am," came the bellow of the second mate as Captain Thorn stepped off the gangplank onto the deck of the schooner *Destiny.*

Hearing Mister Galsworthy's shout, Jane looked up in time to duck as the men swung a bale of dry goods aboard and lowered it into the *Destiny*'s hold. Bracing herself against the mainmast, she leaned over the open hatch and, peering into the darkness below, saw that fully half of the hold had already been filled. It boded well for an early departure the next morning.

"Mister Galsworthy, have we been provisioned yet?" she called up to the mate where he stood at the larboard rail supervising the lading.

"Aye, ma'am, save for the water casks. They'll be delivered by dray this afternoon. By-the-by, Mister Dawkins is hoping to speak with you as quick as ye'r back aboard ma'am. He's down below working the accounts."

"Thank you, Mister Galsworthy. Carry on."

Jane had been ashore since early morning arguing with the apothecary about the medicine chest he was preparing for the vessel's voyage south. The drug maker was adamantly refusing to stock the chest with quinine bark, as he felt it superfluous to the crew's needs. The captain was taking no chances that her men would be laid low with the intermittent fever so common to warmer climes, but the apothecary had scoffed at her concerns, saying that Virginia harbored no dangerous miasma and he needed space for his patent tincture. Jane trusted her instincts on the topic, however, and marched off to the herbalist's shop down the street after verifying that the medicine chest, such as it was, would be prepared, sealed, and delivered on board by noon.

Now that she was back aboard, Jane wasted no time in addressing the remaining items on her lengthy list of things to be done before they could cast off the lines. Hoisting her skirts, she grabbed the edge of the hatch above the companionway and swung below with one big jump. She had expressly forbidden the crew from doing the same as it was a dangerous move when underway. She hoped none of them could see her breaking her own rule.

Jane made her way along the narrow corridor leading to the officers' quarters at the stern of the schooner. As she ducked under the low transom of the saloon entryway she nearly tripped over her chief mate where he sat by the stove with his legs stretched out under the table.

"All well, Mister Dawkins?" Jane pulled off her beaver hat and tossed it through the cabin door onto her berth before settling at the saloon table opposite the chief mate. She waited patiently as he continued to scratch away at the ledgers with his head bent closely over pages and his brow furrowed in concentration. He and Jane had sailed together for many months and Dawkins knew the captain would forgive his taking a few extra moments to complete the task at hand. Finally, he set down the pencil and sat back to run his hands through his thinning hair.

"Aye, ma'am, we look to be loaded by the time the crew goes to dinner, so I've ordered the pilot for seven tomorrow morning. We shall be able to catch the morning tide. Your uncle has the boats arranged in the event we lack a favorable breeze, and the hands are all accounted for."

"Excellent tidings. Galsworthy says you wished to speak with me?"

"Aye, ma'am, it's seaman Singleton's papers giving me some worry. Here, have a look." Dawkins leaned forward and handed Jane a sheaf of papers so ragged the ink was worn away at the fold.

Jane held the pages up to the skylight to read the faded script. It was a proclamation by one Colonel James Singleton of

Tennessee granting freedom to his faithful servant, Henry Singleton, in appreciation for years of good service and selfless acts not further specified.

"Should Mister Singleton become separated from the *Destiny* while we are in a place hostile to his race, he may find himself arrested, and sold into captivity before we are able to rescue him. Those papers may not withstand the scrutiny of someone determined to subjugate all Negroes regardless of their status," Dawkins observed.

"I take your point, Mister Dawkins," Jane said. The many challenges of their long passage the prior year had taught the captain that she could trust the good instincts of her chief mate and rely on him as a friend. "It would indeed be a sore thing to bring him into jeopardy ill-prepared. If Silas can be spared, I shall send him to Uncle Josias for more fitting documents Singleton can bear upon his person while we retain these aboard."

Stepping back out into the passage, Jane climbed the ladder to the deck and went in search of her nephew, Silas Baldwin. At nearly fifteen, her sister's son had grown into a strapping young man a full head taller than Jane. With dark brown hair and deep green eyes, he was the spitting image of his mother, Prudence. Like his aunt, he had joined the family shipping business at a young age and was already an accomplished mariner. This was their first voyage together and she was glad to have him aboard.

Jane found Silas stripped to his shirtsleeves helping to wrestle heavy crates of dinnerware into the hold. She had bought the charming plates and bowls from a factory in western Sweden on her last voyage and thought to do well with them at the auction last fall. To her chagrin, the local buyers in New York had turned up their noses at the simple designs and earthy colors of the wares, saying the refined tastes of the ladies of New York ran more to Chinese porcelain and French enamel. She was sure they were wrong, but her opinion did nothing more than make her huffy with the merchants. They were not budging in their disinterest and she was left to find another market. Perhaps the good wives of Norfolk and Baltimore would appreciate the pottery; Jane hoped so as her portion of the profit from that voyage was largely tied up in the boxes now coming aboard.

Leaving her nephew to his work, she sought out Mister Galsworthy. She found him in the galley drinking coffee and chatting with the cook.

"Mister Galsworthy, if you can spare him, I should like to send Silas to Captain Josias to obtain better papers for Singleton before we depart tomorrow," Jane said.

"Aye, ma'am, we'll make do without him for the nonce; but he'd best return lickety-split as soon as his business is finished. I have need of him here," the mate replied.

"Very good, Galsworthy, I shall remind Silas to keep his mind on his work should he cross paths with Miss Wright at the shipping office," Jane grinned. The charming daughter of her uncle's accounting clerk had been a frequent visitor at the firm these past months ever since Silas had taken up a position there to learn more about the family business. Each time the young lady appeared, he struggled to focus on the work at hand instead of the lace bonnet that floated past his desk more often than was strictly necessary.

Within short order, Jane sent Silas and Singleton off with a letter to her uncle and returned to the quarterdeck to watch over the bustling activity below. The schooner was awash with delivery men, insurance inspectors, customs clerks, and tradesmen busy preparing the vessel for its upcoming passage to the Chesapeake Bay.

This trip had been her uncle's idea but she was still not sure why he had been so adamant that Jane be the one to undertake it. Thorn Shipping and Cargo had been working the shores and estuaries of the Hudson River in fast sloops carrying trade goods and produce up and down the waterway for three generations. In recent years, they bought a fleet of six schooners to carry freight out of New York and took a gamble on the transatlantic trade. The prior year, the family sent one of the schooners, the *Destiny* with Captain Jane Thorn in command, on a run to purchase sugar in Cuba that netted a healthy profit for the firm of over fifty thousand dollars.

After the outstanding success of that voyage, Jane had expected to be asked to repeat the trip in the coming year. She wanted to try her hand again at bringing home a profit for the firm, but she also needed to sort out her feelings and personal affairs before embarking once more on a long, lonely voyage. She knew her uncle was aware of her conflicted emotions and was surprised when he brought up the subject of a new trading trip only a few weeks after her return.

"It will do you good, Jinks, to have something else to think about this spring," he said as they sat together after dinner at her father's house in Newburgh at Christmas. "You've been looking mighty hangdog since that Endeavor fellow took off for Nantucket last month. I hate to see you pining for some sorry pup not worth as much as the end of your little finger."

"He is not a sorry pup!" Jane had fired up, ready to defend her beau from all comers in an instant. She then broke into a smile when she realized her uncle had merely been trying to get a rise out of her and was now grinning at his success.

"All right," she allowed, "I must admit I am feeling a bit down since he left. We had just a few days together before he was called home by his family. He writes that his father is somewhat recovered but anticipates being delayed for many weeks. He must stay to support his mother, but I had hoped we would come to some understanding of things by the new year," she blurted out, then clapped her hand to her mouth.

"Nay, my daughter, you needn't be ashamed of feelings that do you credit," her father, Richard Thorn, remarked from his place near the fire. "He is a fine young man, and we would welcome him into our family should it come to that. It speaks well of him that he is so attentive to his mother in her need, so do not fret at his absence overmuch. He will return to you when he can."

"Come, sweetheart," her mother called from the corner of the divan, where she rested wrapped in shawls to stave off the chill. "Come sit by me and tell me again about the countryside

5

in Sweden, and that lovely Nilsson couple who took such good care of you."

With a sigh, Jane rose and joined her parents in front of the hearth to while away the evening with family stories and roasted chestnuts until it was time to leave for church. As they promenaded down Grand Street to the midnight service her uncle broached the topic of the southern voyage once again.

"Really, Jinks, it would be awfully good if you could see your way clear to taking this on. Captain Albright had some success the first year we sent him to Baltimore, but he was hard pressed to make it pay these last two years. If you and the *Destiny* were to give it a chance, we might find out once and for all if it is worth our while trading on the Bay."

She had put him off that time, and repeatedly over the following two months, as she waited for her childhood friend and erstwhile suitor Endeavor Coffin to return from his travels. But when Endeavor's letters began to arrive less frequently, and the news continued to be less than hopeful, Jane found herself losing heart. She eventually accepted her uncle's offer to take the schooner south to Virginia with import goods for the wholesale market.

Standing now in the shade of the riding sail that kept them floating gently at the dock, Jane was beginning to feel the excitement that always preceded a new venture. She had grown up on her family's boats and now, at the age of twenty-four, was a seasoned sailor and able shipmaster. With her old friend Galsworthy in charge of the fo'c'sle, and her trusted right hand Mister Dawkins attending to the running of the vessel, she was confident the *Destiny* would make a good showing this time out as well. She smiled at the thought of the open water and the feel of a seaworthy vessel under her feet and shook off the lingering sadness at the absence of her dear friend.

Jane rested her hand on the carved ship's wheel as she gazed forward along the *Destiny*'s one hundred and thirty feet of deck. Everywhere she looked, there was evidence of the care that had been taken to prepare the vessel for the upcoming voyage. The smell of freshly tarred rope mixed with the scent of the linseed oil and beeswax that had been rubbed into the brightwork. Newly tanned sails hung in neat rolls below the spars and the deck gleamed from the thorough scrubbing it had received. Turning to the ship's carpenter perched on the taffrail, the captain observed, "She looks polished up and ready for adventure, Mister Koopmans. The *Destiny* always looks her best once you've had a go at her."

"Aye, that she does, Captain. It's been good to have so many months to put her right. She's champing at the bit to cast off now." The old man's eyes crinkled at the corners as he smiled with pride.

"I share the sentiment," Jane replied with a laugh and turned to look out over the wharf. Raising her hand to her brow to block the sun, Jane squinted at a figure in grey making his way down the dock toward the schooner. His broad hat brim shadowed his face, and the large sea bag slung over his shoulder made him stagger a little as he threaded his way through the busy scene, but Jane would have known him anywhere. She felt her heart swell with gratitude as she stepped down to the rail to welcome him aboard.

"You've come," she whispered into the ear of the tall Quaker fellow who had dropped his bag and scooped her into an unseemly embrace in front of the crew as soon as he had vaulted over the gunwale.

"My dearest Jane," Endeavor whispered back, "how could thee ever doubt it?"

II

A Decision

Port of New York
April 17, 1821

"You've arrived just in time; we are due to cast off in the morning." Jane smiled up at Endeavor where he stood in the doorway of her cabin. She had ushered him below as soon as she had signed for the medical chest brought down by the apothecary's boy.

"Aye, my dear Jane, and glad I am to have made New York before thee let go the lines."

Endeavor cut an impressive figure despite his travel-worn shabbiness. His high brow and long nose gave him an air of distinction balanced by a pair of warm brown eyes and a gentle mouth prone more to smiling than to wearing the severe expression favored by his Quaker brethren.

Jane surveyed him from head to toe. He looked weary from the journey with clothes, sea bag and hat all covered in dust. He must have traveled in great haste as it was not like the proper young Friend to appear so dishevelled.

"Come dear Endeavor, sit with me and tell me the news. How fares your father? And has your mother released you willingly to your New York friends?" Jane sat down on her berth and waved her hand toward the bow-backed Windsor chair tucked under her desk. Ignoring the gesture, Endeavor turned to drop his hat on the table and then seated himself next to her on the berth.

"Nay, things are not as felicitous as I would wish at home, but the father seems no worse than he was at the new year."

Jane smiled fondly at the sound of the soft Quaker speech. Formal as it could be at times, the gentle rhythms and old-fashioned terms connected her to her family's past. And perhaps, she thought, to her own future.

"The mother," Endeavor continued, "who sends her fondest greetings, knew that my heart was sore tried by my long absence from thee, Jane, and begged that I leave her to come to thee. Are thee content that I have done so?" he asked as he searched her face for clues to her feelings.

The past year had seen many trials for Jane's heart as she considered her future as a merchant captain who is often far from home and family. Six months at sea had shown her that she treasured a life in the company of her family, and the close friendship of the stalwart young man regarding her hopefully now.

"Oh, dearest Endeavor, I am very much pleased to have you here. It has been far too long since I could see your cherished face and hear your beloved voice. I am so grateful you have come."

Jane was going to say more but Endeavor leaned over and kissed her, passionately, for the very first time. Holding her around the waist, he pulled her to him and held her close as he lingered over the embrace. Finally pulling back just enough to look into her eyes, he gazed at her with clear desire.

"My heart and body are thine, dearest Jane, if thee will have them," he stated with a simple hope.

Jane caught her breath, taken by surprise that he should be so quick to declare himself, and thrilled to her core at the evidence of such strong attachment on his part. She felt in her soul a matching desire and wasted no time in showing him the depth of her own feelings. Throwing her arms around his neck, she kissed him soundly, then drew back.

"If that was a marriage proposal, I accept."

"Aye, my sweet Jane, that it was, and I am honored to hear thee give thy assent," he grinned. "I had not thought what I might do had thee not been willing."

With a wry smile, Jane replied, "But how you do complicate my life, my dear. How ever shall we manage this, since I am off on the morrow and you would rather be hanged in the morning than set foot aboard a vessel going to sea?"

Endeavor dropped her waist to take her hands in his as he

turned soberly to face her fully.

"Aye, I have had much time to consider that question. I can no more contemplate the thought of life ashore without thee, than I hazard thee would be willing to accept a life at sea without me. Surely thee would not wish us to be parted again so soon?"

Jane lifted her hand to his cheek and whispered, "No, dearest man, I would not wish to part with you again. Not in the morning, not next week, and not at any time in the future. My hope is that we are done with the parting and can begin with the joining."

Endeavor's blush rose quickly in his cheeks as his eyes widened at her boldness.

"Ah Jane, thee will be the death of me yet. My days will surely never lack for interest with thee at my side," he laughed, and then took her back in his arms with an ardor that indicated he understood her thoughts and heartily agreed with them.

A hesitant knock at the saloon door brought them back to their senses. Reluctantly slipping from Endeavor's embrace, Jane stood and straightened her skirt before stepping into the outer chamber of her quarters to pull open the door. On the threshold stood her nephew, shyly twisting his cap as he looked down at the floor.

"Auntie Jinks, er, Captain, ma'am," he stammered, "Captain Josias is requesting permission to come aboard."

"Very good, Seaman Baldwin, have him brought on deck where I will join him shortly." Jane closed the door, returning to her cabin to find Endeavor furiously brushing the soil from his clothing.

"I have arrived in a bit of a state, my dear. I hope thee will forgive my lack of tidiness and attribute it to my ardent desire to be with thee as soon as possible," he said with a grin as he stepped toward Jane and took her once more in his embrace.

After a moment, Jane pushed him away with a smile. "Nay, I would rather have you here in this sorry condition than still in Nantucket. But now my uncle waits above. I will send Cookie with tea and biscuits for you while I find out what brings him to the wharf," she said as she scooped up her hat, pushed it onto her head and opened the cabin door.

Jane passed the galley to order refreshments for her cabin, then turned to the foredeck, where she found her uncle standing by the cargo hatch in conversation with Chief Mate Dawkins. As she stepped around the crates piled aft of the opening, Captain Josias turned to her and held out a sheaf of papers.

"Good day, Captain Thorn." The formal greeting and dress uniform made it clear that the head of Thorn Shipping and Cargo was making a business call aboard the schooner.

"I thought to use the excuse of delivering seaman Singleton's documents to give myself the pleasure of seeing you one more time before your departure. Dawkins tells me you are nearly loaded, so tomorrow seems auspicious for setting out. You shall follow Albright in the *Osprey*. Expect the pilot shortly after seven. As we have already cleared you out for the morning, you need merely supply the final manifest to the port Collector as soon as you are fully loaded."

"Aye, aye, Captain," Jane responded with a touch of her hat brim. As she took the papers from his hand, Jane noticed the twinkle in her uncle's eye. "Perhaps you are aware that I have had another visitor today?" she asked.

"Aye, Jinks, I thought that might be the case. Your young man stopped in to my office this morning asking after you. He seemed in a great hurry when he left to seek out the *Destiny*. He has arrived then?"

"That he has, and with a marriage proposal on his mind," she replied. "I have accepted him."

A surprised grunt from Dawkins was accompanied by an enthusiastic "Well done," from her uncle, along with hearty handshakes from both.

"Perhaps you might bring him along to dinner this evening so we may hear more of your plans? Your aunt will be excited to start arranging the wedding party, I am sure."

"Ah, the plans may have to wait since we have scarcely had a moment to consider them ourselves, but I will indeed see to it that we are at your table this evening if he is amenable," Jane answered as she turned to the Chief Mate. "Mister Dawkins, Mister Coffin and I will be going ashore shortly, and expect to return later this evening. Please see to it that the men are aboard by dinnertime and the muster rolls are complete."

Returning below, Jane found Endeavor finishing off the last of the biscuits. He was clearly famished from the journey and in sore need of refreshment. She stroked his shoulders fondly as she rounded the table to sit across from him.

"All well?" he asked.

"Aye, all is well. Uncle asks us to dinner this evening. Are you of a mind to visit with my family?"

He assured her he was and then fell silent as he sat back and regarded her with a serious look.

"May I share with thee my thoughts with regard to our future, then?" he asked.

"I wish you would," Jane replied as she leaned forward to rest her elbows on the table, "as I have no idea how we are to live, dear friend."

"We must establish whether we are to conduct ourselves within the principles of the Society of Friends. I am aware that thy family left the Meeting many years ago." Endeavor paused to assess her reaction. "What is thy thought on the matter, Jane?"

"Ah, a good place to begin." Jane's brow wrinkled as she considered the idea. "Nay, I do not see myself returning to the simple life, Endeavor. It would not suit. My family keep many of the testimonies close to our hearts and seek to live a life that is both pleasing to God and serves our fellow man, but I cannot trim my sails to the opinions of the Friends and don't aim to try."

"Very well. Thy plain speaking and conviction do thee credit. Since I will be disowned for marrying outside, we need not concern ourselves with the Meeting then. Would it dismay thee if we were to perform a simple wedding with thy family at home in the Quaker manner, however?"

12

"Not at all, although my mother will have a spell if she is denied the opportunity to make a fuss about my nuptials. As will my aunt, bless her heart, but that is neither here nor there. We will do as we see fit and I am well content to sign the papers and say our vows to each other."

"The city offices are close by and we can file for our license today, if thee are willing. We could be married this evening after dinner," he suggested with quiet hope.

Jane laughed. "How prosaic the Quaker approach. Yes, yes, yes, dearest Endeavor. Let us make it a simple business and have done with it. And what do you propose we do then? Are you coming aboard or am I leaving you ashore?" Jane held her breath as she awaited his answer.

"Whither thou goest, my dear Jane. My sea bag is already aboard, and I shall gather my courage and tether myself to the mainmast if need be. With thy permission, I thought to speak with thy uncle about some manner in which I might make myself useful to the firm on this voyage."

"An excellent plan, and one of which I wholeheartedly approve. Your knowledge and experience of our business will be invaluable as we assess the trading circumstances in Virginia. A most satisfactory proposal, husband-to-be," she exclaimed.

With that, she jumped up and hurried around the table to plant herself firmly on Endeavor's knee. Wrapping her arms around his neck, she kissed his cheek and rested her head on his shoulder. She gave a deep sigh of contentment as he stroked her hair and whispered into her ear, "I do love thee, Jane, with all my heart."

"Aye," she whispered back. "And I thee, my dearest friend."

An hour later, the pair had sent word to Jane's aunt with the news that a wedding would take place at her home that evening. They waited patiently in the queue at the registry office, then took their freshly inked license with them to the provisioners. There, Jane ordered additional stores for the *Destiny* as their numbers would be increased by one. She also insisted over Endeavor's protestations on a new set of linens for her berth and a lace nightrail in honor of her upcoming marriage. Not extravagant by nature, Jane was not concerned that her personal habits would be a trial to her plain living husband, but she was damned if she would welcome him to her bed on faded yellowed sheets, or in the tatty night dress she had worn since she was fifteen.

As they were leaving the provisioner's warehouse, they nearly ran into Captain Albright of the *Osprey*, the other Thorn Shipping schooner setting out for Norfolk in the morning.

"Ahoy, Captain Thorn," Albright exclaimed as he pulled up short to avoid running into the couple. "I hear we are to make a tandem pair this voyage. What the devil does your uncle mean by sending you to play nursemaid, may I ask? Does he think Albright doesn't know his business, then?"

Taken aback at the belligerent tone of the man, Jane was momentarily speechless. Leaning forward, Endeavor filled the moment by catching Albright's eye and introducing himself.

"Coffin, eh? One of those Nantucket bunch down to learn the trade from us New Yorkers, is that it?" Albright sneered.

"Perhaps, Friend Albright," Endeavor responded evenly.

"Then perhaps you had better stick to your whale boats, Friend Coffin," Albright shot back before stomping off down the street.

"What in blazes do you suppose that was about?" Jane wondered, noticing that Endeavor flinched as usual at her swearing. He would just have to accustom himself, she thought, as she had no intention of acting more ladylike any time soon or curbing her speech to save the tender ears of her Quaker beau. She suspected he would have much to accept during their life together, beginning with the tattoos he had not yet had occasion to see. She grinned to herself as she imagined revealing them to him later this evening, then blushed at the thought of what would follow soon after.

For now, though, she was disturbed by the tone of the encounter with Captain Albright and planned to discuss it with her uncle that night. Surely the *Osprey*'s master did not see her as some sort of rival

III
A Plain Ceremony

New York City
April 17, 1821

Jane turned to look over her shoulder at the image in the looking glass. The gown her sister Prudence sewed for her last fall fulfilled its promise of being "a party frock, and not one of those sea-going creations" Jane usually wore. The deep green silk set off her golden red hair and green eyes and the open bodice and high waist made the most of her tall figure. She smiled with satisfaction as she patted the elaborate braided hairstyle Aunt Meg's maid had pulled together hastily; she looked the part of a bride even with only an hour to prepare. Gazing now at the sheer fabric where it gathered at the top of the sleeves and fell to meet the long white gloves she had pulled on, Jane was confident that her betrothed would find it difficult to keep his mind on anything else this evening.

Her own mind was somewhat distracted with thoughts of home and the dear ones who were not present to share in their joy. Aunt Meg had been delighted at the news of the upcoming nuptials and sent the servants scurrying to prepare a wedding meal, but Jane was sorry that her own parents were so far away tonight. If the *Destiny* were to hold to the sailing schedule, however, there was no time to travel to Newburgh for the ceremony.

As soon as they arrived at the house on Beekman Street, Jane left Endeavor belowstairs to discuss business matters with her uncle and repaired to her chamber to compose a note to her mother. In the midst of her elation at the coming nuptials, she was nonetheless sad not to have her dear parents at her side for the important occasion and sniffed back tears more than once as she wrote.

Dear Mama,

I have the happiest news. This evening I am to marry Endeavor. My only wish would be for you and Father to be present for the occasion, but we sail on the morrow and Endeavor arrived from Nantucket only this morning. I suppose you are not surprised — after his lengthy absence this spring we found ourselves in perfect agreement that such separations are not to our liking. We plan a simple ceremony in the Quaker manner, conveniently suited to the haste in which we find ourselves. Uncle Josias and Aunt Meg will stand in for you and Father, and I shall feel beautiful in the dress Pru made for my last birthday.

Uncle Josias has offered to appoint Endeavor a sort of supercargo for the trip South, which I hope may give him something more to think on than his dread of blue water. I need no other proof of his devotion than his willingness to take ship with me.

Dearest Mama, wish me well and forgive me for robbing you of the opportunity to be part of this important day. My sister will surely be slower to forgive, so please kiss Pru for me, and assure her of my love.

Your devoted daughter,
Jane

Jane left the letter on the hall table to be sent with the morning post and made her way to the drawing room where the family were gathered for the impromptu wedding. As she entered the elegantly decorated parlor, Endeavor came forward to take her hands and lift them to his lips. The cozy fire that burned in the marble fireplace reflected off the gold brocade of the wallpaper and curtains and made the brilliant green silk of Jane's dress shine.

"I would have thee know that thee hast made me most happy, Jane," he said in a low voice as his eyes drifted down over the gown and all it both revealed and hid from view.

Satisfied that she had fixed her groom's attention where she wanted it, Jane took his hand and walked toward the table set out with the license, a pot of ink with a pen, and a Bible. Uncle

Josias, Aunt Meg, Chief Mate Dawkins, and Silas, who had arrived just a few minutes earlier, stood smiling by the window as witnesses of the ceremony.

Turning to each other, Jane and Endeavor joined hands and said their vows.

"I take thee to be my husband and promise with divine assistance to be unto thee a faithful and affectionate wife until death do us part," Jane smiled up at Endeavor, fighting to hold back tears.

"Aye, Jane, I take thee to be my wife and promise with divine assistance to be unto thee a faithful and affectionate husband until death do us part," Endeavor responded, his voice trembling slightly as he made his vow.

With a nod to their witnesses, Endeavor reached for the marriage certificate on the table, signed with a flourish, and passed the pen to Jane. Once everyone present had signed the paper, Josias took up the Bible and read from Colossians.

And let the peace of God rule in your hearts,
to which also ye are called in one body;
and be ye thankful. Let the word of Christ
dwell in you richly in all wisdom; teaching
and admonishing one another in psalms
and hymns and spiritual songs, singing with
grace in your hearts to the Lord. And
whatsoever ye do in word or deed, do all
in the name of the Lord Jesus, giving thanks
to God and the Father by Him.

Smiling through happy tears, Jane joined in the final "amen" as she leaned into Endeavor, feeling the warmth and strength in the arm he had placed around her waist. She lifted herself onto her toes and whispered in his ear, "You know that I am still Captain Thorn, do you not?" she asked with a lifted brow.

Bending to whisper back, Endeavor replied, "I never had a thought otherwise, my dear captain. My wife." And with a broad smile, he kissed her in a most un-Quakerly way.

"Ahoy there sailor, let us eat before you hoist the yardarm," Josias shouted with a clap on the shoulder for his new nephew and steered him away from Jane's side toward the dining room.

"Come, let us lift our glasses to the couple," Josias said once the plates had been filled and the wine poured. The company raised their cups as Josias continued, "May they ever have fair winds to lift their ship and clear skies to find their way. Huzzah!"

A chorus of well wishes followed the toast as Jane and Endeavor held hands under the table and smiled in gratitude at the small group of family and friends who had gathered to mark the occasion. Even the children had been allowed to stay up late and join in the fun.

The meal was eaten and the bride cake cut before Jane had an opportunity to ask her uncle about the strange encounter with Captain Albright earlier in the day. Leaning over to speak quietly, she related the odd conversation. "What say you, Uncle, does he have a grievance against me?"

"Nay, Jane, sooner a grievance against me. I was forced to call him to account for a discrepancy in the logs from his voyage last summer. But his chief mate stood by him and swore the books were correct when handed in, and I had no proof of perfidy. He knows I am on watch and do not trust him, but he has close ties to the merchants in Norfolk and Baltimore and swears they will not give such favorable terms to other captains. I am hoping you can discover if there is profitable trade to conduct even without the connections of Captain Albright."

"So his accusation of nursemaid was perhaps not far off," Jane replied. "Well, I shall keep my ear to the ground and see what might be the chances of our finding good business on the Bay. It is also now clear to me why you were so insistent I lead this voyage."

Josias bowed his head in acknowledgement and gave her a rueful smile.

"Aye, Captain Thorn, you are my eyes and ears. There is no one I trust more, or who better has the interests of the firm in mind. And now, Jane," Josias said, raising his voice so that Endeavor, seated on Jane's far side, could hear him, "we have arranged that you are to spend the night under this roof. Mister Dawkins can manage the vessel this last night before departure, and Silas will return with him. We shall have you awakened early enough to be aboard before the tide turns, but it is fitting you should spend your wedding night in comfort."

"I thank thee, Friend Josias," Endeavor replied with a nod to Jane. "We are most grateful for thy thoughtfulness."

"Aye, thank you uncle," Jane kissed her uncle's cheek. "I believe we are ready to make our way upstairs then, as the morning comes before too long. Good night all and thank you for joining us on this happy occasion."

As the couple made their way hand in hand around the table, Aunt Meg took a moment to pull Jane briefly aside.

"My dear, there is not much time to acquaint you with things but may I be so indelicate as to ask if you are in need of any motherly guidance on, well, bedroom matters?" she whispered in Jane's ear with a meaningful look.

"Nay, Aunt, but thank you for your care. I am familiar with the procedure," she replied, and patted her aunt's shoulder with a smile. Then, taking Endeavor's hand in hers once more, Jane wished the assembled party a final good night and walked beside her new husband up the stairs.

Leaving Endeavor to make his evening ablutions in the bedroom she repaired to the adjacent changing room to remove the evening's finery and replace it with the newly acquired lace nightdress. After brushing out her hair, Jane opened the door to find Endeavor on his knees in prayer. She leaned against the doorframe and watched, content to admire his beloved face and handsome figure from across the room. Soon enough though, he opened his eyes and raised himself to come to her.

"My dear, I am surprised to see you at your devotions so early," she teased him.

"That was because I am sure to forget them later," he grinned back at her and reached for the candle to blow it out.

IV
Heading South

New York Harbor
April 18, 1821

Wednesday, April 18, 1821 Winds brisk NW Passed Sandy Hook at ten o'clock on the morning tide SSW about 2 miles from which I take my departure. Pilot left us. Lat. (chart) 40° 50' N Long. (chart) 74° 00' W. Schooner Osprey left dock at dawn, no further sighting.

"Prepare to cast off Mister Dawkins," Jane commanded the Chief. "Hoist the jib and make ready the mainsail."

"Bring two," Dawkins called down to the deck, where the crew stood by to handle the lines. With a yank, Hitchens released the pin so the heavy hawser could be hauled aboard. One by one, the docklines were set loose, pulled aboard, and hastily piled onto the deck. A proper job of coiling down would be done once they were underway, but for now, the crew worked to get *Destiny* off the dock as quickly as possible. As the final attachment to the wharf was released, Jane turned to the pilot.

"The bridge is yours, Mister Soames."

Standing at the stern rail, Jane watched as the tug boat began the slow turn that would pull the *Destiny* off the wharf into midstream. The schooner would ride the morning tide down the East River and into the bay, releasing the tug as she caught the northwesterly breeze that was even now beginning to make the rigging flap.

Peeking down the aft companionway to her quarters, Jane could see her husband seated at the desk busily making notes in his diary. I suppose, she thought with a smile, those are our quarters now. Jane was grateful that her chosen mate was a man of few possessions as there was little extra room in the cupboards for another person's clothes. However, the cabin had been designed for use by the captain and his wife when the schooner had been built ten years ago so there would be ample room for the two of them although it would mean giving up the privacy to which she had become accustomed over the years.

Jane allowed herself the indulgence of a few more moments of admiring Endeavor while reminiscing about their wedding night. With pink cheeks, she finally straightened and turned to the second mate, who was supervising the helm.

"How do the men look this morning, Mister Galsworthy?" With his broad stance, the stocky seaman stood as firmly on the quarterdeck as a landlubber in his parlor as the *Destiny* rose and fell in the turbulent morning current.

"Aye, they are eager to be off, ma'am," he replied. "And Griggs here says he's got at least one more good voyage in him," he continued as he nodded to the old salt holding the wheel.

Able Seaman Griggs flashed her a quick smile from which most of the teeth were missing, then returned his attention to the lookout at the bow. The river was busy with trading ships and fishing boats competing for passage down the narrow waterway on the receding tide. Young Hitchens, newly promoted to Ordinary Seaman, stood on the foredeck avidly scanning for trouble and making hand signals to indicate where obstacles lay. Jane thought her greenest hand was shaping up nicely and would fulfill his father's hopes by becoming a first-rate sailor in time. He had proven himself a steady hand on the last venture and Jane was glad to have him sign up to sail under her again this time out.

By mid-morning, the *Destiny* cleared Sandy Hook and Jane sent the pilot on his way with the customary bottle of port she gave to show her gratitude. The wind picked up as they rounded the final point of land and made course for the open water beyond the harbor. She gave the command to raise all sails, and the *Destiny* sprang ahead with a spray of mist off her bow and a gentle heel to larboard.

Jane called down to Endeavor to join her on deck to feel the

21

glorious sensation of a lively boat before a following sea under a steady breeze. She smiled as he squared his shoulders and took a deep breath. It really was a trial for the poor man to find himself afloat. He had long been the butt of her jests over his panic at the thought of entering the water. He fully anticipated that drowning would be the outcome of so foolish an act on his part. However, he had declared himself game when he made his proposal to the captain, so he may as well face his new life sooner rather than later.

Jane kept her gaze on the far horizon as Endeavor mounted the ladder to the deck and then, clinging to the rail, made his way to her side. He leaned on the taffrail and held on with a white-knuckled grip as he joined her in looking up at the morning sky to the east. Finally clearing his throat, he allowed as how it was a fine day and the *Destiny* seemed a fine vessel on which to enjoy it.

"That she is, and I hope you will come to take true pleasure in her once you learn to trust her," Jane said.

"Is that what thee do? Trust her?"

"With my life, and the life of every soul aboard her. She's sound and true and I know that she will take us anywhere we desire to go. She has heart, this schooner, and we understand each other."

"Very well, then, I shall learn to trust her as well," Endeavor declared. "Do thee think she will take it amiss if I hold on tightly in the meantime?" he asked with a wry grin.

Jane remained on deck for the rest of the morning as the watch went about their duties under the firm command of Mister Galsworthy and Mister Dawkins. At noon, she called the ship's boys to the quarterdeck to take the sun sight with her and the chief mate, then retired below with the morning's logs to calculate their position.

Descending the ladder to the cabin and pausing to pull the hatch closed behind her, Jane looked about for Endeavor. To her surprise he was neither in the cabin nor the saloon. However, she soon heard sounds emanating from the head that let her know her husband was suffering from a prodigious case of *mal-de-mer*. She waited a few minutes until the worst of the crisis seemed to pass then leaned her head on the door to call softly to him.

"My dear, fresh air and a long sightline will do much to make your stomach settle. I shall have Cookie make you something to soothe your throat and have a seat prepared for you amidships."

His only reply was a groan, and then a renewal of the dry heaving that followed once the stomach was empty. Jane let him be while she left to order tea then returned to coax him above board.

An hour later, a pale but determined-looking Endeavor sat wrapped in a blanket on the hatch cover sipping chamomile tea with honey. His grim visage warned off anyone who thought to commiserate with the poor man, even as he continued to make use of the bucket he clenched to his chest from time to time.

Jane thought it the part of a caring wife to leave the man to his misery, and went about her business below, checking her route, marking her charts, and consulting with Dawkins about their planned landfall in Norfolk. If the wind held they would pass Cape May at nightfall, standing well offshore to keep from being blown onto the rocks should the wind shift overnight. They could then hug the coast tomorrow and look to round Fisherman Island by the end of the afternoon watch. They would anchor there for the night and sail into Norfolk with the morning breeze. Jane wondered if Endeavor would choose to return to the *Destiny* once he got a chance to step onto dry land in Virginia. Were she to ask him now, she suspected he might very well declare his intent to walk back to New York.

As the afternoon wore on, Jane took to pacing the rail with her spyglass fixed to her eye. She scanned every schooner that came within sight for signs of the *Osprey*. Captain Albright had pulled his lines aboard promptly at dawn and was well away before Jane and Endeavor returned to the *Destiny* after their night ashore. He seemed eager to arrive in Norfolk ahead of them.

As Endeavor had asked about making himself useful while aboard, Uncle Josias sent for a large stack of books and papers from the office the night before. He handed them to the still bleary-eyed young man in the morning with the instruction to peruse them carefully to discover anything that seemed amiss, or that would explain why Albright's voyages no longer paid off as they once had. Jane knew Endeavor was eager to apply himself to the task but he would have to wait until he found his sea legs.

Her husband finally staggered below when the first dog watch took over and half the men went to dinner. The smell of salt junk from the galley drove him off the deck and sent him to lie down on the cabin floor where Jane found him when she adjourned to the saloon with Mister Dawkins for her own meal.

"Come on, up with you my friend. The motion down there will do your stomach no good. Mister Dawkins, a hand please."

Together, Jane and the chief levered Endeavor onto the berth, where he sat up long enough to drink a glass of water then lay down again with a faint moan. Setting his bucket next to him, Jane climbed to the quarterdeck in search of carpenter Koopmans.

"Can you look out a hammock for the poor man? We'll hang it on the deck so he gets some fresh air."

Once his place had been prepared, Dawkins and Galsworthy helped Endeavor back onto the deck and tucked him in. Silas was detailed to sit with him and make sure he drank at least a cupful of water every hour. Jane took over that duty in the evening and spent an hour reading to him to take his mind off his trials. At midnight, seeing that he had finally fallen asleep, she reminded the watch to keep an eye on him and retired to her own berth for some much-needed rest.

Off the Coast of New Jersey
April 19, 1821

Thursday, April 19, 1821 Sighted brig El Almirante. Did not speak. Winds steady NNW Noon sight and land bearings place us at Lat. 38° 52' N Long. 74° 45' W. Crew recovering from seasickness.

Jane was roused at dawn by the sensation of a cold, damp person sliding in between the sheets next to her. She smiled as she wrapped herself around Endeavor and held him until he ceased shivering and fell asleep in her arms. Had she ever doubted his love for her, his stoic, uncomplaining acceptance of his miserable fate would have reassured her that he would brave anything to be by her side.

Woken again by the sound of the ship's bell as the night watch came off duty, Jane slipped quietly from the berth and pulled on her clothes, leaving her husband to get what rest he could. She stopped at the galley for a cup of hot coffee then climbed to the quarterdeck.

They had made good time overnight, and the logs showed that they should be approaching the opening of the Delaware River where it joined the Atlantic at Cape May. She directed Mister Galsworthy to have the ship brought to a new heading that would swing them closer to the shore, then went below to enjoy her morning repast. To her surprise, Jane discovered Endeavor sitting up at the saloon table gulping down a cup of coffee and eating her breakfast. Grateful to see him looking more like himself, she sat down across from him and took his hand in hers.

"I have missed you," she said.

"And I thee," he replied with a smile. "It seems that I begin to recover myself. Unfortunately, the cook has not yet remembered that I am aboard so I am afraid that I have made free with thy rations, dear wife."

"No matter," Jane said as she rose to join him on the far side of the table. "A lost breakfast is nothing next to the

25

pleasure of seeing you back on your feet."

They spent a pleasant half hour together as Jane sent for and consumed her own meal then parted ways, Jane to the deck to check on the watch and Endeavor to the desk to begin on the books Josias had sent. On the quarterdeck, Dawkins stood with his spyglass pressed to his eye, intently focused on a brig standing to the east.

"Here, ma'am, have a look. Have you seen that brig before?" He handed the glass to Jane.

Jane scanned the length of the high-sided vessel from bow to stern. The two-masted brig seemed low in the water though not as heavily laden as she would be with a full load of cargo. No ensign flew from her peak, and the stern was angled away just far enough that Jane could not make out her name. Aloft, her square sails flogged in the breeze as the brig sailed off the wind, barely making way.

Lowering the glass, Jane asked, "What do you make of her, Dawkins?"

"Aye, I'm not sure, ma'am. She looks familiar to me, as if I had taken note of her at some point in recent years. She seems to be biding her time out there as if waiting for something but not yet ready to heave to." Dawkins took the spyglass back and put it to his eye again. "I wonder if that is the *El Almirante*? She's got a figurehead like that. Indeed, I think it must be."

"I am not familiar with the name, Chief. How do you know of her?"

Dawkins dropped the glass from his eye and turned to her with a frown. "She was taken by a British frigate in nineteen and the captain was done over for slave trading. He had three hundred souls aboard that he was planning to smuggle in from Santo Domingo, the way I heard it. I saw her when she was towed into Boston as a prize. Wonder who owns her now?"

Over the next few hours, they watched as the brig eventually dropped most of her sails and hove to, finally disappearing astern as the *Destiny* raced south toward Norfolk. Shrugging off her curiosity, Jane set her mind to watching the depth soundings as the schooner rounded Fisherman Island in the early evening. Endeavor had put away the books and joined her on deck to watch the sun set over the low hills to the west. At the bow, Singleton kept a sharp lookout for shoals and they glided without mishap to a shallow anchorage on the leeward side of the island.

Jane remained on deck as the anchor was set and the sails furled, then joined Endeavor and Mister Dawkins in the saloon for a hearty dinner. She was relieved to see that the patient was fully recovered and had regained his ravenous appetite. One more night of sleep should restore him to his normal self she hoped. Soon, they had finished their meal and Endeavor rose. With a nod to Dawkins, he reached out a hand to Jane to lead her to their cabin then paused before she could take it.

"Ah, I forget myself. Jane, I will be in our cabin. Good night, Friend Dawkins." With a warm smile for the company he turned and entered their sleeping quarters, closing the door behind him. Jane, well accustomed to the plain speech and simple clarity of conversation among the Quaker folk, understood and was grateful for Endeavor's care in not seeming to tell the captain what to do or to set himself above her. Dawkins however, sat with a look of surprise on his face, then hurried to rise once Endeavor had retired.

"Good night, ma'am," he said. "I will just check the watch." Jane watched him go with the thought that they all had some adjusting to do before they were at ease with each other.

In their cabin, Endeavor had blown out the lantern and left just a single candle burning in the gimballed sconce above their berth. Already disrobed and in his nightshirt, he helped Jane remove the simple skirt and blouse she wore when aboard ship and then pulled her into his arms.

Later, as they were drifting off to sleep, Endeavor whispered in her ear, "Remind me in the morning to tell thee what I have discovered," and began gently snoring.

V
A Sobering Encounter

Fisherman's Island, Virginia
April 20, 1821

*Friday, April 20, 1821 Overnight mooring in calm cond. at Lat. 37° 06' N Long.
76° 00' W. Frigate Sophie Jones encountered El Almirante. Rescue of frigate crew.*

Boom! Boom! Ba-boom!

The thunder of guns at dawn brought Jane out of her berth
in an instant. Pulling on a muslin skirt over her nightrail and
throwing a shawl over her shoulders, she was out the door
before Mister Galsworthy could call for her. She sprinted up the
companionway to the deck and looked frantically around for the
source of the blasts.

"They're chasing her down ma'am. Look, she's about to go
aground," Hitchens called from the bow where he was jumping
up and down and pointing to the southeast. Out beyond the
channel mouth, Jane could see the brig they had last seen hove-
to off the coast, the *El Almirante*, under full press of sail as she
attempted to elude a huge frigate half a mile off her stern with
all her canvas flying in hot pursuit. As she sped south along the
low-lying shore, the *El Almirante* skirted close to the sandy
shallows extending from the spit of land that marked the
opening to the Bay while the frigate continued firing her guns in
rolling waves, enveloping the scene in acrid smoke that drifted
across the water and turned the sky yellow. Through the haze,
Jane watched in horror as the brig swung sharply away from the
shore but failed to make the tack to port in time. Jane cried out
as she saw it founder on the shoals off Cape Henry and heel
sharply to starboard as it came to a sudden halt. Bearing down,
the frigate maintained a continuous volley that reverberated
across the bay and made the watchers on the *Destiny* cover their

ears. Soon, the hunter and her hapless prey were obscured by billowing smoke, and Jane turned away.

"Mister Dawkins, weigh anchor and prepare to make way. There may be men in the water and we are the closest vessel," Jane ordered and went below to finish getting dressed.

In her cabin, she found Endeavor hastily tying his shoes. She described the scene they had witnessed as she pulled her uniform from the wardrobe.

"She's a privateer, that frigate, mark my words," she said while she pulled the linen shirt over her head and tied the cravat tightly around her throat. "And I would bet my bottom dollar that brig is a slaver. She will be worth a pretty sum to the frigate's crew, so they will want to catch as many of the brigands as they can. It could get hot," Jane observed from the top of the ladder as she climbed back out onto the quarterdeck.

By the time the *Destiny*'s crew had the anchor aboard, the guns were quiet and the smoke had cleared. Jane could make out the frigate, now hove-to with her guns still pointed toward the *El Almirante* and her crew working to lower the jolly boats to row for the brig. Aboard the *El Almirante*, men were running back and forth on the slanted deck, rushing to lower their own skiffs over the side. She caught her breath as she saw several of the men still aboard the *El Almirante* leave their tasks at the davits to line up at the rail and fire their muskets at the approaching captors.

"Dawkins, we'll heave-to well out of range and wait until the situation cools before we seek to render assistance."

As the *Destiny* drifted gently in the swell, Jane and her crew watched the unfolding drama. At the first sign of counter-attack, the crew of the frigate in the jolly boats had shipped their oars and put their weapons to use, firing first at the sailors on the rail of the *El Almirante*, then shooting into the planks of the brig's escaping small boats. Despite their best efforts, they were unable to dislodge the brig's defenders, and three skiffs laden with sailors and officers from the *El Almirante* made the eastern shore, where they splashed in the sandy shallows as they hauled the boats into the marsh grasses that lined the dunes.

Meanwhile, the *El Almirante's* muskets had done their deadly work and holed all of the frigate's jolly boats below the waterline. The frigate's crew had no choice but to turn their sinking boats back as the last of the *El Almirante's* crew jumped overboard from the wrecked brig and swam to join their mates ashore.

"Now, Mister Dawkins. We'll gather up the frigate's men."

In short order, the *Destiny* lay alongside the frigate and put out her own skiff to retrieve the dozen sailors from the frigate clinging to the remains of their jolly boats. Watching from the quarterdeck, Jane was startled to see that the person reaching overboard to haul each man to safety was none other than her husband. She had not noticed him coming on deck, much less climbing into the boat to take part in the action. His long arms and strong back were most welcome and Jane admired his willingness to set aside his fears to help with the rescue.

Within minutes, the *Destiny's* skiff was overloaded and threatened to ship water on the next wave. The half a dozen seamen still in the water grasped the gunwales and swam beside the boat as the men at the oars pulled for the frigate, where a boarding ladder had been thrown over the side. As the skiff drew alongside, the sailors scampered up the ladder to the cheers of their shipmates.

Jane was so intent on keeping an eye on the action below that she was startled to be hailed from the poopdeck of the frigate.

"Ahoy, Captain. We are the privateer *Sophie Jones* out of Savannah. Captain McKnight sends his regards and asks if you would honor us by coming aboard," the boatswain called through a hailing horn.

She turned and nodded to Mister Galsworthy, who took up their own speaking tube and replied that Captain Thorn of the *Destiny* out of New York would come aboard within the half hour.

"Dawkins, let's get the crew aboard and give them a chance to dry out. Take a sounding and throw out an anchor if we have less than fifteen fathoms. I should not care to drift onto that frigate and the tide is carrying us to the southeast," she ordered.

"Aye, aye, ma'am," he replied and then shouted for the sounding man. "O'Reilly. Put the lead out."

By the time the last of the crew were aboard, O'Reilly had reported a shallow depth of four fathoms. "By gum Mister Dawkins, we played our hand a little freely there. All right, let's get the anchor down and keep sounding the depth as she swings. I'll make my visit short and we'll be off again within the hour," Jane said.

Gathering her skirts, Jane looked over the side to see which of her men had been detailed to row her across to the *Sophie Jones*. Grinning up at her from his seat between the oars was a sodden Endeavor. With an answering smile, Jane climbed down the ladder and dropped into the boat. She seated herself in the bow without a word and settled back to enjoy the sight of her husband's muscles through his wet shirt as he pulled at the oars to bring the skiff alongside the frigate.

Jane grasped the boarding ladder and tied off the painter rope, then ordered Endeavor, "Stay with the boat, Mister Coffin. I shall return shortly."

Reaching the top of the ladder, Jane swung her leg over the rail, shook out her skirts, and stepped onto the deck. She returned the salute of a ruddy Irishman in a blue greatcoat and cocked hat who was clearly the master, and asked permission to come aboard.

"Aye, Captain Thorn, welcome aboard. Pardon the impertinence, but am I right in thinking ye're a lass under that coat, then?" he asked with a stern look.

"Aye, Captain McKnight, that I am. And now perhaps you will enlighten me with regard to what we have witnessed here this morning?".

McKnight's frown deepened as he growled in reply, "We've been hunting the *El Almirante* for weeks. We heard she left Santo Domingo last month without declaring her cargo and I have no doubt she is carrying some sort of contraband. God forgive the captain if he has gone back to smuggling human

31

flesh."

Jane turned to look across the water to the *El Almirante*, where the brig was slowly settling onto her side on the shallow bottom. Past the slanted hull, Jane could see the abandoned boats pulled up onto the sand, but no sign of the *El Almirante's* crew. They had made a clean escape over the dunes and into the woods, where Captain McKnight had no authority to continue the pursuit. "Are you thinking there may be Africans aboard her now? We certainly saw no sign of them being taken off in the boats if there were."

"Nay, we suspect she managed to transfer her load before we caught her as she was riding high in the water. Though not high enough to escape the Cape Henry shoals, hah!"

"The tide is running out, so perhaps we should hurry to inspect her before she collapses onto her side. I should not like to think what might happen to anyone chained below if she goes over."

"Aye, if we can use your boat, let us take ourselves aboard. Perhaps the captain was in a hurry and left his papers behind."

The sight that greeted Jane as she opened the access door to the brig's hold was one that would live in her memory forever. As Captain McKnight had guessed, the *El Almirante's* cargo had been offloaded, and the space was empty. However, the signs of human misery were clear. She saw the chains and bars that held the captives prisoner on narrow bunks. The stench of excrement and vomit was overpowering, and Jane and buried her nose in her sleeve. Peering into the dark, she called out in case anyone was still imprisoned in the evil compartment. Hearing no reply, she backed away and nearly tripped over Endeavor, who had come silently up behind her. Looking down at her with shock in his eyes he said, "May God have mercy on us."

Moving quickly, Jane and Endeavor searched the rest of the cargo and crew decks for stragglers, then returned topsides to draw some welcome breaths of fresh air. They were just emerging from the below deck as McKnight emerged. from the captain's quarters.

"Well," Jane demanded, "did the sorry scalawag leave anything behind to tell us what he was up to?"

"Aye, we have his log. I think he meant to take it with him but it was dropped in his haste to abandon ship. I'll have a more thorough gander at it later, but I see that he makes note for the last three days that 'G. atrasado' – G. was delayed."

"We thought she might be waiting for something when we saw her hove-to earlier," Jane said. "Will you turn it in to the garrison commander at the fort? Perhaps they might be able to find the captain and his despicable crew if they haven't disappeared into the swamps by now."

"Perhaps. But in any case, the Portuguese dog will no longer have use of this bloody brig, by God." Captain McKnight's face was grim as he pounded his fist on the capstan.

Jane agreed to follow the *Sophie Jones* into the Hampton Roads and make herself available as a witness should the magistrate have any questions about the events that had transpired that morning. The Act of 1820 had made it clear that anyone engaged in the illegal importation of Africans would be deemed a pirate and sentenced to hang if caught. Their ship would be subject to seizure, making the apprehension of slavers a lucrative business for privateers like McKnight. He would want to make sure there were no questions about his right to the *El Almirante*.

It took another hour for the *Destiny* to get underway once her captain and crew were back aboard. Jane and Endeavor repaired to their cabin to change into dry clothing and recover from the disturbing visit aboard the brig. Endeavor closed the door behind them, then taking Jane in his arms, held her gently as they swayed together. She could feel tears on his cheeks that matched her own, and they grieved together in silence. Finally, holding her hand, Endeavor drew Jane down onto the berth, where they sat side by side in quiet witness for several minutes.

Endeavour broke the silence. "We are called to respond to the evils of the world. We can no more turn our eyes away and believe ourselves to be good, having seen the truth."

"Amen," Jane replied in a firm voice, and stood as she reached for her greatcoat. "I'll see that bastard hanged." Clapping her hat firmly on her head, she marched out the door.

VI
Time for a Change

Norfolk, Virginia
April 20, 1821

"Are you sure, ma'am?" the seamstress asked, looking up at Jane with a worried frown.

"Yes, damn it, I am sure. Tighter, both in the waist and the seat. I'll not have them catching on things as I move about," Jane ordered.

Reluctantly, the seamstress pulled more pins from the corner of her mouth and increased the tucks in the fawn trousers by another inch. She was surprised when Jane entered her shop that afternoon with a set of men's garments and asked to have them tailored to her womanly figure.

"Do you mean to wear them yourself?" the seamstress asked in a puzzled voice, not sure she had heard Jane correctly.

"Aye, that I do. These skirts will be the death of me yet and I see no reason why I should not benefit from the convenience of dress afforded by trousers."

Growing impatient with the fussing, Jane stepped away from the woman kneeling at her feet.

"Come, make haste. I have business to attend to before the end of the day," she said irritably as she stripped the trousers off and pushed them into the waiting hands of the seamstress' assistant.

"And thank you," she remembered to say before rushing out the door and letting it slam behind her.

Jane had been in a foul mood since they arrived at Norfolk. Walking down the gangplank to the city dock, she caught her skirt on a loose nail and nearly somersaulted into the water. Only a quick grab from behind by Mister Dawkins saved her from a thorough ducking. She immediately turned and marched back aboard to seek out her husband's wardrobe.

"He always says we should have fewer possessions," she

muttered to herself as she commandeered his one fine pair of breeches from the bottom of the drawer. Slamming it shut, she marched back up the ladder, across the deck and down the gangplank past the waiting chief mate.

The near fall she experienced was not the first. Many times over the years she had been caught in the rungs of ladders, stepped on a hem and tripped, had her skirt obscure her vision when blown over her face in a high wind, and nearly drowned once when she slipped off a dock. On that occasion, the yards of heavy wool became waterlogged and entangled in her legs, making it impossible to swim. She struggled to keep her head above water until someone reached out to pull her ashore. This morning's close call was the final straw and Jane was determined to leave her skirts behind when she was aboard.

Feeling much happier at the thought of her new uniform, Jane was in a better mood to carry on a conversation about their plans for the cargo with Mister Dawkins as they proceeded to the courthouse.

"What say you, Dawkins? Do you think the ladies here will like my plates? They live closer to nature, surely they will appreciate the simple motifs and sturdy weight of them."

"Aye, ma'am, they might. Perhaps you'll do better selling them off the dock directly instead of at the auction. Shall we try putting a notice in the morning paper that a special load of unusual Swedish pottery is available in limited quantities to discerning ladies only? That should draw their curiosity, and they'll compete with each other to have the latest European goods."

"You old fox." Jane laughed. "I reckon you are right on that score. Let us give it a try. We'll stop in at the Herald once we've done our civic duty."

Near the steps of the courthouse, they found Endeavor waiting for them in the shade of a large oak tree. He had gone ashore that morning to seek out their local agent. Judging by his grim visage, the information gleaned from MacAndrews & Co. was not encouraging.

That morning, Endeavor had shared what he discovered in the *Osprey*'s logbooks.

"Come have a look at this," he said, spreading the books out on the saloon table. Jane pushed aside the breakfast plates to make room and leaned over to follow along as Endeavor turned the pages.

"Here, thee can see in the latest two logbooks where the first mate records sales and purchases. He makes a right muck of it, keeping notations only when the goods sell or are brought aboard, never making a proper accounting of the totals; and he uses various weights and measures, never accounting for things the same way twice," Endeavor pointed to a number of suspect entries in the books.

"Now," he said, "look thee at the log from three years ago. It appears to be written in another hand. Why did Albright have a different first mate for that voyage, does thee know?"

"I recall Uncle Josias mentioning that Albright did not get on with Mister Timmons, and Uncle moved the mate to the *Hawk*. I remember it because Uncle seemed put out over the whole affair, thinking that the fault lay with the captain and not the mate. In any case, Captain Albright brought his own man aboard and things settled down," Jane replied.

"The records from that first voyage are clear and concise. They show a well-managed trading trip with a tidy profit returned to Thorn Shipping. If we do as well this time out, we shall count ourselves a success. The new man, Markham, seems part of the failure of the following two years, does he not?" Endeavor observed.

"Aye, I take your meaning. What do you aim to do?" Jane asked, looking up at him.

"Look thee here," he said, as he pulled a paper covered with neat columns and numbers from the bottom of the pile. "I have re-figured all of the cargo carried and sold with a uniform accounting of weights and measures. If my calculations are correct, his cargo weights are light by over five tons, sometimes by as much as nearly ten."

Jane scanned the row of totals he was pointing to and could

see that Albright had been sailing with a partially empty hold for the last two summers. What was the blasted man up to?

"I shall pay a visit to Friend MacAndrews when we arrive in Norfolk and see what our agent has to tell us about his dealings with the *Osprey*," Endeavor said.

At the courthouse, Jane halted in front of her husband as he stood under the tree in an attempt to stay cool in the afternoon heat.

"What did MacAndrews say? Did he have an explanation for the shortages?"

"Pray let us wait until we are aboard again, if thee does not mind, Jane," Endeavour replied. "There is much to consider and I am not sure I have a full understanding yet."

Frustrated and impatient to know what had been going on, Jane nevertheless saw the wisdom in his words. "Aye, let us complete our business here before we undertake consideration of the confounded dealings of Captain Albright." With a nod to Dawkins, she climbed the steps and strode into the cool darkness.

Clustered outside the door to the magistrate's chambers were Captain McKnight and his officers, along with several members of what appeared to Jane to be the local press.

"Captain McKnight," Jane nodded as she passed him on her way into the courtroom. The poor man looked harried by the news-hungry writers pestering him for details of the morning's encounter.

"Nay, I shall relate the tale but once, and that to the magistrate, ye buggers," McKnight growled as he returned Jane's greeting with a slight bow.

Inside the chambers, Jane was asked to state her business to the clerk perched at a desk behind a low counter that partitioned the public area from the magistrate's realm.

"Captain Thorn of the *Destiny*, here as a witness to the capture of the *El Almirante* this morning."

"Please wait to be summoned," the clerk replied, waving her party to a bench set along the wall. "Judge Glennan will be with you shortly."

Nearly an hour elapsed before Jane was called and her patience wore increasingly thin as the minutes ticked by. When they were finally summoned, she bristled as she walked behind the clerk into the magistrate's private chambers, fighting to keep her exasperation in check. There was the customary surprise and consternation on the face of the magistrate as he realized that Captain Thorn was a woman and she nearly exploded in irritation. As she drew her breath to express her feelings, she felt Endeavor's warm hand on her shoulder. Looking up, she caught the flicker of caution in her husband's eyes and held her tongue.

"Captain Thorn, I presume?" Judge Glennan asked as he rose from his seat behind a large desk piled with papers and stacks of law books.

"At your service, Judge," she replied with a nod as she removed her hat. "And this is Mister Coffin, representing Thorn Shipping and Cargo, and Mister Dawkins, Chief Mate of the *Destiny*."

"Thank you for attending this informal inquiry into the events of this morning, ma'am," the magistrate said as he guided them across the room to a large table set about with chairs in front of a row of large windows open to the afternoon breeze. "Please, have a seat and tell me what you saw and heard."

In a few words, Jane related their role in the encounter, closing her eyes in pain as she described the condition of the brig's hold. As he listened to her story, Judge Glennan shook his head, then threw down his pencil.

"Captain McKnight has been on the trail of the *El Almirante* for many weeks, he tells me. A pity he did not come upon her earlier when she was still fully laden with unfortunate captives. It would have been a simple matter to make the case for trafficking and impound both the vessel and all aboard her. We Virginians run things fair and square. The importation of Africans has been illegal for twenty years, and we mean to make it hot for any crooked sea captains who think to flout the law."

Quelling an urge to make a comment about the relative fairness of the slavery still practiced in the Tidewater region,

Jane stood and held out her hand to the Judge.

"Well sir, I hope we have been of service, and that you catch the renegade master. Have you news of his whereabouts, or that of his crew?"

"That we do not, but the militia are scouring the swamps and woods and I am sure we will find them soon enough. And then they will all hang, Captain Thorn. You have my word on it," he replied with a firm handshake.

As Jane's party left the Judge's chambers, they were accosted by a short fellow in a frayed linen coat and battered hat.

"Captain Thorn, is it? William Sykes, publisher of the Norfolk Herald. I've had the story of the morning's chase out of McKnight over there," he said with a nod to the fuming captain who had been left to cool his heels while the judge pondered his case. "Have you anything to add to the facts, ma'am? Any thoughts on where the *El Almirante's* cargo may have been taken off her?"

Jane stopped to consider the question.

"We are new to these parts, Mister Sykes, but I reckon he had a contact that helped bring them ashore somewhere distant from any settlements. It seems there must have been dozens of captives from what we saw; it would not have been a small number of souls at any rate. And he could not take that brig very close to land for fear of running aground. Someone had a boat big enough to carry a lot of people, but shallow enough to bring them safely in along the coast. Find that boat and you have your answer," she declared.

That evening, Dawkins and Galsworthy joined Jane and Endeavour in the saloon to share a glass of cider and debate the motives of the perfidious Captain Albright of the *Osprey*.

"How has he done it, Mister Coffin, sir?" Galsworthy asked. "Tried to hide the shortfall, like?"

"Simple obfuscation, Friend Ezra," Endeavor replied. "By having the mate record the amounts in various ways and scatter them about in the log, they tried to keep it secret that the hold was not full. And I say 'they' because the captain must have approved the log keeping."

"What had MacAndrews to say on the matter? Has he had dealings with Albright?" Jane asked.

"Yes, and he was relieved that someone from Thorn Shipping had finally turned up to ask questions. He has noted discrepancies in the *Osprey*'s actions these past two years and had determined to cease doing business with our firm over them. Whenever he questioned Albright about why he had not brought a larger load, or why he had taken so long to reach port, the captain apparently refused to explain and allowed as how he knew his own business without oversight from any jackanape of an agent. The man was right insulted and vowed he would write to Friend Josias to terminate the relationship should Albright take a similar tone with him in the future," Endeavor reported.

"What can he be up to?" Jane repeated her thought from earlier in the day.

"Not Thorn business, that is quite clear," Endeavor responded. "MacAndrews is further frustrated that Albright seems to be in a hurry to sell and offload any cargo he carries and is not concerned with getting the best sale he can, nor negotiating the lowest price when seeking a load.

"Where has he traveled, do you know?" Dawkins asked.

"Not yet, Friend Dawkins, but I aim to plot that as my next task."

"Surely our other agents have noticed something is amiss," Jane said.

"Aye, they may have a similar tale to tell," Dawkins observed. "Perhaps one of them may have an inkling of the truth."

"I suspect thee are correct, and I shall certainly seek them out as we continue our journey," Endeavor replied.

"Say," Galsworthy sat up. "Shouldn't the *Osprey* be here in Norfolk by now? Captain, ma'am, wasn't he headed for Virginia same as us when he left New York? I haven't seen her in the moorings, or at the dock."

"Aye, you are right on that score. I was just about to mention that myself. Where the devil do you suppose he has got to? He wasn't many hours ahead of us, yet we never saw him again once he rounded the bend on the East River. Let us keep a sharp lookout for him as we unload in Norfolk. We shall see what tale he tells if he dares show his face," Jane said with a grimace.

The conversation continued for another hour as the lamps burned low but they could not throw any light on the strange behavior of Captain Albright. Finally, they doused the lanterns and retired for the evening.

As she began to undress in the cabin, Jane suddenly remembered that she had not yet informed her husband of the loss of his trousers. She thought she had best make short work of it and let him express his feelings on the matter now, before he actually saw the altered garment on her.

"Dear husband," she began.

Endeavor looked up with the buckled shoe he had just removed in his hand.

"Dear wife," he said, sitting back to take her in more fully. "It has been but a few days since we wed, and yet I have come to understand certain things about thee to which I was not privy in our earlier dealings."

"I see," she smiled. "And what, aside from my inclinations in certain delicate matters, might those be?"

"Ah, thee seek to distract me, then?" He grinned back at her as he stood to pull her close.

"Nay, but I do find myself curious as to what revelations you have come to with regard to my character," she said as soon as he had finished kissing her.

"Most relevant for the present instance is that thee seek to soften a message thee fear I will dislike by addressing me in tender tones at first. In this case, "dear husband" will surely be followed by unpleasant news, will it not?"

"Aye, that remains to be seen," she said. "What say you to the thought of me garbed in your trousers?"

"I should say the sight would be most interesting. Why? Am I likely to be blessed with such a thing?" he asked with a bemused look.

"Aye, that you shall. Tomorrow, in fact." Jane said. When he looked at her in confused silence, she continued. "I have given your best breeches to a seamstress in town."

"Jane dear, I feel thee are making a muddle of something quite simple. Perhaps thee could be plain in thy speaking on this matter? My head would welcome the attempt."

With a sigh, she stepped back to put a little space between them and declared, "I have stolen your trousers and had them made over to fit me. I am tired of being nearly killed by my blasted skirts and have decided to wear men's clothing on board. There, that's the truth of it and I am sorry I did not ask you first. I was so upset when I nearly fell in the water again this morning that I may have acted rashly, and for that I am repentant. Why are you laughing?"

It took Endeavor a moment to bring himself under control as his wife looked on with her hands on her hips and a defiant glare on her face.

"Ah, my sweet Jane, thee has done me a great favor. I have carried those particular breeches with me for many years with the idea that I must at some point present myself in a more fitting manner among good company despite my strongly held principles in the matter of plain clothing. Thee has removed the temptation to sin, and for that I thank thee," he grinned.

"Well then, perhaps I am good for you in more ways than one," Jane replied, and dropped her hands to step to his side once more. Reaching up to caress his cheeks, she smiled as she said, "I shall try them on especially for you once they have arrived in the morning."

With a groan, Endeavor rolled his eyes, then scooped her up and deposited her on the berth.

"I see that my prediction that life in thy company would be endlessly interesting seems to have been prescient," he said, as he reached down to take off his other shoe, then blew out the lantern.

VII
A Good Business

Norfolk, Virginia
April 21, 1821

"Have you no more presentable garments with you, Seaman Baldwin?" the captain asked with a frown. The tattered young man in front of her shook his head with a grin.

"No, ma'am, these are my best duds. Mother would not allow me to pack my new Sunday clothes as she reckoned I would leave them 'moldy, wet and shoved in a corner'." His aping of Prudence's severe tone when one of her children failed to meet her exacting standards brought forth a laugh from his aunt.

With a sigh, Jane realized she would be ransacking her husband's wardrobe again. She could only hope he did not come to regret sharing quarters with someone as frequently light-handed as she was turning out to be.

Silas was soon outfitted in one of Endeavor's shirts which, though it hung from his slender frame, was at least clean and more fitting to his role as a seller of fine pottery. Jane had decided that her nephew's fresh young face and innocent air would give him an advantage with the ladies of Virginia and detailed him to man the tables that had been set up on the dock. Piled high with colorful plates and hand-painted bowls, the display was inviting. To further entice customers, Jane reserved the finer pieces, including a set of puzzle jugs, and set them out in her cabin. Silas was instructed to whisper an invitation to view the "Captain's Special Selection" to any buyers who seemed flush with coin. Jane would take on the task of showing these wares to the customers, many of whom were sure to be as curious about the "lady captain" as they were about Swedish clay goods.

Jane dressed in her frock coat and the fitted trousers

delivered earlier that morning by the seamstress' assistant and had scarcely finished putting a brush to her hair when the first visitors knocked at the saloon door. Endeavor, who had been given the job of footman, opened it with a flourish and begged the ladies to step into the captain's quarters. The saloon was immediately overtaken by a gaggle of Norfolk's first ladies, done up in their finest satins and lace and clamoring to meet "Captain Jane".

"Lawd almighty, aren't you just the cutest thing?" a portly matron in a flamboyant maroon gown adorned with yards of ruffles exclaimed as she caught sight of Jane. "Olivia, isn't she just darling? All dressed up like a captain and everything! Oh lawd, you must come to tea with us tomorrow, mustn't she, Olivia?"

This outburst was met with an emphatic nod from the young woman at her side who was less garishly dressed but equally enthusiastic in her greeting.

"Indeed Mother, she must. Oh, dearest Captain, say you will," she pleaded as she took Jane's hand in her eagerness.

Charmed by the warm Southern welcome, Jane was pleased to accept and vowed to attend the Williams family at their home on Granby Street the next day. Soon, the other ladies had likewise extended invitations and extracted promises from Jane that she would not leave port without gracing their drawing rooms and entertaining their guests with tales of her seafaring adventures.

Gently turning the conversation to the main purpose of their visit aboard, Jane related her adventures during her visit to Sweden the prior summer, including her meeting with the proprietor of the Falkenburg pottery whence the ceramic pieces had come.

"A most charming man, and the fifth generation of his family to fire the kilns. When I asked to see a sample, he rushed to his rooms to bring out the plates he carried with him everywhere. He is immensely proud of their product, as is only right. Look how cleverly he has disguised the secret of the puzzle jug. Come, see if any of you can solve the mystery."

The ladies crowded around the saloon table and each tried her hand at pouring from the pitcher without spilling water into the ewer Jane had set out to catch the overflow. In the end, it was the young Miss Williams who took a methodical approach, testing each opening and examining the surface minutely to locate the hidden the hole.

"Voila!" her mother cried in satisfaction as Olivia demonstrated the trick. "Isn't she wonderful! Captain Jane, I must have one of them for each of my three brothers. We shall see if her uncles are as cunning as my dear Olivia."

The other ladies were equally enamored of the charming jugs and purchased the rest of Jane's stock on the spot. Within the space of an hour, Jane sold every last piece of pottery from her special collection and had given her word to make an appearance at a musical evening on Tuesday next at the Town Hall.

Closing the door behind the final customer, who could be heard exclaiming to her companion over the "clever little jug and even cleverer captain" as they made their way up the stairs, Jane leaned her back against the planks and blew her hair out of her face.

"Lawd have mercy!" she said in her best imitation of the town ladies. "What a perfectly wonderful, if exhausting, batch of hens."

"Thee has done well, my dear," Endeavor smiled back. "It appears we shall be quite busy the next few days, and I shall have the opportunity to play the role of the captain's gallant husband. It is unfortunate that I do not own a pair of suitable breeches," he grinned.

With a playful poke, Jane hugged her husband and made her way to the dock to alert Silas that her cabin had been laid waste by the horde he had sent below. She found him surrounded by a crowd of customers desperately bidding to acquire the last of the plates and bowls. Silas was masterfully playing them off, one against the other, as he sought ever-higher prices for the remaining goods.

"Thank you, ma'am, these plates will be the envy of your friends," he said, as he looked over the crowd after accepting the latest bid. "Shall I wrap them for you?"

The suggestion brought forth a new round of offers, and the final sum was more than triple the opening amount. A smug Silas waved his hand over the cleared tables as he bowed to his captain. "We appear to have run out of wares, ma'am."

Jane clapped him on the back and vowed that he would henceforth be given the job of sales clerk in every port. "Aye, ma'am, I would be pleased to take on the work. And am I to understand that the customary commission for such sales is two percent on the gross?" he smirked back at her.

"A true Thorn, I see," she laughed. "Aye, you shall have your well-earned share, nephew."

Pleased at the takings from the venture, Jane handed off the accounts to Dawkins and went in search of cargo to fill the newly vacant space in her hold. While she knew that tobacco, cotton, and rice would bring a good price in New York, she was also adamant that Thorn vessels would not carry plantation goods. The successful voyage to the Chesapeake Bay undertaken by the *Osprey* three years earlier had relied greatly on slave commodities, but Jane was determined to make a go of things without trafficking in exports produced by people in chains. Her visit to a sugar plantation in Cuba on her last voyage had opened Jane's eyes to the conditions of slavery in a way that all of her father's lectures and uncle's pamphlets had not.

"We cannot, must not, live one way at home and another at business," she had declared at the most recent Thorn family gathering. "We say we believe that all persons are of equal worth, and that slavery is wrong. Yet we consent to carry on the business of those who perpetuate the evil practice. Surely that makes us complicit in their shame."

"Aye, Jane, you speak for all of us and put a name to that which we have only whispered to ourselves," her father avowed.

"It is our disgrace that we have been slow to place our morals above our pocketbooks," Josias agreed. "While we do not transport or sell many plantation goods, we have nevertheless made a great deal of profit when we have chosen to do so. It is a seductive business, and it is easy to turn a blind eye when the return is so high."

It seemed almost a relief to her family that Jane had broached the sensitive topic. Men of goodwill and staunch principles, her father and uncles had nonetheless been less than upright in not taking a public stance against trade with the South that depended on the enslavement of Africans. They talked often around the dinner table about abolition. But until now, they had avoided taking a position on whether the company could ethically engage in trade with southern slaveholders.

Before the meeting concluded, Jane insisted, in traditional Quaker fashion, that they come to a consensus on the issue. It was swiftly done and Josias agreed to place an advertisement in the commercial papers that Thorn Shipping and Cargo was no longer in the business of carrying slave-produced cargo.

"It may cost us customers in the short run, as there is no shortage of sympathy with the southern way of life even here in New York, but we will sleep better at night," Prudence declared.

As Jane made her rounds of the Norfolk warehouses, she was reminded of the constraints of this new policy many times over. Each building was packed to the rafters with bales of cotton, bags of grain and rice, sheaves of tobacco, and boxes of sugar. Surely the South had produced something else. Alas, there were no goods on offer that were unequivocally produced by free labor, and the captain returned empty-handed to the *Destiny*.

"It seems our principles have put us in a rather tight spot," she announced to her officers and Endeavor that evening. "We have done a good business today with the pottery, and market prices are high for our other goods, so we should do well here in Norfolk. However, our hold will be more than half empty as we make for Baltimore and points beyond, and I hate to return home with nothing to sell."

"Are there no crafts on offer?" Dawkins asked. "I have seen

many fine pieces of furniture for sale in New York that were produced from southern timber, ma'am."

"Aye, we can expect to find cabinets and other furniture in Baltimore and may make up the load there. It will take a keen eye to find pieces of good quality and low price, but that is certainly one possibility. I will also seek out MacAndrews tomorrow to inquire about paid freight, should there be any contracts available for goods not from the plantations. In the meantime, I have another proposal," Jane said. "What say you to our carrying passengers for hire?"

"To New York, you mean?" Galsworthy was astonished. "Where would we put them, Captain?" Her second mate was clearly worrying about her plans for his cabin.

"Nay, we'll take them from here to Baltimore. It is only a short voyage of a few days, and we ought to be able to take advantage of our social whirl in the coming days to recruit paying customers. What say you all?" she asked as she looked around at three surprised faces.

Dawkins cleared his throat as he ventured to follow up on the second mate's question, "And where will they sleep, ma'am? Are ye thinking we will put them in the officers' quarters?" He looked just as worried as Galsworthy at the thought.

"We shall build them cabins in the hold," Jane said. "I shall go over my plans with Koopmans in the morning, but I think we could construct at least four single cabins in the center of the hold where the vessel is steadiest. With a simple berth and storage together with a fold-away table and clothing rack, we ought to be able to make our guests comfortable enough to pay us the going rate for the passage. Even with the cost of the lumber, we should be able to turn a profit."

Looking relieved and far more enthusiastic, Galsworthy slapped the table as he allowed that the captain had a "right fine idea" that might work for the legs of the voyage that had limited cargo.

Later that evening as they were preparing for bed, Endeavor brought up the issue of catering to passengers.

"They shall require feeding and entertaining. And shall we

share the head with them?" he wondered.

"Aye, it will be all hands to the guns for this if we are to make it work," she agreed. "But I reckon Cookie will be pleased. He always says seamen are a bunch of Philistines with no palate and his fine cooking is going to waste. He will be glad to have an appreciative group of diners."

For all her brave talk however, Jane was worried that she had taken on more than she could comfortably handle. Her well-run vessel would be disrupted by the presence of guests, and the demands on the captain for socializing with the passengers would take its toll on her sanity, she was sure. However, it was up to her to make this voyage pay, and she could see no other alternative on offer at the moment. As she blew out the lantern and curled herself into Endeavor's embrace, she said a short prayer that the Lord would bring her an abundance of patience in the coming days.

VIII
A Day of Rest

Norfolk, Virginia
April 22, 1821

The captain and her husband spent Sunday morning in quiet reading and reflection in their cabin. Dawkins released the crew ashore.

"Mister Galsworthy, they are to be back aboard by first watch. Should Mister Singleton decide to go ashore, please make sure he is accompanied by another crew member at all times and suggest to him that he not wander far from the port," Jane had warned as she conferred with her mates at breakfast.

In the early afternoon, Jane and Endeavor dressed in street attire and made their way down the gangplank. Kicking her skirts out as she walked, Jane reflected how quickly she had become accustomed to the ease and comfort of her husband's pilfered trousers. The couple set a sedate pace as they strolled arm in arm past the closed shops that made up the mercantile end of Granby Street near the port and were soon standing on the front stoop of the Williams house.

"Captain Thorn and Mister Coffin," Jane announced to the young woman who answered their knock.

Leaving their hats with the maid, the pair stepped into the elegant drawing room where the Williams family welcomed them boisterously. The company, composed of Mistress Williams and all three of her daughters, including the clever Olivia, along with a large gentleman of great girth and enormous whiskers who turned out to be the *pater familias*, were gathered around a table set out with a set of china Jane recognized as coming from the finest English kilns. Clearly, Virginia was not the cultural backwater Jane had expected, which cheered her immensely as she intended to do a good business in these waters.

"Welcome to Norfolk, Captain. And Mister Thorn... er,

Coffin," Archibald Williams exclaimed as he grabbed Endeavor's hand before her husband could gracefully avoid having it shaken. Jane watched Endeavor out of the corner of her eye as he politely turned down the offer of a libation from their host and deftly turned the conversation to the sights and attractions of the town. It was a challenge for him to keep to his Quaker customs in society settings, Jane knew, and she admired his tact. As Mister Williams attempted to steer his guest toward the brandy bottle on the sideboard, Olivia came forward to pull Jane toward a divan by a low fire that warded off the slight chill of the spring day. The misses Williams were eager to hear how she had come to be captain of her own vessel, and whether the life was as thrilling as they imagined it to be.

"Indeed," Jane assured them, "most of my days are filled with matters of business and other monotony, but there is nothing as glorious as the wind in my face when the bow lifts in a freshening breeze. My travels bring me to so many intriguing places where I meet such interesting people," she said with a meaningful smile at the ladies.

"Aren't you afraid of pirates?" the youngest girl, who could be no more than six, asked.

"No, Miss Abigail, the *Destiny* is swifter than most pirates, and I am fierce when cornered," Jane replied with a growl and a menacing glare.

Her eyes grown wide in wonder, Abigail sat in rapt silence staring at the captain for the remainder of the brief visit. As Jane and Endeavor took their departure amidst promises from the family to pass the word among their acquaintances about the passage to Baltimore in the new cabins, a soft hand was slipped into Jane's palm. Looking down, she saw the upturned face of Miss Abigail and knelt to give the girl a swift embrace and whisper in her ear.

"Don't you forget to be fierce, too, Abigail Williams."

"I promise I won't, Captain Jane," Abigail whispered back as she threw her arms around Jane's neck for a final embrace.

Jane was deep in thought as she walked at her husband's

side back to the wharf. Eventually, Endeavor broke into the silence to ask if she would care to share her thoughts.

"Home and hearth, Endeavor, are on my mind. Our home and hearth, to be more precise. And the children who will surely gather there, my husband," she replied.

"Ah, yes, dear one. We should perhaps begin to think about how we shall conduct our lives when we are no longer just a pair," he smiled.

"Indeed, although I think not quite yet. Let us continue to be careful for a while still, and see how we get along with our life aboard."

"Agreed for now, Jane. Although surely events may catch up with us and it is best to be prepared with a plan, is it not? However, let us talk of this another day when we have had time to consider." Endeavor squeezed her hand as he tucked her in tighter to his side.

Grateful for his understanding, Jane knew that she could not put off for long the question of making room for children. Their efforts to delay the day when she would conceive were likely to fail at some point and Jane found herself panicked at the thought of giving up her life to land ashore keeping house for a growing family. She would just have to find a way to follow her own path, she decided, wherever it might lead.

Given the fine weather and early hour, Jane suggested they take a stroll along the harbor before returning aboard. Although crowded with ships of all types and sizes, the docks were nearly deserted as the crews found entertainment ashore. It would be many hours yet before the streets filled with inebriated sailors seeking their berths to snatch some sleep before morning muster. The few seamen they saw intrigued Jane; many of them, even more than in the ports of New York and New England, were clearly of African descent.

"Do you suppose they are slaves, Endeavor?"

"Perhaps. But many will be former slaves, loosed from their bondage and making a life for themselves and their families here in Norfolk. Some are fishermen, or captains of the coastal vessels thee can spy around the Bay. And of course, there are a great number of freemen among the sailors in the merchant and whaling fleets, as thee knows."

"Aye, and they make able seamen, such as Mister Singleton," Jane observed.

"Thee has seemingly called him forth with thy words," Endeavor teased as he gestured to two men standing outside a low brick building that faced the waterfront. A painted sign hung from an iron bracket over the door showed it to be an ironmonger. As they watched, the two shook hands and Mister Singleton turned away to walk toward the dock where the *Destiny* lay. The other man, of similar appearance to the retreating seaman but dressed in a dark suit and felt hat, turned to open the door of the shop and disappeared quickly inside.

"How strange that Singleton should have an acquaintance here in Norfolk," Jane remarked.

"Aye, although perhaps not unexpected since the brotherhood of negro freemen is tightknit of necessity," Endeavor observed. "Still, one does wonder what business our man had with that merchant. And I wonder where his escort has gotten to."

"Well, he appears to be safe and on his way back to the *Destiny*, so all is well at any rate."

They dropped the subject for the moment but Jane was nonetheless perturbed by the meeting they had witnessed. There was something furtive about the actions of the men, and she did not care for unexplained events that touched her vessel or her crew. Vowing to address the matter with Singleton soon, Jane put it out of her mind and enjoyed the remainder of her stroll at the side of her husband in the sunny warmth of the southern afternoon.

Later that evening, Mister Galsworthy stopped by the captain's quarters to report that all the hands had returned in more or less good order. Young Mister Hitchens had apparently been jollied into drinking more of the local rum than was strictly good for his health and had ended up partaking in a round of fisticuffs with a cabin boy off the *Endurance*. The mate had patched him up and put him to bed with a stern warning about accepting a dare, and the fo'c'sle had settled in for the night.

As Jane lay in her berth listening to the soft tramp of the watch as he paced the deck, she wondered where the *Osprey* had gone. If Captain Albright did not make an appearance in the Roads by the time they were ready to set sail, she would be forced to report him missing to her uncle. Surely the man had not absconded with vessel and crew. More likely he had run into trouble and was holed up in some port in New Jersey making repairs. At least she hoped so, even if that meant a loss for the company.

And what was she to make of Mister Singleton's odd behavior? She had asked Mister Galsworthy to bring him to her cabin after dinner, where she queried him about his visit ashore. Singleton strongly denied having met anyone and swore he had spent his hours in port at a tavern that catered to sailors like him. He assured Jane and Endeavor that they were mistaken and would not be moved from his testimony by the captain's sternest look.

"What do you make of it?" she asked Galsworthy once Singleton had been sent forward to rejoin the crew.

"Could you be wrong, ma'am? Mister Coffin? Perhaps the light was playing tricks, and one seaman looks much like another at a distance."

"I very much doubt it, Mister Galsworthy. But it seems we are not to be given an answer, so we must let it rest. Let us, however, keep an eye on Mister Singleton in the future. As to which, what happened to the seaman sent to accompany him ashore?"

"Gave him the slip, short and sweet, ma'am. Told Griggs he would meet him on the dock as they were setting off, then never showed. Griggs waited a while and then searched the vessel, but there was no sign of him. Didn't think it worth reporting, ma'am, and so he made off for his own diversions ashore," Galsworthy replied with a rueful tone.

"All's well that ends well, I suppose, but perhaps things may become clearer in the coming days."

Her troubled thoughts kept Jane awake for a long time, and it was well after she heard the changing of the watch at midnight that she finally drifted off to the sound of her husband's even breathing.

IX
Return of the Lost

Norfolk, Virginia
April 23, 1821

Koopmans scratched his head as he looked over the sketches spread out on his workbench. Hastily drawn up by Jane that morning, they laid out a plan for converting the aft section of the hold into four tidy cabins with single stacked bunks and a small wardrobe each. The captain's design featured movable walls that could be knocked down and stowed when the space was needed for cargo.

"It will not be luxurious accommodations," Jane pointed out, "but we can make the cabins cozy and bright with a lick of paint and some chintz. Seeing as the captain is a woman, I thought to cater to the needs of ladies traveling on their own. I might function as the unofficial chaperone, as it were."

"Huh," was the carpenter's reply as he continued to study the designs. He took up a pencil and began busily making notes in the margins of the drawings while muttering to himself about board feet and fittings. Leaving him to work out the details of the job, Jane returned to the saloon to consult with her mates and Endeavor about the day's business.

"We're off to Baltimore on Friday," Jane announced as she seated herself at the table, "and I aim to make this voyage pay right the way along. We did well with our sales on Saturday and have cleared much of the hold. Let us continue as we have begun, gentlemen. Our first item of the day is to visit the Herald offices and let Mister Sykes know that passage aboard the modern schooner *Destiny* is available for ladies or couples wishing to travel to Baltimore this week. I'll pay that call myself."

Nods from the other three around the table showed they agreed.

"Mister Dawkins. Take yourself down to McAndrews this

morning and consult with him about finding an acceptable load to fill the rest of the hold. Koopmans can tell you how much room we will have once the cabins are built. Surely there is something we can find to help pay the way to Maryland."

"If thee have no need of me this morning," Endeavor said, "I shall be nosing about the waterfront and attempting to catch a whiff of Albright's scent."

"Aye, that is a good plan," Jane agreed. "I note this morning that the *Osprey* is still conspicuous in her absence. Perhaps someone can tell us more about her prior comings and goings."

"Thee might have a word with Friend Sykes on that subject too," Endeavor suggested. "Surely he has his ear to the ground and must know more of what happens in this town than most of its inhabitants."

Within the hour, Jane was on her way to see Mister Sykes at the newspaper. As she rounded the corner onto the street where the Herald's office lay, she nearly collided with Captain McKnight.

"Ahoy, miss. Captain. Ma'am. Oh blast, whatever it is ye' like to be called," he growled. "Was on my way to send a word of thanks to ye'. The magistrate has just laid down the case and awarded me the *El Almirante* as a prize. We are off to float her on the high tide and bring her into port. 'Twas your word that did the trick and I am most grateful for your assistance Captain Thorn."

"My pleasure, Captain McKnight and no more than should be expected of any mariner who knows his duty, sir."

"There are many who would have turned tail and run, mark my words. Not everyone wants to run afoul of the miscreants who make it their business to smuggle slaves and other contraband up the Bay. Captain Carvalho will have powerful friends who won't take kindly to the loss of his ship."

"Be that as it may, we could hardly stand aside and watch your crew drown. Have you heard anything more about the renegade captain and his men?"

"It appears they got away. The search party picked up their

trail, but it led back to the shore five miles south of here, where it seems they were taken aboard a vessel. We have no hope of finding them now, and the scum are most certainly on their way home to Portugal."

"Any news of the captives they had aboard?"

"Nay, and my crew will be out the bounty unless we find them. At twenty-five dollars for each African, the men are quite eager to trace them, Captain. We'll do our best."

Jane bid the captain good day and watched his back as he lumbered down the street toward the wharf. She felt troubled by the smoke of lies and criminality that seemed to permeate the atmosphere on the Bay. Where in all of this did the missing Captain Albright fit? For she was as sure as she was standing there, the *Osprey*'s master was up to no good. She was more anxious than ever to make contact with the man and find answers to her questions. She could only hope that he would make an appearance soon.

A bell jangled above the door as Jane stepped into the newspaper office, startling her so that she jumped. Annoyed with herself for being so flighty, she slammed the door closed harder than she had intended and turned with a frown toward the long bench at the center of the room. Perched on a high stool behind it, Mister Sykes was busy dropping lead slugs into a wooden frame with a pair of pincers gripped in his ink-stained fingers. He looked up quickly as Jane approached, then turned his attention back to his work as he greeted her.

"A fine day, Captain Thorn. To what do I owe the pleasure of your visit?"

"A notice for your publication, Mister Sykes, if you please. Is that this morning's edition you are assembling there?"

"Indeed it is, Captain. You are just in the nick of time if you wish to have your notice included today." Sykes set down his tool and pulled off his spectacles as climbed down from the stool.

"Have you the notice written out?"

"Here it is, although you might take a glance at it in case the wording could be improved. I wish to make it clear that the

Destiny offers safe passage for ladies traveling on their own to Baltimore without emphasizing that the captain is also a woman."

Sykes glanced up at her from the paper in his hand then fished out a pencil from the pocket of his printer's smock. With a few swift strokes and scribbled words, he edited the notice and handed it back to Jane.

"There, that should do it. A penny a line per day to run it for four days. Paid in advance."

As Jane pulled the coins from her pocket, she asked for news of the *El Almirante*.

"The garrison still has scouts out," Sykes said, "but no one expects to find them. Looks like they made a clean escape."

"I understand the people in the hold have not been found?"

"No, and not bleeding likely they will be, if you pardon the expression, ma'am. Too many rivers to run up into on the Bay where they could be brought ashore and no one the wiser."

"Can they be traced from the other end? If the buyers could be located, they could answer for the smuggling."

Sykes smiled sadly at her as he replied, "Not likely, Captain. There are few around here with the interest or the will to enforce the trafficking laws. The magistrate's puffery notwithstanding, most officials will turn a blind eye to the smugglers either because they disagree with the law or they are looking to make a profit from the awful business in some way. Bribes can turn a good man bad very quickly, Captain Thorn."

"And make a bad man worse," she countered, as an image of Albright rose in her mind. "Perhaps you may have heard rumors about one of our own men, Mister Sykes. A Captain Albright, who sails for Thorn Shipping on the schooner *Osprey*."

Caution came into the newspaper man's face as he gave Jane his full attention. "Ah, I think perhaps we have come to the real reason for your visit today, Captain Thorn. Please, step into my office."

Closing the door behind them, Sykes lit a lamp to dispel some of the gloom and pulled out a cigar from the top drawer of a large oak desk. Before he could light it, he threw it back into the drawer with a sigh.

"Dirty habit that, and I promised the missus I would quit. Calms my nerves though."

Sykes waved Jane into a chair across from him, then sat down behind the desk. From a large stack of papers on a table to his left, he pulled a roll of documents tied with twine and marked "Vessel Movements" in a large, spidery hand.

"I make it my business to know what is happening in the Roads, Captain. My morning stroll takes me past the docks and the customs house. I make note of the vessels that come and go. Sometimes, something seems a little off, and I am nosy by nature. So when your Captain Albright put into port more often than he should have were he hauling goods to New York and back, I sat up and took notice."

Passing the roll of papers to Jane, Sykes continued. "Go on, have a look. I've marked the arrivals and departures of the *Osprey* so you can see her pattern."

Jane smoothed out the papers on the desktop and bent to look them over. It took a few minutes to see it, but eventually the dates next to the entries marked *Osprey*/Thorn swam into focus.

"He's been arriving in port every two weeks, more or less, all summer long," Jane exclaimed. "Where the devil does he go in between? And why does he put in here?"

"As for the first, I have no idea. Not far, I would say. Certainly somewhere on or near the Bay. As for the second, the answer is 'provisions.' Miller's has been supplying his schooner with basic foodstuffs and corn in large quantities while Albright has gone about his business, whatever it is."

Is he smuggling grain and produce under the guise of crew provisions, Jane wondered? Or perhaps he was picking up more than corn from the Miller establishment. Whatever it was, these vessel records would be a vital clue for Endeavor as he sought to unravel the mystery of the *Osprey*'s voyages.

"May I borrow these, Mister Sykes? I should like to make a copy of them to look over more carefully."

"My pleasure, Captain Thorn. On the agreement that you will share with me any information that might prove pertinent to my own investigations."

"Agreed, although I hardly think we are likely to uncover anything of interest, Mister Sykes. Thank you though, and I shall send someone to return these today."

Jane gathered up the papers from the desk and shoved them into the worn canvas holdall she carried. Shaking hands with Mister Sykes, she turned and left the office and its clanging bell with a thoughtful air.

Back aboard the *Destiny* after her errands in town were complete, Jane laid out the scrolls for Endeavor and shared Mister Sykes' information with him.

"Miller's." Endeavor pulled at his ear and frowned down at Jane. "We placed our own order there, but they said nary a word about us being the second Thorn vessel they supplied."

"I hardly know what to make of it, truth be told," Jane said. "It seems every answer leads only to more questions, and all of them lead straight back to Captain Albright. Oh, where is the confounded man?"

"Until we know for certain, we should assume that he has encountered difficulties. We must notify the authorities and thine uncle that the vessel is missing, last sighted in New York. We cannot delay any longer."

"No, I don't suppose…"

Jane was interrupted by a shout from above that brought her and Endeavor topsides at a run. Standing in to the Roads from the north was a schooner flying the Thorn pennant, her name picked out in gold on the bow.

"It's the *Osprey*, ma'am." Dawkins' voice was quiet as he stood at the rail watching the missing vessel as she hove to and boarded the pilot.

"That it is, Mister Dawkins, and glad I am to see her."

X
A Mystery Deepens

Norfolk, Virginia
April 23, 1821

Jane ran her eyes over the *Osprey* as she stood on the dock watching the schooner approach. She could see no evidence of damage that would explain Captain Albright's delayed arrival and grew increasingly angry as the vessel dropped her sails to glide into the harbor. On the quarterdeck, Jane could see the rotund little captain as he shouted instructions to his crew who jumped to obey his orders. Clearly, George Albright was a master who expected obedience from his men.

At her side, Endeavor stood calmly as Jane waited for the vessel to be secured to the wharf and for the harbormaster to go aboard with the Collector. Fidgeting impatiently, she watched the captain as he marched about the deck, pointedly ignoring her presence at dockside. Eventually the business of clearing into Norfolk was complete and the captain had little choice but to acknowledge the representatives of his employer.

Standing at the rail midships with his feet spread wide and his arms crossed, Captain Albright scowled down at Jane and her husband, waiting for them to speak first. Behind him, a short man whose rigid demeanor and polished uniform marked him as the *Osprey*'s chief mate, stood with a frown on his face as he listened to the ensuing conversation.

"Permission to come aboard, Captain Albright," Jane began.

"Nay, permission is not granted, Captain Thorn," Albright replied with a sneer, then stared silently down at her again.

"Perhaps you would care to join us here on the dock then, Captain Albright," Jane tried again.

"Perhaps I would not, Captain Thorn. If you have no further suggestions, I plan to be about my business," he said as he started to turn away.

"About Thorn business, you mean," Jane called to his back.

"Aye, about Thorn business, though it is no concern of yours miss," he replied over his shoulder and disappeared down the companionway with Chief Mate Markham hard on his heels.

"Thee look rather like a fish at the moment, my dear," Endeavor whispered in an attempt to lighten the moment. Indeed, Jane could feel that her jaw was wagging up and down as she struggled to draw breath in the face of such hostility.

"Heard you that?" she exclaimed in a low voice. "The impudent bastard."

"Aye, it was not politely done, but the man has the right to say who comes aboard, Thorn captains and all. I suspect there is more to the story than mere bad manners, however. Come, let us return to the *Destiny* and think on the matter," Endeavor suggested.

Back aboard her own vessel, Jane let loose a tirade that made clear to her listeners her opinion of the character and unsavory origins of the *Osprey*'s master. By the time she wound down, her husband and the two ship's mates were left in no doubt that Captain Albright's days as an employee of the family firm were numbered.

"Endeavor, please draft a letter to Captain Josias detailing the state of affairs here. It is high time we alerted him to the questions that have arisen, and our suspicions of the man."

"Ma'am, I certainly agree with the need for the Captain to be made aware of the situation but do we really have much to go on?" Dawkins asked. "After all, he is but two days late and may well have a perfectly acceptable explanation for the delay which he simply refuses to share with you. In point of fact, we have nothing more than a short absence and Sykes' record of unusual activity to add to his logbooks, which were not falsified but simply poorly kept. The man has been clever in committing no outright crime."

"Aye, perhaps it is better to wait and see what he does here in Norfolk before we report to thine uncle," Endeavor agreed. "Galsworthy here might pick up some gossip from the crew when they come ashore."

Frustrated, Jane stared around the saloon at the watching men. She knew they were right, but it galled her to think Albright would be free to make continued use of Thorn company assets for his own hidden purposes as she stood helplessly by.

"So be it. Galsworthy, detail the men to follow Albright every time he comes ashore. I want to know where he goes and whom he makes contact with here in Norfolk. He is not to know that he is being watched, though he may suspect it now that he knows I have the cut of his jib," Jane said. "Endeavor, let us send word to my uncle that the *Osprey* has arrived in port with no explanation as to the delay and no success in conversing with her captain. Pray inform him of what you have discovered with regard to the logs and that we intend to investigate his activities further as we put into ports around the Bay. For now, we will hold our suspicions to ourselves until we can put facts to theories."

With a quick touch of his cap, the second mate ducked out the door of the saloon to set about organizing a clandestine watch on the *Osprey*, while Dawkins excused himself to return to the warehouses and continue his search for goods to carry to Baltimore and New York.

"I shall have just enough time to dash off a message before we are expected at our afternoon social calls," Endeavor reminded Jane.

"Perhaps we can make good use of the time, and nose about to hear any news of Albright among the good citizens of Norfolk," she replied.

"It will be most interesting to watch thee play the bloodhound, my dear," Endeavor smiled back.

The day's first call was at the home of the mayor and his wife. Mister and Mistress John Holt lived in a splendid mansion above the main street of the town, from which they reigned over Norfolk society. A perennial candidate for the city's top office, Mayor Holt was nonetheless barred by law from serving more than one term at a time, he explained to his guests as they sipped tea on the veranda behind the house.

"Lord knows what they were thinking," he smiled, "but I am too clever by half to be held back by such narrow-minded legislation. I simply put forward one of my associates to run for office when my time is up. He resigns after two or three days, and back we go for another election, which I always win."

Astonished to hear of such goings-on in a backwater like Norfolk, Jane could not help but laugh. "It sounds to me like you Virginians have taken a page from our own New York politicians," she remarked, thinking of the decades of Tammany Hall scandal that had rocked her native state all the way to the governor.

"Or perhaps they have learned from us," Holt smirked.

"No doubt. A man with strong ideas and a loose interpretation of the law would appear to have a fair chance of making a success of things here on the Tidewater." Jane delivered this rather incendiary remark with a sweet smile and a lowering of her eyelashes.

Holt looked taken aback for a moment as he worked out whether he had been handed an insult by the captain, and then threw back his head to laugh out loud. Turning to Endeavor, he remarked, "That is a right handful of a wife you have there, Mister Coffin. Mind you keep her in check lest you find yourself no longer the master of your own ship."

"Ah, thank thee for thy concern, Friend Holt. I find my wife both perceptive and clever, however, and am well assured that our ship runs true to course as we steer it together," Endeavor answered with a wink to Jane.

The couple concluded their visit a short while later and were soon walking down Main Street toward their next port of call.

"What did you make of him?" Jane asked as they paused to search out the next calling card on their list.

"That thee had best be careful lest thee gain an enemy in high office," her husband replied.

"Aye, he seems a rum one, and you are probably right to caution me. Mark my words, I will not be at all surprised to find him mixed up in whatever unsavory business Albright has gotten into."

The rest of the afternoon's round of visits was soon accomplished with Jane none the wiser with regard to the *Osprey*'s doings over the past two years. Introduced casually into the conversation as another of her family's interests in the Chesapeake, no one seemed to have heard of the vessel or its ill-tempered captain. Clearly, Albright had made no attempt to ingratiate himself with the local society. Despite her failure to elicit any information about the schooner's doings, Jane was nonetheless well pleased with the day's work. She had gently promoted the new cabins aboard her vessel bound for Baltimore, and was lucky enough to have found passengers to fill three of them. When they returned to the *Destiny* at suppertime, Dawkins was eager to relate that the fourth cabin had been booked as well and Jane poured a glass of port for herself and her officers to celebrate.

Over dinner, Galsworthy reported that Captain Albright had left the *Osprey* in the late afternoon to visit Miller's store. He was overheard by O'Reilly, who had been detailed to follow him, as he ordered a large quantity of corn to be delivered aboard first thing in the morning.

"It appears he is in a hurry to shift loads as he then called on McAndrews and demanded that his cargo be offloaded immediately into a warehouse. The agent was most reluctant to comply as the warehouses are full and space is dear, but Albright was adamant. O'Reilly reports that the *Osprey*'s cargo is being unloaded this evening, ma'am. I sent him to watch."

Before they had finished the meal, O'Reilly returned and was shown into the saloon.

"Well, man, what have you to say?" Galsworthy demanded.

"Ma'am," O'Reilly said, with a tip of his hat to the captain, "it would appear the *Osprey* has mislaid some of her load. Either that, or she left New York light, though it puzzles me as to why she might have done that."

"What do you mean?" Jane asked with a frown.

"Just that it took but a half hour to empty the hold ma'am, and there was but three horse carts needed to carry it away."

Jane thanked him for his good work and sent O'Reilly to the cook for a belated evening meal.

"What do you think, gentlemen?" she asked as she returned to the table.

"He has offloaded elsewhere, as I know for certain she was fully loaded when the *Osprey* left New York," Galsworthy replied. "We were made to wait while Peterson's men finished her lading and they were about it for many hours. She was well filled when she left, I swear it, ma'am."

"Very well, we have an explanation for where she has been these two days," Jane said. "Ridding herself of the cargo to take on corn. Now we have but to figure out why. What was she carrying?"

"Flour and nails," Endeavor said. "Easy enough to sell anywhere, although he was expected to bring the load to Norfolk before picking up tobacco and other goods for New York."

The remainder of Jane's evening was spent transcribing the vessel movement documents she had obtained from Mister Sykes. Working together, she and Endeavor were able to create a chart of the arrival and departure dates of the *Osprey* at the Hampton Roads. Pulling out his transcriptions of the *Osprey*'s logs, Endeavor then added the cargo information to their notes. Soon a pattern emerged. Twice a month from May through September, the *Osprey* would arrive in Norfolk with a small load of goods for sale, after which she would take on a nearly full load of grain stores before leaving again for one or another of several small towns along the southern shore of the Bay.

"Look thee here," Endeavor said as he pointed to yet another document he had been working on earlier in the day. "I have begun to plot his voyages on this map, along with the dates indicated in the log for his arrival. In nearly every case, the time reported to make the transit is one or two days longer than would be strictly needed. If he consents to talk with us, I would like to question him on that. How is it that his ship is so slow? Or where does he go on his way there?"

"And what does he do with all that grain?" Jane wondered as she finally blew out the lantern in the saloon for the night, and banked the small fire in the stove to stave off the damp Bay air that seeped down the companionway.

XI
A Hurried Leavetaking

Norfolk, Virginia
April 24, 1821

Jane leaned on the rail watching the sun rise over the hills to the east. The flat land of the Tidewater lay open in every direction and it was sometimes hard to see where land became sky. The breeze that set the marsh grasses along the shore swaying blew away the sharp tang of the sewer that emptied into the harbor and Jane filled her lungs with the scent of the sea. A troubled night's sleep had driven the captain from the warm cocoon of her husband's embrace to wander the deck in the pre-dawn quiet. Now, she sought distraction in conversation with Silas, who had come off watch and was drinking a cup of coffee before heading below.

"What do you make of the voyage so far Mister Baldwin?"

With a shake of his head, Silas cast a troubled look over at the *Osprey* where she lay moored further down the wharf. "The trip is to my liking right enough, Captain. But something is amiss with the *Osprey*, ma'am. There were folks coming and going all night long, and it seemed they were keeping as quiet as they could so as not to be heard. What is going on over there, Auntie Jinks? Is it trouble for Thorn Shipping?"

"You're a smart lad, Silas. I don't know and that's the truth of it. But we aim to find out, rest assured. Good man for keeping your eyes open. Let me know if you see anything else that troubles you, aye?"

"Aye, aye, ma'am, that I shall. I don't like people playing fast and loose with our family's property."

Jane smiled at his eager tone and reflected that the company would be in good hands as the next generation of Thorns came of age. "And how do you like being away from home for so long?"

Silas paused a moment before answering. "Well, I miss my

friends."

"Any particular friend?"

Silas looked sideways at her then turned back to look out over the rail, blushing as he hid his face in the coffee cup.

"Ah, as I suspected. From what I hear, she is missing you as well and will be pleased to see you return safe and sound. And with coin in your pockets to boot," Jane observed with a grin. It was not so many years ago that she herself had pined for a young man who seemed not to know that she hoped to be more than just friends.

The *Destiny* came to life over the next hour as the crew mustered for morning call and breakfast. The deckhands were busy with daily chores while Koopmans oversaw the delivery of wood and nails for the new partitions and the sounds of sawing and hammering soon rose from the open hold. As Jane stood by the hatch to watch the progress, she glanced up to see a sight that sent her running to the open companionway, shouting for Dawkins and Endeavor.

"Look there! The *Osprey* has cast off and is making for the Roads! She'll be looking to catch the early tide. Blast the man, where is he going?" Jane shouted in frustration.

The crew of the *Destiny* could do nothing but stand and stare as the schooner hoisted her sails and sped out of the harbor with the morning breeze behind her.

"Koopmans! Koopmans!"

The carpenter's sawdust-covered head popped up out of the hatch. "Aye, ma'am?"

"How quickly can we be underway? Can you finish the cabins today?"

"No, ma'am, not with all the will in the world. It will be two days' hard labor and that's without the furnishings. No, we'll not be ready for our passengers before Thursday."

Furious, Jane marched to the quarterdeck to cool down and ponder her next move. Dawkins and Endeavor, who had followed their captain aft, stood silently awaiting her orders.

"Mister Dawkins, we must follow as closely behind Mister

Albright as we can. I must know what he is up to, and where he is going. Unless he can prove his honesty and allegiance, I aim to relieve him of his command as soon as I can catch him ashore. Do what you must to have the *Destiny* ready to sail by tomorrow night. We will look to catch the morning tide Thursday. Please see to it that Mister Koopmans is given all needed assistance to complete his work in time."

"Aye, aye, ma'am." Dawkins turned sharply on his heel, calling the ships' boys to him as he made smartly for the companionway.

"Endeavor, would you send word to our passengers that they must report aboard no later than seven in the morning in two days' time? Please make it clear that we sail with the tide whether they are aboard or no."

Over the following days, Galsworthy and Koopmans drove the crew hard to complete the construction of the new cabins and load the remaining cargo into the hold. Dawkins had come upon a warehouse filled with fine mahogany logs from Florida destined for the construction of a great mansion in Baltimore. The owner had gone bankrupt, leaving the timber unclaimed at the wharf. Jane was pleased with the purchase and knew it would fetch a good price in Baltimore, or even New York.

Lower Chesapeake Bay
April 26, 1821

Thursday, April 26, 1821   Passed Old Point Comfort Light at just after noon from which I take my departure. Lat. 37° 00' N Long. 76° 18' W. Good sailing cond. P'gers settled, crew adapting to new routine. No sign of Osprey.

As she stood on the quarterdeck next to the harbor pilot early on Thursday morning, Jane was satisfied that her hold was filled with valuable cargo and paying passengers that would all but guarantee a profitable voyage to Maryland. Despite her frustration with the elusive Captain Albright, she was pleased with the success of the trading voyage thus far.

The only sour note during the visit to Norfolk had occurred at the musicale on Tuesday evening. As Jane and Endeavor left the hall in the company of their new friends the Williamses, a drunk patron accosted them, blocking their passage to the exit.

"It's the captain and her fancy man, I'll warrant," he slurred as he struggled to hold himself upright. "Come to stick your nose in our business, eh? Well you can just take yourself back off to where you came from up north. We don't need your interference in our matters down here. Your Captain Albright knows better, he does," the man shouted.

"All right, Weston, you've said enough." Mr Williams, chided. Stepping forward to steer the man away, he bent down to whisper in Weston's ear. The man snickered in reply and threw a nasty sneer toward Jane then staggered out to his waiting carriage. When questioned by Jane as to what Weston meant, Williams merely shrugged his shoulders and begged that they forget the incident.

Now, as she watched the dock slide away astern, Jane vowed to uncover whatever dirty business Albright had been conducting behind their backs, and to haul him up before the magistrate if any of his doings had broken the law.

By the noon bell, the *Destiny* had made good time out into the Bay and was sailing strongly before a freshening breeze from the east. The morning mists had cleared, and Griggs had predicted they would have clear skies for the remainder of the day, which the steady barometer reading confirmed. As they passed the lighthouse at Old Point Comfort, Jane ordered all sails raised and the topsails shaken out, while lookouts were posted to find and identify any vessels they passed in the faint hope they might locate the *Osprey*. Jane's plan was to make toward Baltimore at the north end of the Bay and unload cargo and passengers in all haste so they could point the *Destiny* south to scour the shores of the Bay in search of Captain Albright and his command.

The fine weather and brisk wind provided a thrilling ride up the Bay. In all directions, the sparkling waters of the Chesapeake stretched to low-lying shores covered in deep green forest. With no hills to interrupt its passage, the ocean breeze blew in a steady line that filled the *Destiny's* sails and heeled her onto her starboard beam as she crossed the wide expanse of the lower Bay. The schooner seemed to revel in the favorable conditions and kicked up her heels as she skimmed through the waves. The passengers, three middle-aged sisters returning to their home in Baltimore after an extended visit with relatives in Virginia, and a young couple on their marriage tour, petitioned the captain to have their luncheon served on deck so they could enjoy the fine weather, much to the consternation of the ship's cook.

"You shall just have to make the best of it," Jane declared when confronted by an irate Cookie. "We want to keep our guests in good humor. And if that means cold meats on the larboard deck, so be it. Get Koopmans to lash a table to the rail."

In short order, Cookie had Singleton and Hitchens scurrying to set up dining accommodations on deck. Jane watched bemused as they struggled to keep the chairs and table settings from pitching over as the schooner heeled. Her only hope was that the guests would finish their meal before they needed to tack to stay on course. She smiled as she watched Singleton attempt to maintain his dignity as he crab-walked from the galley with a loaded tray. They had much to learn yet about the passenger business.

By nightfall, the *Destiny* made Tangier Island and dropped anchor in the shallow waters off the western shore. The island was barely discernible in the dusk as it rose but a few dozen feet above the water, and Jane wondered how long it would be before the whole thing blew away in a spring storm. Watermen soon rowed out to meet them in square-ended boats, offering fresh oysters and handwoven baskets for sale. Cookie's efforts at the stove that night were rewarded with a round of applause from the appreciative diners in the saloon, which went a great way toward soothing his ruffled feathers.

Before retiring for the night, Jane left strict orders with her second mate that she was to be roused when the tide turned in the morning. "We'll make way as soon as she swings to the north, Mister Galsworthy. The glass is falling and I don't care to be caught on the shoals should it turn out to be a real growler on its way in. I want to be well in the deep channel should we need sea room to keep our course."

Galsworthy, with a tip of his hat to the captain, marched off to locate the larboard watch leader. Soon, the lanterns were extinguished and the quiet tramping of the watch was the only sound that disturbed the peace of the moonlit night.

XII
Strangers in Our Midst

Chesapeake Bay off Tangier Island
April 27, 1821

Friday, April 27, 1821   Strong squalls in the a.m. followed by fresh breezes, choppy cond. Lat. 38° 37' N Long. 76° 20' W. Unexpected discovery in cargo bay. No sign of Osprey.

Shortly before dawn, Jane was roused by a gentle knock at the cabin door. Cookie, bless his soul, had arrived with hot coffee and breakfast. Stuffing most of a warm biscuit into her mouth, Jane rushed to dress in warm clothes, taking care not to waken Endeavor. As she lifted her oilskins from the hook on her way aloft, she paused to smile at her husband where he lay sprawled across the berth. Had she been the praying sort, she would have thanked her Maker every day for the blessings their union had brought her.

Hurrying now to join her mates on the quarterdeck, Jane threw a hasty eye toward the barometer as she climbed the companionway. The pressure had fallen further overnight and she knew they were in for a blow.

"Mister Dawkins, have Mister Baldwin alert our passengers to stow their gear and be prepared to stay below this morning. Inform Cookie that breakfast must needs be only what can be held in the hand. I want no spills in the saloon today."

Jane turned to scan the horizon, studying the clouds lit from below as the sun slowly rose in the east. To the north and west, banks of dark thunderheads were rolling in and she could see curtains of rain slanting down to obscure the view of the Virginia shore. The weather would soon be upon them and she buttoned her slicker tighter around her neck with a shiver. These Chesapeake storms were notorious for driving vessels onto the shallow bottom and Jane had no intention of becoming one of the Bay's many shipwrecks.

"Mister Dawkins, let us weigh anchor with all due speed. I should like to meet this gale with room to manoeuvre. Have the crew check the hatches and prepare the deck for weather."

Jane stood with her back to the helm as the men sprang into action, running to stow the extra sails below and lashing down the boats. Within minutes, the *Destiny* was ready for action and the crew wrapped in oilskins and boots. No sooner had the captain pulled her own hat down over her ears than the storm enveloped them with howling winds and driving rain. Waves rose around them in choppy peaks as the northward current of the incoming tide battled with the driving winds from the northwest. Leaving the crew to maintain course on a port tack, the captain hurried across the heaving deck and ducked below to check on her guests. She found them huddled around the stove in the saloon, rubbing their hands by the dying embers to keep warm as they sipped hot coffee from tall tankards. To her surprise, they greeted her cheerfully.

"It is a fine morning for sailing, Captain Thorn," Miss Evans, the eldest of the traveling sisters, called out with a laugh.

"Indeed, if one does not mind a little excitement," Jane replied. "Now, I am glad to see you all smiling. I assure you that the *Destiny* is quite up to the task of bringing us through the weather to our evening's anchorage. However, please remain here in the saloon while we are underway today as we will need to keep the deck clear."

"Aye, ma'am, we are well prepared with amusements as my sister Anne has brought her divination cards with her. She will be pleased to provide readings from the ancient art of the tarot for everyone this morning. Captain, would you care to be first?"

"Ah, I fear I must decline as I am needed above but do carry on. Just a word of caution, however. Should the waves pick up further, you may find it more comfortable to retire to your berths for a while, at least until the storm blows out. You will find buckets stowed under your bunks in the event you find the movement difficult for your digestion."

Leaving the passengers to their meager breakfasts, Jane passed through the far door into her private cabin. There, she found Endeavor perched at the desk, his arm splayed over the logbooks as he held a kerchief to his lips. He looked up as Jane closed the door, then promptly leaned over to deposit the contents of his stomach into the pot he held between his feet. With a moan, he righted himself again and smiled wanly.

Jane put her hand on his shoulder with a gentle pat. "And how fare you, my husband?"

"*Oh, that I had wings like a dove, for then would I fly away, and be at rest. Lo, then would I wander far off, and remain in the wilderness. I would hasten my escape from the windy storm and tempest.*"

"Ah, and does the Good Book suggest an alternative for the earthbound?"

"Unless, like the Master, thee can rebuke the wind and calm the raging of the water, I fear we are doomed to cling to our raft as it is tossed by the tempest and hope for the best." Upon which pronouncement, Endeavor renewed retching into the bucket at his feet.

"I would counsel you to come out into the open air, my dear, should you find the strength to do so. You may indeed need to lash yourself to the rail as you once threatened to do, but you will find the deck more congenial for your stomach."

With a last tender smile at the poor man, Jane mounted the aft ladder to the quarterdeck, taking care to leave a crack in the hatch to provide much-needed fresh air to the fetid cabin. She hoped Endeavor would soon find his sea legs, for she feared that many more bouts of upset would render him unwilling to follow her aboard on future voyages. Jane was at a loss to know what they should do in that case.

Luck was with the *Destiny* and the storm blew past by the end of the morning watch. As the sun peeked out through broken clouds, the wind swung around to the southeast and pushed the schooner from behind. The tide had turned too and was running south to the sea into the face of the breeze again, creating choppy waters that bounced the vessel from side to side. Jane hoped the passengers would not be too put out that luncheon was a simple meal of cold meats and sliced bread. It would be this evening, once they had safely anchored in a calm cove, before Cookie could fire up the galley stove and provide hot victuals for everyone aboard.

Jane swept her gaze around the rigging and deck. She was pleased to see everything well battened down with the lines properly hung on their pegs and the boats tightly tarped. The captain demanded order and neatness even, or perhaps most importantly, during foul weather, when the slippery deck heaved and threatened to pitch unwary sailors over the rail. A loose barrel or neglected rope could spell death for anyone unlucky enough to be struck by it in a raging storm.

As she cast her eyes forward, she was surprised to see Endeavor emerge from the forward hatch and stagger his way toward her. She was doubly surprised when she saw Mister Singleton emerge behind him, then follow Endeavor aft to stand at the foot of the ladder.

"Captain Thorn, permission to speak on a delicate matter, if thee have a moment."

"Of course, Mister Coffin. Join me on the quarterdeck," Jane called down to him with a frown.

"With all due respect, Captain, perhaps the saloon might be preferred." Endeavor's calm voice and bland demeanor gave no hint as to the issue at hand, but Mister Singleton's downcast mien and sloped shoulders indicated trouble might be brewing. Crew discipline was the responsibility of her officers, and she called to Mister Dawkins.

"Send the passengers to their cabins, Mister Dawkins, with instructions that they will be served their meals there for their comfort. Then sort out whatever the devil is going on here and send Baldwin to make arrangements with Cookie."

Jane watched as Dawkins followed Endeavor and Singleton down the companionway ladder, then returned to watching the horizon for signs of a storm.

A short while later, she was surprised to see Mister Dawkins emerge from the forward hatch. What mysterious circumstances were taking everyone to the cargo hold today? There was nothing more interesting stowed under the fore hatches than several tons of sawn planks.

Dawkins stalked aft and climbed to the quarterdeck. "Ma'am, would you be so good as to join us in the saloon?"

Jane opened her mouth to ask what in tarnation was afoot but held her tongue when the chief gave a small shake of his head and a meaningful glance at the sailor holding the wheel. Instead, she nodded in reply and turned toward the ladder.

As Jane swung open the door of the saloon, the *Destiny* swooped to leeward, sending her flying into the room to sprawl across the table. Dawkins leaped to catch the door before it could swing back to catch her from behind, then closed it firmly as he started to speak.

"It would appear we have stowaways, Captain."

Jane's thoughts flew immediately to her last trading voyage, where one of her crew had smuggled illicit cargo aboard without her knowledge, but this was far more serious a concern. She suspected that her hidden passengers were not simply desperate travelers without the means to pay their passage.

"Go on," she demanded.

"It would appear that Seaman Singleton has been the means by which certain individuals, whose ownership is claimed by a planter in Georgia, have attempted to escape to freedom, ma'am. They are…"

Jane's anger mounted, becoming white fury as she ordered the mate, "Show me. Now. Mister Singleton, you are to remain here with Mister Coffin. Consider yourself in custody."

She quickly followed Dawkins's bent back through the narrow walkways of the forward hold until they came upon a family crouched in a small chamber that had been left between the furthest stack of lumber and the forward bulkhead. The heaving of the vessel had upended the buckets which they had been using for their privy, and the contents were now liberally dispersed about the cramped space. Two children, whimpering in fear, hid their faces as their parents sought to shield them from view. Gently, Jane knelt and beckoned them forth, then led the way silently back to the cabin with the stowaways behind her and Dawkins bringing up the rear. By the time they were assembled in the saloon, Jane had cooled enough to consider her next course of action.

"Mister Dawkins, please deliver Seaman Singleton to Mister Galsworthy with instructions that he is to be kept under watch until called for. Mister Coffin, be good enough to explain what has transpired aboard my vessel."

In short order, Endeavor related how he came across the family, whose name was Calloway, when he visited the hold to check the condition of the cargo in the wake of the storm. He heard the younger child, who could be no more than three or four, crying softly in fear. He soon discovered their place of concealment, and which of their crew had made the arrangements for their clandestine trip aboard the *Destiny*.

Jane shuddered as she listened, struck by how the miserable conditions of their passage, however brief, echoed the plight of those aboard the slave ship they had recently encountered. Was there no end to the suffering? And to think that they had been brought to this by one of their own.

She turned to Mister Dawkins, who had returned from his errand, and instructed him to have hot water and towels brought so the family might clean themselves. "And show them to my cabin, Dawkins. They shall at least be able to put themselves to rights."

"Captain, thank you, ma'am," Mister Calloway said as he stepped forward now and held out his hand. "We are mighty grateful for your hospitality, and I did mean to pay our way."

Jane looked down at the bundle of banknotes clutched in the man's hand. "Why did you not simply purchase tickets, then? It would appear you have the means."

"And would you not have asked why we were in such a hurry to leave, or whether we were, in fact, free to do so? Had you knowingly sailed with fugitives aboard, you would have been stopped and charged under the laws of Virginia with assisting in the theft of property. Most captains will not take such a risk."

"Indeed, Mister Calloway, you are quite right in that." Jane paused as she felt the discomfort of realizing that she may well have left the desperate family ashore had she been asked to assist in their flight. However, since they were aboard, she would make the best of things. "We will discuss this further, but for now I hope that you and your children will be comfortable in my quarters."

Turning to Mistress Calloway, a tall woman in a dark gown holding her children behind her skirts, Jane extended her hand. "I am sorry you have been put in this position, ma'am. I am Jane Thorn and am pleased to make your acquaintance. Please accept my apologies for your treatment aboard my vessel."

"Bess Calloway, and you have my thanks Captain. We have been many days on the road and these trials are but minor concerns should we finally make our way to safety."

Leaving orders with Dawkins that the family was to be made comfortable and fed, Jane climbed to the deck and set to pacing the starboard rail. Eventually, finding no relief for the turmoil in her mind, she mounted to the quarterdeck and joined Endeavor where he stood at the taffrail. The wind had calmed and the blue waters of the Bay were now sparkling in the afternoon sun. Endeavor appeared much improved from his morning's distress, but his brow was furled in concern as he watched her approach. Jane leaned her back against the low rail, shoulder to shoulder with her husband, who waited quietly for her to speak first.

"He must be disciplined."

"Aye, I can understand that he must."

"Even though I think he was in the right, to want to help, to bring his fellow man out of bondage."

"Aye, I would agree that he was, in the eyes of the Lord."

"And in your eyes?" Jane looked up at Endeavor as she asked.

"I confess I would like to think I might be as brave and be willing to risk my livelihood and my life in the service of others."

"I cannot have my crew risking my vessel, my cargo, perhaps even our own freedom, however high-minded the intent."

"Nay, that thee cannot."

"He must go ashore, at any rate. I cannot keep him among the crew."

"Aye, that seems clear, albeit a harsh outcome. However, Friend Singleton knew the risk." Endeavor voice was sorrowful as he acknowledged the rightness of her decision.

"That he did and must face the consequences." Jane looked down. "Oh, how I hate this world where good men do wrong in the service of justice and I am forced to punish them for it. But I see no other way forward."

XIII
The Cost of Courage

Upper Chesapeake Bay
April 27, 1821

Later that afternoon, Jane opened the door to the saloon to find her chief mate at the table hard at work calculating their position and marking the charts.

"We have been put fairly off our course, ma'am," he informed the captain. "We are well south of where we reckoned to be this evening, and much to the east. I put our position at 38 degrees north and 76 degrees west. We have traversed a scant 24 miles this day."

With a shake of her head in frustration, Jane shifted around the chart to see where Dawkins held his finger off the shore of a large island.

"That must be Bloodsworth Island off our starboard beam. The chart shows small settlements here and here," Dawkins said as he pointed to two sheltered coves on the north shore.

"Oystermen, or I miss my guess," Jane observed. "Let us anchor off the closer one and if any of the inhabitants offer us their catch, a good dinner will go a long way towards making up for the discomforts of the day."

"Aye, ma'am, that it will."

Turning now to her husband, who had followed close on her heels, Jane beckoned him forward as she made to knock on her cabin door. She halted in surprise at the sound of children's laughter and heard someone singing a silly song in a falsetto voice. Marvelling at the resilient spirit of the young, Jane gently rapped her knuckles against the planks.

She nearly fell backward as the door was yanked open and a grinning Miss Evans threw out her arms.

"Captain Thorn, welcome to our fairy kingdom." With a lavish curtsey, she motioned to Jane and Endeavor to enter what had so recently been their humble accommodations. Now, the room was draped with colorful scarves and gaudy baubles hung from about the necks of the smiling children and adults.

"My goodness, what have you all been up to? And Miss Evans, however do you come to be here?"

"I heard the children when I went on deck and came to investigate. My sisters will tell you that I have a bad habit of pushing myself in where I am not invited. I hope you do not take it amiss that I have intruded here, dear Captain."

"You are clearly welcomed by the children, Miss Evans. What a lovely place you have made."

"We must take their minds off of their recent trials, Captain Thorn," she replied with a sorrowful frown. A second later, she broke into a radiant smile and turned to the girls who were spinning in circles to make themselves dizzy. "Come, it is time for you to put our playthings away while I visit with Captain Jane. Mister and Mistress Calloway, please excuse me."

With a gentle push, Miss Evans manoeuvred Jane and Endeavor back into the saloon before they could respond and then motioned to them to join her in the passageway outside. Jane was so taken aback by the whole affair that she followed the older woman obediently. However, once the door had been shut behind them, she demanded an explanation.

"I knew at once what they must be," Miss Evans replied, "as soon as I saw them and knew they had not come aboard with the other passengers. It is a dangerous mission you have taken upon yourself, Captain Thorn, though I applaud you for your courage."

"Nay, you misunderstand the situation. This is none of my doing although it is now my responsibility. May I first ask how many other passengers are aware of the Calloways' presence?"

"None at present. I did not see my sisters when I went to my cabin to fetch my things to entertain the children. I believe all of the passengers are on deck enjoying the sunshine after the storm today."

"It must remain so for the safety of everyone," Jane demanded.

"Yes, I agree. You see, my dear, I am a member of the Maryland Society for the Abolition of Slavery. My sisters and I are close acquaintances of Elisha Tyson and have provided help to many people who are escaping their masters. We send them to Friends in Philadelphia as the Georgia men have been known to snatch people off the Baltimore streets. What is your plan for the Calloways once we arrive?"

"I have no plan as I did not bring them aboard," Jane burst out. Catching herself, she continued, "But it is high time to make one. What can you tell us of the situation in Baltimore? Would you be able to help them on their way?"

"Most assuredly. But I am curious, if you did not bring them aboard, how did they come to be here?"

Jane paused to consider the implications of sharing such information with the well-meaning, but unknown, Miss Evans. For all Jane knew, she might not be who she was representing herself as. No, it was better to remain cautious until such time as the Calloways were safely out of danger.

"That is neither here nor there," Jane replied. "However, if you would be so kind as to guard the secret until we arrive, I shall see to it that they are sent ashore with enough resources for the next stage of their journey. Will you help them, ma'am?"

"That I will, Captain. Now please allow me to return to the Calloways and set their minds at ease."

As Miss Evans returned to the saloon, Jane climbed the companionway ladder deep in thought. Behind her, Endeavor held his peace as he waited for the captain to speak.

"We shall have to follow through, you know," Jane observed to Endeavor as they paced the rail. "We cannot leave them to their fate, nor turn them over to the authorities in Baltimore. If we are boarded here in Virginia, as we may yet be, we must hide them. I accept full responsibility for this decision and for the consequences should we be caught."

"Thee has the right of it, to my mind, my dear. And while the burden is thine to bear, know that I would willingly shoulder it if I could."

Jane smiled ruefully up at her tall husband. "Aye, but such is the price of command. The heavier burden is Mister Singleton. The captain seeks your advice, Mister Coffin. What would you do with the man in my place?"

"Put him ashore with the others. I see no other way."

"And what explanation to the crew?"

"Illness. Let us place him in Mister Galsworthy's quarters as sick bay. And let it be known that he has come down with the intermittent fever."

"A lie? I hardly thought you capable, Friend Coffin," Jane teased with a smile. "But it is a sound notion. Please ask Mister Dawkins to join me on the deck when you go below."

The *Destiny* was moored in a quiet cove on the north shore of the island. The air had cleared and the balmy temperatures drew everyone into the open where supper was served on deck. Moreover, Jane wished to keep the passengers clear of the saloon until she had settled her stowaways more securely for the remainder of the voyage. The schooner rocked gently at anchor in the night breeze as the passengers enjoyed a lively meal while the Calloway family silently followed Jane forward to the hold whence they had emerged that morning.

"I apologize deeply for the need to return you to your confinement," Jane said. "But we must keep your presence known to only a few. However, Mister Coffin will see to it that you are as comfortable as you can be."

Jane waved her hand to show the mats and bolsters that had been laid down in the cramped space in the hold where the family would continue their journey.

"We are grateful, ma'am. My wife and I will never forget your generosity."

Jane nodded and bid them goodnight, leaving them with her heartfelt wishes for a successful passage to freedom.

The scene that met Jane in the saloon on her return was of an irate and quivering Ezra Galsworthy relieving himself of a strongly-worded dressing down to Seaman Singleton. Chief Dawkins had brought his second into the secret at the first opportunity, and Galsworthy had the greater part of the evening to work up a head of steam over the deception by his trusted crewman. Having covered the duty of an employee to his employer, the recklessness of setting all of them in danger, and the blatant disregard for honor and obedience, Galsworthy wound up with a growled demand.

"What have you to say for yourself, man?"

"That I stand guilty as charged, sir."

"Were you paid, then? Has someone compromised your ethics with filthy silver, is that it?"

"No, sir. It is a question of honor. Ma'am," Singleton said as he turned to the captain. "I heard tales of seamen like myself being approached to help bring people away aboard their ships. It was no surprise when I was given a note in New York pleading with me to go to the proprietor of the ironmonger in Norfolk upon my arrival. I could not turn my back, ma'am. I simply could not."

"Your dereliction of duty has made you unfit to serve aboard my ship. You understand that, I take it?" Jane asked.

"Yes, ma'am, I knew the risk."

"While I regret the circumstance, I cannot have people I do not trust under my command. I recognize the moral quandary you have been subjected to, but your first duty is to the ship, and to me. I will not turn you over to the authorities, and we will look to the welfare of the family you smuggled aboard, but your employment with our firm, and aboard the *Destiny*, is at an end. I do not wish to see you again. Mister Galsworthy will explain the arrangements we have made for you."

With a final nod to her officers, Jane withdrew to her cabin where Endeavor waited. He gently folded her in his arms as she finally allowed herself to cry for the people in bondage, for the unfairness of the justice she was compelled to mete out to Singleton, and for the children who suffered the most.

A short while later, she pulled away to look up and declare, "I did not ask for it, but I accept the task now as my own. We shall not fail these people. Do you stand with me?"

"With all my heart and strength, dear Jane. Forever."

XIV
Lives in the Balance

Upper Chesapeake Bay
April 28, 1821

*Saturday, April 28, 1821   Anchored off Bloodsworth Lat. 38° 12' N Long. 76° 04'
W. per chart. Heavy fog delayed morning departure. Revenue cutter interception. Picked up
Baltimore pilot and made port. Many ships, no Osprey sighting.*

Eager to make port in Baltimore and offload her cargo, both
people and goods, Jane had been up since dawn pacing the rail.

"This blasted fog. How long till it clears, do you reckon?"
she fumed as she passed Galsworthy at the bow.

"This time of year, it could be many hours yet, ma'am, but
we dare not haul in the anchor until it does. The channel is too
narrow, and there are too many ships making their way through
for us to take a chance and run for it, Captain."

"Aye, and well I know it. But the waiting does not sit well."

With a final frustrated glance at the wall of white that
enveloped the *Destiny* on all sides, Jane made her way to the
galley for a fresh cup of coffee. Joining the back of the line to
wait her turn at the steaming urn, she looked at the handful of
crew gathered in the mess to have a hot meal before going on
watch. Around her, men who had been on duty since the middle
of the night sat wrapped in their warmest jackets with their hats
pulled low and their hands wrapped around warm coffee to
stave off the morning cold. As Jane listened to the chatter, she
noted that the men's voices were unusually subdued and more
than one sailor glanced her way before quickly lowering his eyes
to his plate. Even Cookie, normally talkative at this hour of the
morning, limited himself to a simple good morning salute.

"Something is amiss with the crew, Mister Dawkins." Jane
set her mug down on the saloon table where her chief was

hurrying through his breakfast before taking up duty on the deck. "What has them stirred up?"

Dawkins looked up in surprise, "How do you mean, ma'am?"

"They've got ahold of something and it is making them uneasy. Find out what it is and report back to me this morning, chief. We need to get to the bottom of this before we have trouble on our hands."

"Aye, aye, ma'am." With a final bite of biscuit, Dawkins rose from the table to jam his watch cap over his ears and shrug into his peacoat. "I shall have a nose about and see what is what."

Jane watched as her chief mate ducked through the door into the passageway. She knew Dawkins would ferret out the problem and just hoped it was something they could fix. Reaching over her head to turn up the lamp, Jane set about working over the charts for the day's passage. If the wind held, they should make Baltimore on Sunday, and the crew could take their Sabbath ashore. But they would need to take things cautiously as they wound their way around the shoals and up the river into Baltimore. Best to try that in the morning light with a fresh wind, so they would drop anchor tonight at the mouth of the river. With luck, they could pick up a pilot as soon as the morning mists cleared and be tied up at the wharf in time for church.

Engrossed in scanning a map of the Baltimore waterfront, Jane jumped in shock when a warm hand landed gently on her shoulder.

"Bless me, but you scared the daylights out of me," Jane cried, then rose swiftly to wrap her arms around her tousle-headed husband. "We are fogged in this morning, so I thought to let you sleep. How is the head today?"

"Nary the worse for a few hours at rest, but I must profess that the idea of going ashore on the morrow is a most pleasant one," Endeavor said with a smile.

"Come, let me clear away this mess and we shall have some breakfast. Cookie has sent down fresh berries this morning and the biscuits are still warm. Go fetch yourself some coffee while I set things to rights," Jane suggested as she began gathering together her charts and tools.

Later, as they picked at the last of the crumbs, Jane shared her concerns about the crew with her husband. He often had an insight into people that eluded Jane, who was more of a straightforward person and inclined to focus only on what was in plain sight.

"What does Friend Dawkins make of it?" Endeavor asked.

"Ah, here he is to tell us. Mister Dawkins, what have you discovered?" Jane turned to her chief as he ducked back into the saloon and shook the drops of fog off his hat.

"The crew knows we have runaways aboard, ma'am. Someone heard voices from the forward hatch and put two and two together. They suspect that Mister Singleton is involved and we are holding him separate. That he is not at all ill. What they don't know is if the situation has your blessing or if you were privy to Mister Singleton's actions."

"And would it make a difference if I were?"

"Aye, that it would ma'am. For it makes them part of the crime, as it were, and they don't like that at all. Even if most of them are sympathetic to the case."

"Very good. Mister Dawkins, please muster the crew in the foc's'le immediately, including Cookie and Koopmans. Set Mister Baldwin to stand deck watch while I have a word with the men."

Ten minutes later, Jane looked around the hot confines of the forward hold where her crew kept house. A dozen sweaty faces stared back at her, some questioning, some curious, but none openly hostile yet. She hoped to get them all on her side but knew that she must not break their trust in her as the captain in whose hands they had placed their livelihood and well-being. A low muttering could be heard as the crew found places to perch, shouldering between their mates to claim a spot on the edges of the lower berths.

"Ahoy, men, let us have your ears for a moment. The

captain wants a word," Dawkins called out, and the voices were stilled.

"All right, men, here is how things stand," Jane began. "Mister Singleton has been the instrument of people ashore who wish to aid our enslaved brothers to escape their bondage. Without the knowledge of the officers aboard this vessel, he arranged for a family to travel with us to Baltimore concealed in the hold. Mister Singleton is no longer employed on this vessel and will be going ashore as soon as we make land. There is no place under my command for anyone who seeks to make use of my ship or my crew for their own purposes, however laudable they may be. I hope I shall never need to make that point again, men," Jane continued in a stern voice that made clear her feelings about those who might think to take advantage in the future.

"No, ma'am. Quite right, that," and other assenting comments could be heard from the men as they nodded their heads in agreement.

"However, I have offered my assistance to this family and they are now under my protection. I expect to send them on their way with the help of their friends and will do my utmost to prevent their being hindered by any who wish to return them to their former masters. Are there any among you who would be unwilling to render such aid under my responsibility?" Jane looked around at the assembled faces, waiting for signs of dissent. When none was forthcoming, she spoke again into the silence.

"Very good. We make port in Baltimore in the morning. Mister Galsworthy, over to you."

Jane climbed back to the deck then made her way to the bow where her nephew leaned over the side, peering into the mist.

"Is it starting to clear, do you think?" she asked.

"Yes ma'am, I think I see the trees over there to the east. And a breeze is coming up the Bay from the south. We should be ready to haul anchor within the hour. Captain?" Silas paused for a moment. "Were you telling the crew about the runaways, ma'am?"

"Ah, I see there are no secrets aboard, Mister Baldwin. Aye, they deserved to know. It was Singleton's doing, but I have taken on the responsibility. You are to think of them as my guests now."

A moment or two passed as Silas processed this, then asked, "What will you do, Aunt Jane? Will they bring us trouble?"

"Yes, Silas, they might. But that is my concern and nothing for you to worry about. If trouble comes, I will be ready, I hope."

Two bells had been rung on the forenoon watch before the fog had lifted enough to see their way out of the cove where they had moored. As soon as she could make out the low-lying headlands, Jane gave the order to weigh anchor and set the sails. The *Destiny* swung smartly about in the freshening breeze and was soon making good speed toward the channel north.

On the quarterdeck, Jane stood with a glass to her eye, scanning the water on all sides for vessels. While she did not expect to see the *Osprey*, she wanted to make sure she did not miss the schooner should it happen to pass them going south. She was determined to set out in search of the errant captain and find out what he was about as soon as she cleared her hold in Baltimore and found a new cargo. She would send a report to Uncle Josias via the mail coach from Baltimore and ask for orders should she locate him.

Meanwhile, Jane's eye was drawn back to a swift cutter that seemed to be tracking them up the Bay. Since entering the main channel, she had seen the small craft take up a position on her stern and pile on sail to overtake them.

"What do you make of her?" she asked Dawkins as she handed him the glass.

"She is in an all-fired hurry this morning, that is for sure, ma'am."

"Aye, I thought the same. Where is she headed, do you suppose?"

"Unless she plans to put into some village, I dare not hazard a guess. It would be an awfully long voyage to make Annapolis or Baltimore in a dinghy like that, ma'am," Dawkins observed as he kept watch on the cutter.

Over the next hour, the pursuing vessel drew nearer as it made use of the shifting winds to cross waters too shallow for the *Destiny's* deeper keel. Soon they could make out a dozen men on deck and two swivel guns mounted at the bow. As it closed to within half a mile, the cutter suddenly fired its starboard gun in their direction, and the men aboard her began to shout and wave.

"Everyone down!" Galsworthy bellowed as the *Destiny's* crew sought shelter behind the rails.

"Hold your course!" Jane yelled to Griggs as he ducked behind the wheel but kept a hard grip on the spokes to hold the schooner steady.

"Dawkins, to me!" she shouted and scrambled behind the galley wall. Peering around the corner to watch the cutter, she yelled to Endeavor to go back below when she saw his head pop up out of the companionway in response to the ruckus.

"Right, Dawkins, looks like they mean to catch us and I doubt it is for a friendly chat. Pirates, do you suppose?"

"Nay, ma'am, not in these waters. More likely it is the law, or anyway those who profess to serve it. My guess is that someone has put them on our trail as we are carrying fugitives aboard."

"Damn, man. I suspect you are right. What happens if they catch us?"

"I don't rightly know. Certainly, they will want to recapture the runaways. But I don't know if they can make trouble for us too. They do have the law, such as it is, on their side as long as we are in Virginia."

"And are we?" Jane shouted over her shoulder as she watched the cutter load and fire its starboard gun again.

"No, ma'am, but just barely," Dawkins shouted back. "With no witnesses, they could put us anywhere they like."

"All right, let us make a run for it. Put up all sail and let us see what speed we can make. Keep everyone low in case their aim improves before we are away."

Shielded from the view of the pursuing craft by the billowing mainsail, the crew made quick work of changing out the headsails and running up the topsail. Alas, the wind chose that moment to shift to the northwest and then die back to a light breeze. The booms swung to starboard, then banged about amidships as the *Destiny* lost forward motion and began to drift.

Soon enough, they saw the cutter put out its oars and make headway toward them. Two men were busy flaking out the boarding lines and the helmsman brought his heading up to come alongside the *Destiny*. Jane could do nothing but stand at the rail and watch as they approached.

"Ahoy, Captain. We are the revenue cutter *Tidewater*. Captain James Petty. Heave to and put out your ladder. We are coming aboard."

Jane peered over at the man with the speaking horn and noted that he wore neither uniform nor badge of office. Nor did any of the other men in the cutter as far as she could discern. A motley group of rough-looking sailors, they were dressed in clothing more suited to hunting than boating, right down to the guns holstered in the leather belts holding in the waists of their woollen riding breeches. As she looked them over, she realized one of the faces was familiar.

"On whose authority?" she shouted back.

"The Commonwealth of Virginia. You have sailed through our waters carrying cargo without proper inspection. We wish to come aboard and verify your papers, then you are free to go."

"Are you in the habit of firing on merchant vessels in need of paperwork, sir?" Jane shouted back.

"Aye, when captains attempt to avoid us, we are empowered to take whatever means necessary to ensure compliance. I am sending over our lines now." With a wave to his crew, Petty soon had his lines snugged to *Destiny*'s rail, then waited impatiently as the schooner's crew dropped the boarding ladder over the side.

Behind her, Jane could hear the exclamations of her

passengers as Dawkins sought to reassure them. The sound of the guns had brought them out of their cabins on the run, then sent them to cower behind the hatches as the pursuit heated up. Now, they were assembled by the ladder to the quarterdeck peppering the chief mate with questions.

"It is a simple misunderstanding, sir. We will have everything sorted out soon and be on our way," Dawkins replied to John Rumpole, the young groom, who demanded an explanation as he sought to shield his bride from the turmoil on deck.

"What do they want from us? What has the captain done?" Rumpole demanded belligerently. "I knew we should have waited for the steamer! No good comes of women in command, I said, and here we are!"

"Please sir, mind the ladies. Perhaps you might all prefer to wait in the saloon while we deal with these gentlemen?" Dawkins urged as he directed them toward the companionway.

"I will be damned if you push me out of the way, sir," Rumpole shouted. "We have a right to know what she has gotten us into."

Right then, Dawkins' attention was drawn away to the side deck where Captain Petty and four of his men were climbing over the rail, including the man who Jane now recognized as the one who had accosted her at the theater, Mister Weston. Within short order, the party had formed up behind their leader, who addressed himself to Jane.

"Captain, please provide us with your lading manifest. We will then make a brief inspection of your hold, and if we find that all is in order, you are free to continue on your way."

"No sir, I do not intend to provide you with papers or allow you into my hold before you show me credentials certifying your right to board me and make such demands." Jane stood with her arms crossed and stared the captain down.

Silently, Petty opened his jacket and pulled out a sheaf of documents. Unfolding one, he passed it over to Jane. Printed across the top was the seal of the Virginia General Assembly, and the wording below made it clear that the cutter *Tidewater* had been duly commissioned to enforce the trading and export laws of the commonwealth. It further stated that the captain had the power to impound and hold in lieu of fines any vessel deemed to have evaded the proper declaration and payment of taxes to the commonwealth. Jane was well and truly stuck. She knew that the fugitives in her hold would be considered real property under Virginia law, and that she was, in fact, smuggling undeclared goods. Her only hope lay in delaying the search long enough for her to hide the Calloways somewhere below.

"Mister Dawkins, it would appear that Captain Petty is in need of our papers. Please take him below to my cabin and show him our cargo manifest. I will then meet you in the cargo hold," Jane said as she gave the chief a meaningful nod.

"Wait, wait! I know where they are." This shout came from Rumpole as he broke free from his wife and rushed toward Petty and his men. Dawkins stepped in front of him with an arm outstretched to halt his progress but Rumpole swerved to avoid him, then pulled up short in front of the boarding party.

'I heard them, in the forward hold. Last night, there was the sound of a child crying down below, and we have no young 'uns among the passengers." Rumpole, his face red from emotion, jabbed his finger toward the forward hatch. "I warrant they are stowaways. And we knew nothing about it."

"Captain, perhaps you could take us directly to your hold and have your chief meet us there with the manifest instead," Petty said as he turned to Jane. His tone made it clear that the suggestion was in fact an order.

Seeing no alternative to compliance, Jane silently led the way forward and motioned for Koopmans to break the seal on the forward hatch and shove the butterfly doors open. With a prayer that the family had found a hiding place at the first sign of pursuit, Jane led the way down the ladder and into the hold.

As she stepped off into the gloom of the timber-filled space, Jane was startled to find Endeavor emerging from the shadows. He nodded quickly, then disappeared behind the lumber stacks toward the interior door that led to the passageway below decks.

With a sigh of relief, she moved aside to allow Petty and his men room to join her, then led the way forward along the cramped aisle between the lockers and the lumber secured in neat piles amidships. Waving her hand as she ducked underneath the beams, she called behind her,

"You can see that we are fully laden with fine timber. You are most welcome to inspect the seals on our lockers and count the lumber if you please."

Petty edged past her and pointed his men forward into the dark hold. "Use your flints, men, and look for anything amiss." Petty paused and looked at Jane. 'Unless you are carrying powder, ma'am?"

Jane shook her head, then leaned carelessly against the bulkhead as they waited for Petty's men to return. Shortly, they filed back into the aisle, shaking their heads.

"Well, Captain, it would appear that all is in order here. Perhaps we could look over that manifest now," Petty said with a frown.

With a nod, Jane led the way to her cabin, where Dawkins and Endeavor were ready with the ship's papers laid out on the table. Petty spent a number of minutes reading carefully through them, then looked up at Jane.

"Passengers, ma'am? Where are they housed?"

"In our new cabins, aft of the cargo hold. Would you like to see? They really are quite nice, if I do say so myself," she offered innocently.

"Search them," Petty commanded.

Jane and her officers spent the next few minutes in quiet contemplation of the ceiling as Petty and his band made a thorough inspection of the passenger accommodations. Miss Evans had been forced to open her trunks, which earned the men a thorough dressing down from the enraged lady. Jane could hear the refined voice raised in anger as her passenger followed them back to the saloon. Putting out her hand at the door to prevent Miss Evans from entering, Jane gave a slight shake of her head and a smile to reassure her that everything was under control then closed the door.

"Everything would appear to be in order, Captain," Petty said after making a cursory reading of the bills and handing them back to Dawkins. "We had a report that you were carrying undeclared cargo and were obligated to follow up on the information. You are free to carry on your way."

"One moment," Jane said as Petty turned to leave. He turned back to her with a questioning look.

"What information, may I ask? And from what source?"

"From me, Captain Thorn." Weston stepped forward and pushed Petty aside as he glared at Jane.

"We keep an eye on who comes and goes in the harbor, and when Prentice Calloway came looking for his property, two escaped slaves and their children, we checked the shipping records. You were the only Northern vessel that left the harbor recently. Albright told us you might be looking to meddle in things, so I figured it was likely your schooner they were on."

"Clearly, we have no children aboard. Now good day to you sir." Jane nodded at Petty and motioned for Galsworthy to open the door and allow the men to leave. As the last of them passed through, the air was rent with the sound of a child's piercing wail emanating from the captain's quarters.

XV
Baltimore Bound

Upper Chesapeake Bay
April 28, 1821

Jane stood at the rail in helpless fury as she watched the cutter pull away. Powerless to stop Perry from taking the Calloways into custody, she had been forced to step aside as they broke down the door to her cabin and hauled the protesting family into the saloon. Endeavor stepped between them and Mistress Calloway as Weston reached out to throw her to the floor.

"Nay, Friend," Endeavor said as he placed his body in front of the weeping woman, "there will be no violence here. Thee must treat them as human beings even as thee does thy work." With a gentle hand, he himself led the terrified family onto the deck, and paused a moment in prayer with them before Petty's men took them away to board the cutter.

In despair, Jane rounded on the Rumpoles.

"Please bear witness to the fruit of your actions, Mister Rumpole, and may God forgive you."

A deeply discomfited Rumpole had no reply to give the captain but instead gathered his wife to him and led her below to spend the remainder of the voyage in their cabin.

As the distraught family was herded down the ladder, Jane could see Weston and Petty arguing in low voices as Weston stabbed his finger in Jane's direction. It appeared that the captain had the final word though, as Weston finally gave in and made his way over the rail with a final glare for Jane. Before climbing down the boarding ladder himself to return to his boat, Captain Perry paused a moment and addressed Jane.

"Consider yourself warned that we will brook no interference in the affairs of our people, Captain Thorn. I have shown great forbearance in not impounding your vessel, ma'am, but we will not be so forgiving next time."

It had taken all of Jane's will to bite her tongue and maintain a steely silence in reply.

As soon as the cutter pulled in her lines, Dawkins directed the *Destiny's* crew to make sail. The wind picked up again as the heat of the noonday sun penetrated the shallow waters of the bay, and they were shortly making good speed northward. Heartsick, Jane nevertheless remained on deck to oversee the course. When she was ready, she would have to speak to the crew. But that could wait until they arrived in Baltimore and offloaded the passengers. It would give her time to think about what she wanted to say.

Galsworthy set the men to work as soon as they were underway in an effort to keep their minds, as well their hands, busy. Standing on the quarterdeck, Jane could see her nephew down on the foredeck where he was hard at work scraping the bottom of an upturned boat. From the force with which he wielded his scraper, Jane could tell that Silas was angry, and exercising his feelings on the hull he was cleaning.

Meanwhile, Jane directed Dawkins to have supper served to the passengers in their cabins. She did not think there would be much conviviality in the saloon this evening and personally could not have stomached sharing a meal with Mister Rumpole.

"And push the *Destiny*, Mister Dawkins. If we can make Baltimore harbor this evening, we shall have the passengers taken off in the lighters. Let us bring this voyage to an end as quickly as we can manage."

"Aye, aye, captain." He acknowledged the order with a sad shake of his head. "I shall have the passengers made ready to disembark tonight."

A favorable wind hummed in the rigging that afternoon and the schooner passed Annapolis as the first dog watch sat down to supper. Hitchens was stationed at the bow to keep a lookout for a pilot's boat, which was not long in making its appearance.

"Pilot ho!" Hitchens came running aft to report.

Jane was relieved to see the little schooner but did not let herself relax. The Patasco River shoals, an ever-shifting morass of sandbars and rocky outcroppings, were a challenge even for mariners familiar with the waters. She was glad to take on the pilot well before entering the channel, but as sunset was in less than three hours, Jane worried that she might be too late to make the inner harbor that evening.

"Good afternoon, ma'am," the pilot saluted as he clambered over the side. A tall man impeccably turned out in navy blue wool with polished boots and a neat cap, Avis Bailey introduced himself and asked for the captain.

"Good sir, I am master of this vessel and I welcome you aboard," Jane replied. Pausing to shake his hand, she continued. "We hope to drop anchor off Seven Foot Knoll and disembark our passengers this evening. What say you to that, Mister Bailey?"

The pilot looked up into the rigging to sense the wind. "Aye, the tide is running in, and we have a following breeze. We should make Baltimore harbor as the sun sets. You will pay more for the lightermen after dark, though. They will be sure to charge a Sabbath premium, the scoundrels. Perhaps you had better wait until the morning?"

"Well," Jane said, "let us see what time we make, and I shall gladly pay up if it comes to that."

Over the next hour, Bailey showed himself to be a fine navigator as he steered the *Destiny* safely up the treacherous river crowded with vessels moored along both banks and even in the middle of the main channel. Jane breathed a sigh of relief as they let go the anchor near the eastern shore, and she got her first look at the city. In the gathering dusk, the shoreline was still filled with traffic along the busy waterfront. Behind the rows of warehouses and shops, imposing buildings of stone and marble dotted the rising landscape, including the new Merchant's Exchange. Finished just a year earlier, the largest structure built in America dominated the view with its domed rotunda and reaching arms. Jane looked forward to exploring it during their brief stay in Baltimore, along with several other famous landmarks in one of the young country's oldest cities.

For now, though, she would be content to put her passengers ashore and settle the *Destiny* for the night. As Bailey climbed back over the rail to drop onto the deck of the pilot's vessel now waiting alongside, Jane handed him her customary bottle of port. Dawkins had already settled the bill but this was her personal way of showing thanks.

"Much obliged, ma'am," Bailey lifted the bottle in a mock toast. "And I will be sure to send along the best lighterman in the harbor if I can find him before he pours himself into the tavern." With a final grin, he slipped over the side and soon disappeared into the night.

"Mister Galsworthy, please present my greetings to our guests and have their baggage brought up. And send Miss Evans to me in my cabin if you would."

"And Mister Singleton, ma'am?"

"He can cool his heels where he is for the moment. But have him gather his things, for I shall have him off my vessel as soon as it can be arranged. The chief has already prepared his pay packet. You can give him that, anyway."

As Jane climbed the ladder below, her belly gave off a low growl. She hadn't eaten since breakfast in the mess. Once she completed this piece of business she would just have to throw herself on Cookie's mercy for a small handout or starve until morning. Opening the door to the saloon, a mouth-watering aroma greeted her, however. Endeavor was in the middle of setting out the plates and cups in preparation for serving the meal.

"Bless you, my husband." Lifting the pot lid, Jane closed her eyes and breathed deeply in delight. Beef stew, her favorite. "And bless Cookie."

Endeavor smiled then reached over to open the door again at Miss Evans' peremptory knock.

"Ah, thank you for joining us, Miss Evans," Jane said as she came back around the table to grasp the older woman's hand. "I shan't keep you as the boats will arrive soon, but I wanted to beg a favor of you."

"Of course, my dear Captain. Ask away!" Dressed in her straw hat and lace shawl in preparation for departure, Miss

Evans looked the part of a kindly grandmother. Jane knew her to be a far more formidable personage and hoped that she could find her way clear to helping with the serious matter at hand.

"With regard to my man Singleton, Miss Evans. I must put him ashore, but I feel an obligation to make sure that he comes to no harm. I have written him a letter of recommendation should he choose to seek out a berth on another vessel. But I fear he will find himself at a disadvantage, and perhaps in danger of apprehension, if he is set loose in Baltimore without friends to watch out for him."

"Say no more, Captain Thorn. It will be my pleasure to offer him a place in my household until such time as he chooses to leave. Rest assured that he will be well looked after."

"Thank you, ma'am. You have set my mind at ease."

"Well, I bid you farewell then. Should you also find yourself in need of a friend in our fair city, I hope that my name will come to mind and you will call on me. Good-bye, Captain Thorn. Mister Coffin." With a nod of her head that set the feathers in her hat dancing, Miss Evans swept out the door and closed it firmly behind her.

"Well. I shall miss her, despite everything," Jane observed, turning to her dinner.

XVI
A New Plan

Baltimore Harbor
April 29, 1821

"Five more minutes. Just five. Then I shall just *have* to scratch."
Jane thought.

Try as she might, Jane was finding it hard to keep still as she
sat with Endeavor in silent meditation this Sunday morning, or
rather, First Day, as he referred to it. Never much interested in
spiritual matters, Jane had attended church services with her
family out of a sense of duty rather than conviction. No longer
associated with the local Society of Friends, the Thorn family
had found a welcoming congregation in the Presbyterian church
just down the street, and Jane made regular appearances in the
pews out of habit. However, her marriage to Endeavor had
brought the issue of religion to the fore. At first, she had simply
left him to his devotions, knowing how important the life of the
spirit was to her dear husband. Lately, though, she had thought
to join him at least on Sundays as he sat in silent witness for an
hour. A lifetime of practice had accustomed Endeavor to long
periods of quiet contemplation of the "still, small voice within."
Jane, however, was finding it increasingly difficult to keep quiet,
particularly since she could see no purpose in the endless sitting.

Finally, she could contain herself no longer. With a deep
sigh, she stood up and stretched, then reached behind to scratch
the infernal itch.

"Endeavor, my dear, my still, small voice tells me that I am
bored, famished, and ready to be about my day. I will be on
deck," she said to the top of his bowed head and turned toward
the ladder.

Emerging into the sunshine, Jane breathed deeply as she
looked around the deck of the schooner. With the exception of
Hitchens on watch, the rest of the crew had gone ashore, as the

cargo would not be offloaded until after the Sabbath. The passengers had all disembarked in the moonlight last night, leaving the *Destiny* peacefully rocking in the harbor swell cloaked in blessed silence. Jane strode forward, nodding to Hitchens where he sat on the forward hatch, and peered out over the bow toward the city laid out before her.

It was time to make some decisions, and to communicate with her uncle about her plans. The *Destiny* would spend a week in port here as she made arrangements to carry out her mission, and she just hoped that Josias would agree. She was not sure what she would do should he order her back to New York, but she knew that he would have to approve any deviation from the charted voyage. With a sigh, she turned away from the view and went below to write the letter that would determine her next course of action.

Settling herself at the saloon table with the biscuits and coffee she had purloined from the galley, Jane began to write.

Dear Uncle Josias,

There is much news. We have concluded profitable transport and sale of the pottery trade goods. They were well received and the transaction was handled in large part by Silas. He has the makings of a fine businessman! We have also been fortunate in the acquisition of a load of fine mahogany, which we will sell directly from the ship and avoid the warehouse fees if at all possible. The load is valuable enough that we will bring it to New York if we do not find a suitable buyer in Baltimore.

A quickly conceived and carried out notion has also suggested a possible source of revenue, the transport of passengers. We constructed removable quarters in the hold, which were quickly engaged, and passengers delivered safely to Baltimore. I fear there is not a great future in this business, however, as Captain Weems and others of his ilk have invested heavily in steamboats and are making a great success of transporting passengers and goods around the Bay. However, should we otherwise fill our hold with merchandise for trade, we might carry on with a small number of paying passengers for a while yet. However, I fear that the steamboats are highly suited to conditions here on the Bay, and it will not be long before they replace all sail traffic in these waters. Even now, most of the sailing vessels we see are bringing in passengers from across the Atlantic to Norfolk and on to Baltimore. Perhaps it is time we begin to think about steamships, uncle, as it appears to be the new way of things.

A full accounting for these items will be found in the enclosed documents from Mister Dawkins, and Endeavor is sending you details of his discoveries with regard to the activities of Captain Albright. The Osprey made a brief and belated appearance in Norfolk, but I was unable to question Captain A about his actions, as I was denied permission to board, and the ship made a quick departure the following day. I have been unsuccessful in locating her since leaving Norfolk. With your permission, I aim now to seek out the Osprey, wherever she may be, and to take her under my command after dismissing the master and mate should I uncover evidence of wrongdoing. In that case, I will send the Osprey straight home to New York with Silas in command along with Mister Galsworthy to keep order in the crew. Please advise if this course of action meets with your consent.

And finally, we find ourselves in a complicated situation as the result of our Mister Singleton being the means by which a family of runaways was secreted aboard the Destiny. Despite my best efforts, the family was captured and returned to Virginia although no harm has come to the Destiny or her crew. I will provide details once I see you at home, but my conscience prevails on me to not let the matter rest. Uncle, if you could but have seen the terror in the eyes of the little girls as they were taken back to captivity, your heart would break as did mine.

Despite their presence aboard being not of my making, once having offered the Calloway family my protection, and seeing them brutally dragged from my ship, I feel personally obliged to seek their release or rescue, as conditions permit. The Thorn family having already made the decision not to profit from the labor of enslaved persons, I find it morally incompatible to have participated, however unwittingly, in the re-enslavement of these persons - children!

106

Bearing in mind the need to make this voyage pay, I nevertheless feel compelled to follow my moral compass and bring these poor souls to freedom if the thing can be done without loss of vessel or crew. I know not what this will entail and ask your forbearance in giving me license to pursue this goal even as we continue in our trading activities. I cannot give you more details or assurances at this time beyond your knowledge of me as master of the Destiny, and the guidance you have given me over the years.

Dear Uncle Josias, I greatly anticipate your instructions. The Destiny will remain here in Baltimore until I hear from you.

Affectionately,
Captain Jane Thorn

As she put down her pen and scattered sand on the paper, the door to her cabin opened and Endeavor stepped through. Jane rose to embrace him, then tilted her head back with a smile.

"I hope I did not disturb your thoughts by taking my leave so abruptly."

"Nay, Jane, thee could not disturb me no matter the cause," he smiled back at her. "I am, as William Penn would have it, 'rested in mind and spirit from the silence.' And am likewise famished. Have thee kept aside any biscuits for thy poor husband?"

Jane sent Endeavor to the galley to search out his breakfast as she tidied up her papers and pondered her next moves. It would take a day for her message to reach New York by the mail coach and another for it to return with her uncle's reply. They could use the time profitably to seek a buyer for the lumber in her hold, and to find a load for transport back south. For she meant to head back to the Tidewater, and points beyond if need be, in search of the errant Albright. She also meant to get word of the Calloways and bring them back to New York with her if at all possible. From there, they could easily take passage to New Bedford or one of the other New England towns where escaping slaves could find liberty and a new life. But first, she would have to find them, and her best hope for that lay in Norfolk.

When Endeavor returned from his foraging mission a short while later, he found Jane with her charts spread over the table and a deep frown on her face.

"There are so many places to look. Here," she jabbed at the chart in frustration. "And here. And here! There are dozens of rivers and creeks and bays where a shallow bottom boat might take refuge on the Chesapeake. And I daresay many more that have not been mapped. However shall we find the *Osprey*?"

"What do thee believe he is about?" Endeavor asked as he swallowed his first bite of breakfast. "Perhaps that might guide thee in choosing a place to look."

"Slaving, or I'll eat my hat. There is much money to be made in trafficking Africans now that the law forbids it. And Albright strikes me as just the sort of man who loves money and lacks principles that would be attracted to the sorry business. I've been thinking about the *El Almirante*. Her log says they were waiting for "G" who had been delayed. Am I correct that Captain Albright is, in fact, George Albright? Could it be he they were waiting for?"

Endeavor took a moment to consider as he polished off the last of the biscuits and jam he had liberated from the galley and brushed away the crumbs from the front of his shirt. "Aye, thee may have the right of it. It would explain where he had been during his absence if it was he that took the human cargo off the brig for transport ashore. His boat would be well suited to the task."

"Precisely," Jane exclaimed. "And think on all of the corn he has been buying. It would feed a great number of people cheaply. He might well be provisioning the transport ships as well as feeding any people he carries himself. I think our sighting of the *El Almirante* was no coincidence. I think she was waiting for a Thorn schooner leaving New York on our schedule."

"If he is engaging in that illicit trade, we would find him in the lower bay, would we not? I doubt he would be landing captives in Maryland."

"Aye, that stands to reason," Jane agreed. "So let us track him there. We'll ferret him out like a terrier after a rat, and I will see to it that he is put ashore to stand trial for his crimes."

Whether they were right in their theories about the elusive *Osprey* or no, Jane was glad they at least had a plan. If Josias gave the order, they would load up with flour and other basic foodstuffs for trade with the isolated towns that dotted the southern shores and islands of the Chesapeake. Sooner or later, they were bound to catch a whiff of the *Osprey*.

When the crew returned aboard that evening, Jane sat down with her officers and Endeavor to discuss the problem of finding the errant schooner.

"What do you mean to do if we sight her, ma'am?" Galsworthy asked.

"Follow her, if I can. I want to catch her captain ashore where I can relieve him of his command."

"And if he resists, Captain Thorn? What then?" Dawkins looked worried.

"Have you got your pistol with you Mister Dawkins?" Jane grinned at him.

Dawkins leaned back in consternation before realizing that the captain was attempting a joke. "Aye, it would not do to shoot a countryman ma'am, no matter the provocation.

"Nay, I suppose not. Well, we shall just have to use our wits then. In any case, I aim to see to it that the *Osprey* is headed home under new command before the summer is out."

As for her other mission, Jane decided to wait for word from her uncle before laying out the issue for her men. Should Josias not approve of her seeking out the Calloways for clandestine transport to the north, she would have to decide how to square her actions with her principles. Her hope was that Josias would stand behind her, but for now, she could only speculate and wait for a reply to her letter.

XVII
A Visit in Baltimore

Baltimore, Maryland
April 30, 1821

The tramp of the watch overhead woke Jane early on Monday. Peering out through the deadlight overhead, she could see that the sun was barely up. With a groan, she pulled the quilts over her head and tucked herself around Endeavor as he slept soundly on the bulkhead side of the berth. Just as she was drifting off again, the footsteps on the deck above her resumed their pounding and someone set a tin plate down on the cabin roof. When it was knocked to the deck a moment later with a ringing crash, Jane decided she had had enough.

"Ahoy sailor," she whispered through the slats of the companionway door at the top of the ladder that led from her cabin to the quarterdeck. "What are you about out there?"

"It's me Aunty Jinks," came the voice of her nephew Silas in a low murmur. "Sorry to disturb your sleep Ma'am. But I..." Silas' voice petered out as he seemed to lose his nerve.

Jane took another step up the ladder and opened the door to see Silas huddled on the deck with his back against the cabin wall. A light mist blew across the bay making everything damp and causing the young seaman to shiver where he sat.

"All well, Silas"? Jane asked as she reached out a hand to brush his hair off his forehead. Sometimes it was more important to be an aunt than a captain, she thought, and this seemed to be one of those times.

"No, ma'am," came the miserable reply.

"Wait right there, I shall be out in a moment."

Jane slid back down the ladder to find her greatcoat and a shawl. As she turned again to climb back to the deck, she saw that Endeavor had awakened and was watching her with a puzzled frown.

"It's Silas," she whispered. "Go back to sleep." With a quick kiss on his forehead, she gathered her nightrail around her knees and started up the ladder.

"Come, let's see if Cookie has some coffee on the boil yet," Jane said as she led Silas down to the main deck and into the galley. Finding the dregs of the pot still warm, they each poured a mug and returned to the quarterdeck to sit on the taffrail where they could talk and watch the dawn.

Jane waited patiently for Silas to speak as she sipped from the strong brew in her mug. Finally, with a deep sigh, he began.

"You shall most likely think I am silly."

Jane continued to wait as the silence stretched out again.

"I have so many things that I am thinking about, Aunt Jane, and I can't seem to settle my mind to anything. It just keeps going round and round and I feel so angry sometimes, and others so sad."

A few minutes passed as they sat in silence watching the seabirds on their early morning search for breakfast. Finally, Silas cleared his throat and asked, "What will happen to them, the Calloways?"

"I wish I knew, Silas, I surely do. I suppose they will be turned over to their master."

"It's not right," Silas burst out in a loud whisper. "Those little girls, that family. How can people do that?"

"I do not know," was all Jane could think of to say.

"We have to do something, Aunty Jinks. I can't sleep for thinking about them. We have to find them." Silas jumped off the rail and turned to face Jane, his expression earnest. "We have to save them."

Jane contemplated the passionate young face for a moment and was deeply moved to see Silas' moral outrage and sense of justice.

"Aye, you have the right of that, Silas. Will you trust me for now that I aim to do what I can to help?" Jane asked in a calm voice that made it clear that the conversation was at an end.

Silas looked to be on the verge of another outburst but caught himself in time. "Aye, ma'am. And thank you." With a touch of his hand to his hat, Silas turned away and set off on his next walk around the deck and to ring the half hour on the bell.

Mid-morning found the captain and her officers huddled in front of the saloon stove making their plans for the week in Baltimore. The early spring chill in the air had them bundled in their coats with their hands outstretched toward the small fire.

"I will take Cookie ashore with me in the boat this morning, Captain," Dawkins announced. "I can place the notice in the tradesheet about the mahogany, and Cookie will want to reprovision."

"Aye, and Endeavor and I will join you. I can carry the letters to the post if you have your reports ready, Mr. Dawkins?" Jane waited for his nod, then continued. "We will wait here in Baltimore for our orders from New York as I need to take counsel from Captain Josias with regard to the *Osprey* and other matters. I reckon we will remain until the end of the week. Shall we give the crew shore leave?"

"Aye, ma'am, by watches, and only by day," Galsworthy replied. "We'll keep 'em aboard for the evening watches. Keep 'em out of trouble. Koopmans and I will have 'em plenty busy, Captain."

"All right, you can let the men know. And give them some of their wages so they have something in their pockets, though Lord knows they will just drop it all in the first tavern they find," Jane observed with a wry smile.

The walk from the harbor to the post office took but a few minutes once the boat put Jane and Endeavor ashore. They waved to Dawkins and the cook, who were headed in the opposite direction along the wharf, and made their way up the hill, arriving shortly before the noon mail carriage for New York was ready to depart. Jane handed in her packet marked for the offices of Thorn Shipping and inquired about arrival times for the return post on the following day.

"Dinnertime, or thereabouts," the postmaster announced from behind a barred window. "Although it may be delayed if we need to send a guard to meet it. We had a driver killed and robbed last month, and now the men are asking for special protection."

"Good heavens," Jane exclaimed. "Have they caught the perpetrator?"

"Oh yes, ma'am. The very same day. Two men out of New York who planned the whole thing. Seems one of them had been a stage driver and knew the poor fellow they shot and stabbed. Got away with over ten thousand dollars, they did. But we caught 'em with the proceeds and they confessed soon enough."

With a shake of her head at the avariciousness of man, Jane handed over the coins for the packet and thanked the postmaster for his assistance. "And may we hope that the mail arrives safely."

"Whither now, my captain?" Endeavor asked as they stepped back into the street and he tucked Jane's hand under his arm.

"I wish to call on Miss Evans," she replied. "If Uncle Josias agrees that I should seek out the Calloways, she is my best hope for guidance in how to find them I think."

A delighted Miss Evans opened the door to them later that afternoon. "Captain Jane. And Mister Coffin. What a pleasure." She beamed at them as she stepped back. "Come in, come in, we are all in the parlor," she exclaimed as she waved them over the threshold.

The tidy little house in a shady neighborhood just off Light Street welcomed them with the smell of baking bread and the heady scent of an early spring bouquet on a stand in the entryway. Pale pink wallpaper made a charming backdrop to the white furniture in the little parlor where the sisters had just sat down to afternoon tea. At Jane's entrance, two of the women rose and came to greet the couple with warm smiles.

"My goodness, what a pleasure." Eliza Evans, the youngest of the three sisters, was sensibly dressed in a severely tailored skirt and simple lawn blouse with a black ribbon at the neck, a style Jane much admired. "Have you come to see how your Mister Singleton fares?"

"Yes, we should like to hear news of him. I am most grateful that you have taken him under your care," Jane said as she seated herself on the divan next to her husband and accepted a cup of tea from her hostess.

"He is well, though saddened at the circumstances of his dismissal, of course," Miss Evans replied. "And do call me Polly, as we are all friends here."

With a nod to Jane, Endeavor picked up the conversation. "Does he intend to make his way back to New York soon, does thee know?"

"Yes, I believe that is his intent, though I fear he is uncertain of his future there as he is not welcome aboard Thorn vessels," Miss Polly replied with a severe glance toward Jane.

The captain felt no need to justify her decision to remove the seaman from her crew, and brought the talk around to her main purpose.

"I have not yet thanked you for your assistance with the Calloway family, Miss Polly. Your efforts to cheer the children were much appreciated, though things did not turn out as we had hoped."

Jane leaned forward to set her cup on the table as she paused to consider how to broach her dangerous topic.

"What do you think has happened to them? Would they have been returned to their master?" she asked.

"Possibly." It was Miss Anne who took up the thread. "But our contacts in Virginia tell us that many recaptured slaves are no longer trusted by their former masters and are sold off at the next opportunity. They might be anywhere at this point. Most likely though, they are still in Norfolk awaiting a decision."

"And would someone be able to locate them there?" Endeavor asked, revealing their intent to the sisters. Jane drew in her breath as she looked around to judge their reactions.

Miss Polly set down her own cup in surprise and sat back to regard the couple. "What is it you think to do, Mister Coffin?"

"If it can be done, I mean to provide them passage to New York aboard my schooner," Jane declared. "I hope I have not misjudged that you all might be sympathetic to such a plan and willing to provide us information and assistance."

At these words, Eliza Evans rose and walked over to a rolltop desk under the window. She pushed up the cover and reached into a cubby to pull out a sheaf of printed leaflets. Returning to her seat, she handed one each to Jane and Endeavor without a word.

"Minutes of the Adjourned Session of the American Convention for Promoting the Abolition of Slavery," Jane read out loud. She looked up as Eliza spoke.

"In there, you will see that we are listed as the sponsors of a proposal to dedicate funds to the active rescue of Africans from their bondage. Please tell us what you need."

Relieved, Jane glanced at Endeavor as she replied, "I do not rightly know yet. We are awaiting word from New York on our further orders, but with your permission I will return in a few days' time to consult with you."

As they rose a short while later to take their leave, Anne laid her hand on Jane's arm. "I know that he was in the wrong, but if there is a way that Mister Singleton could be useful in your venture, I think he would welcome the opportunity to redeem himself, Captain."

Jane paused as she considered Anne's words. "Perhaps. But please do not discuss the matter with him until we are sure of our path."

Anne nodded. As she stepped aside to allow Jane to pass, she picked up the leaflets from the table where Jane and Endeavor had left them and pressed them into Jane's hands. "Please read them."

XVIII
Trade Goods

Baltimore, Maryland
May 2, 1821

Wednesday morning brought a heavy downpour that threatened to last all day. Aside from the men on watch, Galsworthy kept the crew below variously employed in making new mats for the berths, repainting the companionway ladders, scraping tar from the anchor locker, and other pursuits well suited to keeping bored young men occupied and out of trouble.

In the saloon, Jane sat with Dawkins and Endeavor by the stove and mulled over the problem of the load of mahogany sitting unsold in the cargo hold.

"Just the one offer, then?" Jane asked for the third time.

"Aye, ma'am. At less than the price we paid for it in Norfolk," Dawkins answered yet again.

Jane tilted her chair back and scratched her head as she pondered her options. "We can take it to New York but I had hoped we might sell it here in Baltimore. Do you suppose we might piecemeal it out? Look for many buyers instead of one who wants the whole load? I know we thought a builder would be interested, but if there are none who want to pay our price..."

As Endeavor opened his mouth to reply, the *Destiny* suddenly rocked violently from side to side, and Jane had to grab for her breakfast dishes to keep them from being dashed to the floor.

"What in tarnation?" she muttered, as she dumped the plates in the bucket under the table and made her way hand over hand into the passageway and up the companionway ladder to the deck. Holding tight to the opening, she looked around the crowded inner harbor. Steaming rapidly away, Jane could see the stern of the *Chesapeake* as it made its way at full speed through the mooring field. With her paddlewheel churning up great gouts of water and smoke belching from her smokestack, she made a prodigious noise as she set every vessel in the harbor yanking at its anchor chains.

"Damn his eyes." Jane shook her fist at the swiftly retreating boat. Around her, she could hear similar oaths being shouted from other decks when several vessels looked to nearly cross masts as they swayed violently in the steamboat's wake. "I'll have his hide, I will," she thought, and stamped her way back below.

"It was that damnable Trippe fellow," she reported as she resumed her seat. "He is so all-fired worried about his schedule he takes no care for other vessels in his path. Someone will have to do something before he causes a collision."

"Aye, I heard talk at Bowley's Wharf that so many competitors have been gnawing away at the Frenchtown run that he is hard pressed to make the best speed he can so as to keep his advantage," Dawkins remarked. "He is gaining a reputation for being a bit of a dare-devil."

"Be that as it may, someone should put a stop to his antics before he kills someone," Jane groused.

Leaning forward, Endeavor turned the talk back to the issue of the languishing cargo. "Thee mentioned Baltimore furniture once, if I remember rightly, Jane. Would the cabinetmakers perhaps be induced to purchase portions of the load if we were to deliver it to them as part of the price?"

"Mister Dawkins, what say you? It would be a prodigious amount of work and bookkeeping, but perhaps we could make it pay?" Jane asked her chief mate.

Dawkins lifted his hand to rub his chin as he stared at the beams over his head in thought. "We would be forced to offload at a warehouse ma'am, since we could hardly bring the *Destiny* to the dock each time someone wanted a delivery." He looked back down at Jane. "If we could get orders for much of the load before we begin, however, we might at least limit the footage needed. How would we find our buyers, Mister Coffin?"

"I shall pay a call on my cousin Hepzebeth on the morrow.

Her father is my uncle, and she followed her husband down to Baltimore from Nantucket on her marriage three years ago. She and Friend Ashael will help us make the right connections," Endeavor assured him.

Jane smiled as she thought how fortuitous it was that her Quaker husband had shipped aboard. The tightly knit religious clans of the Society of Friends preferred to do business with each other, and Endeavor was the key to opening the door to their vast network of contacts. She did not mean to take advantage, but any help she could get would be most welcome.

"I am agreed, then! Mister Dawkins, please draw up the wording for a handbill we can print to distribute among the furniture workshops. Leave off the price, as we shall negotiate that separately."

"Aye, aye, ma'am." Dawkins got his feet under him and stood. "I shall just have a word with Mister Koopmans, who may have some idea of how best to talk up the merits of the lumber."

After Dawkins had ducked out through the saloon door, Jane inched her chair closer to Endeavor and rested her head on his shoulder. He kissed the top of her head and asked, "Are thee worried, dear Jane? Thee seem uncommonly perturbed this morning."

"Aye, that I am. It is most vexing that a letter from Uncle Josias did not come by the mail yesterday. Without his instructions, I am unable to set in motion the plans for finding Captain Albright, or the Calloways for that matter. It is most unsettling merely to wait."

"Come." Endeavor pushed himself out of his chair and pulled Jane with him. "Let us row ashore and see about finding Ashael and Hepzebeth. The post office will have a city directory."

The postmaster did indeed have a copy of Matchett's and Endeavor soon located the address for Ashael Hussey on Howard Street.

"Here, they have opened a dry goods store."

Endeavor pointed to a listing halfway down the page. Flipping back to the street locators at the front of the book, he made a note that Howard Street ran north from Hill Street. "And look," he pointed to the address of the printer at the back of the book, "Matchett's is on Gay and Water streets. We might stop in on our way to discuss the printing of the handbills."

Well satisfied that they had a sensible plan of action, Jane and Endeavor stepped back into the street to make their way to the printshop. As she gathered her skirt to keep it out of the muddy lane, Jane glanced back toward the harbor. To Endeavor's astonishment, she suddenly gave a yell and took off running down the sidewalk with her skirt hoisted up to her knees and her hair flying loose as her hat fell off.

Endeavor had barely caught up with her when she stopped at the corner and twirled around as she looked frantically about. "He was just here," she panted. "Albright. I saw him. Oh, where did he go?"

The sidewalks were filled with the noonday crowd as people rushed home to lunch. Tall as he was, Endeavor could not catch a glimpse of the wayward captain over their heads, and Jane, even on tiptoe, could not see through the milling crowd.

"Oh, damn, I saw him, as sure as I am standing here."

"I doubt thee not, Jane. Did thee see where he came from?"

"No," she shook her head in frustration. "But that means the *Osprey* must be here, or at least nearby. Back to the boat."

Jane ran back to pick up her hat, then sprinted down the hill to the dock where they had tied up the *Destiny's* skiff. She jumped down into the bow as Endeavor untied the dockline and dropped onto the rowing seat. With Jane as lookout, he grabbed the oars and started pulling for the mooring field.

Half an hour later, they admitted defeat and turned the boat toward shore. There were too many vessels in too many harbors around the city to search them all. Jane slapped her hand on the gunwale in frustration.

"The best we can hope for is that the harbormaster has registered his arrival. I shall send Mister Dawkins to speak with him tomorrow. All right, let us pay a visit to your cousin and hope for better success."

The Hussey mercantile establishment was prominently situated on a busy corner where Baltimore Street crossed Howard. As Jane and Endeavor approached on foot, it was evident that the shop was doing a brisk business. On entering, they were obliged to wait a number of minutes before one of the harried clerks turned to them.

"Good day, Friend," Endeavor said as he stepped forward. "My name is Endeavor Coffin and I seek Ashael Hussey."

As he finished the introduction, a cry came from the back room and a rosy-cheeked young woman dressed in the plainest Quaker garb came rushing from behind the counter. "Endeavor Coffin! Here in Baltimore!" Abruptly, she stopped short and settled her demeanor into one more fitting for a Quakeress, but nonetheless came forward to embrace her cousin with a warm smile.

"The father wrote that thee were in Nantucket but recently. How comes it that we see thee here?"

Endeavor gestured toward Jane. "May I present my good wife, Jane Thorn, who has brought us in on her trading schooner."

Jane began to reach out her hand to shake with Hepzebeth, then remembered that the Friends frowned on such formal practices and gave a quick nod in greeting.

"A pleasure to make your acquaintance, Hepzebeth Hussey."

"And thine, Jane Thorn. Please, come to the back while I find my husband. He will be so pleased to see you."

Soon after, the young couples sat facing each other across a long wooden table that took up most of the floorspace in the workroom at the back of the store. At one end of the table were piled an assortment of dry goods in the process of being rebagged for display in the shop, while a simple snack of weak cider and dry biscuits had been set out in a small cleared area at the other.

Ashael Hussey proved to be a stalwart man of middling

height and broad shoulders with the long face and high brow of his Nantucket kin. His open demeanor radiated goodwill toward the visitors and Jane's hopes for his assistance in their business began to rise.

After a number of minutes spent sharing family news, Jane brought the conversation around to the purpose of their call.

"Ashael, we are hoping to make some connection with the furniture makers in the city. We have some prime mahogany to sell. As we passed Gay Street on our way to Matchett's, it looked like many of their establishments are located in that neighborhood."

"Aye, thee are right, Jane. The Finlays produce all of their Fancy furniture there and others have set up shop near them. "

"Think thee it would be profitable to call on them?" Endeavor asked.

Ashael paused as he considered the question. "Aye, I have had some dealing with Hugh Finlay and can recommend him as an honest trader, though I do not care for his taste in decoration," he observed with a wry smile. Indeed, the rage for painted Baltimore furniture was at its peak, and the local cabinetmakers were churning out hundreds of intricately painted sideboards, chairs, tables, and desks to meet the growing market. Cheaper to produce than fine wood inlay, Baltimore Fancy pieces were in high demand in the midwest and even in some of the drawing rooms of Boston and New York.

"He may not himself be in the market for exotic wood, but he might be able to introduce thee to the cabinetmakers who specialize in that sort of thing."

Jane looked at Endeavor. "I wonder if we might wish to bring some of the Finlay furniture to New York? It had been my thought to find some of the finer pieces here for transport north, but perhaps we would do better with these cheaper goods? There will be more of a market for them."

"If thee drop a hint to Hugh Finlay that thee are interested in such a purchase, I am sure it will go a long way toward gaining his assistance with the other manufacturers," Hepzebeth observed.

"And what of thy further plans?" Ashael turned to Jane. "Will you sail straight for New York?"

"Nay, we aim to spend much of the next month trading on the Bay." Jane did not mention their hunt for the missing *Osprey* or the captive Calloway family. Best to keep such information close to her chest for now.

"With what cargo? If it would suit, I have just brokered a goodly shipment of patent medicines and ointments, far more than I can sell here in the shop."

"The *Celebrated Panacea* has been very popular in Philadelphia," Hepzebeth said, "and we are getting a great number of the ladies here requesting it. We thought to become the main source for it in Baltimore, but we perhaps have more than we can easily sell at the moment," she continued with a wry smile.

The Husseys led their visitors to a small warehouse at the back of the lot. When they stepped inside, Jane could see that it contained a large number of wooden crates marked "Swaim's".

"Do you think there might be a market in Norfolk?"

"Aye, there might indeed," Ashael replied. "We know that word has spread of its efficacy, but I do not think Swaim's are shipping to the Tidewater yet."

Jane turned to face him squarely. "Would you give us a contract to carry it for you? A flat rate for the shipment, sold or not, and a percentage of the profits to Thorn Shipping for any amount over your minimum price."

"Done. I will show thee the accounts so we can determine a fair price. Once thee has met the gross revenue amount, thee may negotiate freely so as to sell the rest of the shipment."

Jane knew that no further paperwork was needed to secure their interests. A Quaker's word was as good as any written contract. The load in front of her would nicely fill the Destiny's lockers and would give them a good reason to return to Norfolk. She was well content with the deal. After arranging for them to receive Mister Dawkins the following day to work out lading and other details, Jane and Endeavor took their leave of the Husseys. The afternoon was wearing away and they had still to walk back to the harbor and row out to the *Destiny*. Finding her schooner in the dark would be much more difficult, and Jane liked to be back aboard well before the lanterns were lit.

Although they made good speed on their walk through town, it was nearly dinnertime before the couple reached the dock. Making haste to ready the skiff for casting off, they were so concentrated on the task at hand they did not take notice of the small group of people approaching rapidly from the end of the dock until one of them spoke.

"Captain Thorn?"

With a start, Jane swung about, then burst out, "Mister Wright, good heavens."

XIX
Orders from Home

Baltimore, Maryland
May 2, 1821

"And Miss Wright!" A puzzled Jane leaned over to catch a glimpse of the tall young lady standing behind her father. "What brings you here?"

The last time she had seen her uncle's accounting clerk was in the company offices in New York. Jane was astonished to see him on a dock in Baltimore.

"Greetings from Captain Josias, ma'am," Wright replied with a slight bow as he held out a letter to Jane.

Quickly breaking the seal, Jane scanned the contents of the letter. "He says you are to look over the documents with Endeavor and evaluate the losses caused by Albright these past three summers." She looked up at him. "What does he intend to do with the information?"

"My guess is that he will sue Captain Albright as well as remove him from his command. I have a letter to that effect here." Wright patted his pocket.

"Let me see it."

Taking the letter, which was addressed to George Albright, Jane read Josias' brief instructions to the captain. Albright was to turn over command of the vessel *Osprey* to Captain Jane Thorn immediately upon receipt of the letter, and to return to New York to answer questions about his trading activities on behalf of Thorn Shipping and Cargo.

"I doubt he will heed that latter instruction," Jane observed with a smile as she handed the missive back to Wright. "He won't dare show his face in New York again."

"Aye, you are probably correct, Captain Thorn. However, we won't know until we find him and hand him his orders."

"We?" Jane opened the letter from her uncle again and read a little further. "Ah, I see he means you to sail with us, Mister Wright." She looked up. "And will Miss Wright also accompany us?"

Wright smiled fondly at his daughter, then turned back to Jane with a shrug. "She was most insistent that she be allowed to travel south with me and I did not have the heart to leave her behind. I understand that you have passenger cabins aboard the *Destiny* now and Captain Josias thought we might occupy one of them if it is not too much trouble."

As she took a moment to consider this new plan, Jane looked down the dock and saw that the Wrights' luggage was piled on the shore, ready to come aboard.

"Very well, Mister Wright. We can take you aboard now if you are quite ready."

The Wrights lowered themselves into the skiff while Jane stood on the dock holding the painter line. Mister Wright, a short, fussy man of middle age, was remarkably spry, and made his way off the pier with little trouble. To her surprise, the elegantly dressed Miss Wright refused assistance from her father's outstretched hand, gathered her skirts, and jumped nimbly down into the center of the boat. She seated herself quickly next to her father on the stern bench and looked eagerly out into the harbor where the *Destiny* rocked in the gentle swells.

"Oh dear," Jane thought as she climbed down and seated herself at the bow.

It took Endeavor nearly twenty minutes of hard rowing to bring the skiff to the schooner's side. Silas was on watch and shouted out that the "Captain is inbound," as soon as he caught sight of the boat's approach. Jane could hear Galsworthy call for the ladder to be sent over, and she caught it as the skiff bumped the schooner's side. Picking up the painter from where it lay coiled on the seat next to her, she rose and, with one great heave, threw it over the *Destiny's* rail.

"Bowline fast," Jane heard Silas call, and she climbed as quickly up the ladder as her skirts would allow.

"Mister Baldwin, we have guests coming aboard. Please send down an extra line to Mister Coffin so we may hoist the luggage. Mister Baldwin!" Jane raised her voice to get her nephew's attention. *"Mister Baldwin!"*

Silas leaned over the rail to catch a glimpse of the other

passengers and now stood frozen with his mouth agape and his eyes fixed on the lace bonnet that fluttered lightly in the harbor breeze

"Mister Baldwin, you heard the captain. Fetch a rope." Galsworthy's voice was enough to finally break the spell and Silas ran aft toward the rope locker.

Within short order, the Wrights were installed in their quarters to unpack and freshen up before dinner. Jane sent word to Cookie to add two more plates to the evening mess and then sat down at her desk to read Josias' letter in full.

Dear Captain Thorn,

Your letter contains much to consider.

First to matters of your cargo. The mahogany is of particular interest. I have a buyer here who is most desirous of obtaining a lot, so please reserve five thousand board feet to return with you to New York. For the remainder of the voyage, your judgment has proven sound in choices of goods and their disposition and I leave it to your discretion.

As to George Albright and the Osprey, the news is indeed distressing. I am dispatching Mister Wright to consult with Mister Coffin and make further examination of his calculations. Based on the information already received, I enclose a letter of dismissal for Albright, and authorize you to relieve him of command, placing Osprey in the charge of Messrs. Baldwin and Galsworthy. She is to sail for New York at the earliest opportunity with whatever cargo she currently has aboard. Mister Baldwin's orders are enclosed.

The final matter is indeed of a most distressing nature. As you are aware, the safety of ship and crew are at all times the primary factor. I can understand and share your abhorrence of the entire situation. Should you have occasion to aid in the family's release and assist them in their further journey, please bear in mind that your ship and its voyage must remain your first priority, and you are not to divert from your trading mission to carry out such assistance.

126

There are at times difficult decisions to be made, and which is the correct path is yours to determine.

Fondly, your Uncle
Josias Thorn

Putting the letter down, Jane sat back in thought. Clearly, the first order of business was to find the *Osprey* but she was loathe to sail the Bay on a hunt for the missing schooner without making the time pay. They were losing money on account of Albright and she didn't see why she should dig the hole deeper by keeping the *Destiny's* hold empty as well. They could play hide-and-seek with the *Osprey* for weeks, Jane thought. "We might as well do some business while we are about it."

"Gentlemen," she announced as she stepped into the saloon to find her mates and husband chatting by the stove while they waited for their guests. "We have new orders and some decisions to make."

Jane was interrupted by the arrival of the Wrights along with Cookie and the dinner platters. Talk of miscreant captains and missing schooners was delayed while the company enjoyed their meal and were entertained by the lively Miss Wright. It was not until Galsworthy went above to supervise the watch change, and Miss Wright retired to her cabin for the evening, that Jane found an opportunity to bring up the new sailing orders again.

"Mister Wright, please remain if you would." Jane reached out a hand to stay the man as he rose to leave. "What we have to discuss involves you as much as any of us and we would welcome your thoughts."

"It seems we are to play cat and mouse this summer," Jane began. In a few words, she laid out the gist of the instructions from Captain Josias. "We must find the *Osprey* as soon as we can but I will not neglect our main purpose. We must return a profit from this voyage." The captain was adamant on this point.

"If we are to be successful with any of it, we must divide up the work. Endeavor, I am giving you and Mister Wright the task of locating the *Osprey*. As we saw her captain ashore today," Jane paused as Dawkins and Wright exclaimed, then continued "we think she may well be here in Baltimore. Check with the harbormaster tomorrow, Endeavor, and with the harbormaster in every settlement and town we visit over the coming weeks until we find him. In the meantime, you and Mister Wright must dedicate yourselves to the task Captain Josias has set you."

Endeavor and Wright nodded as Jane paused again for their agreement.

"Mister Dawkins, you and I will deal with the cargo. Please arrange for a warehouse large enough for the entire load as I wish to have an empty hold by the end of the week. We will sell what we can piecemeal, setting aside the quantity Captain Josias has reserved for his New York buyer."

"Aye, aye, ma'am. We will need to return to Baltimore later in the summer then?"

"Aye, that we will. We will be carrying goods on consignment from Hussey, so we may need to offload any unsold cargo as well."

Jane did not mention the final task, which she intended to reserve for herself. Josias had expressly forbidden her to make use of the *Destiny* or her crew in pursuit of freedom for the Calloway family. She refused to simply walk away from her promise though and would have to figure out a way to find and rescue them before she left the Bay.

An hour later, the company prepared to retire for the night. Jane was so tired from the exertions of the day, she could scarce keep her eyes open, and rose from the table to indicate that the evening had come to a close. In her weariness, she simply dropped her outer clothing on the cabin floor and climbed into the berth in her shift. She was softly snoring even before Endeavor blew out the lantern and opened the companionway hatch to let the soft night breezes blow into the cabin.

"Good night, dear Jane," he whispered as he crawled beneath the quilt and wrapped himself around her.

The sound of the watch crossing the quarterdeck roused Jane in the middle of the night. She lay awake for a few minutes, counting the footsteps and willing herself back to sleep. As she finally dropped off again, she thought she heard voices that sounded like Silas and Miss Wright.

"I shall investigate in the morning," was her last thought as she drifted off.

XX
Thorn Mercantile

Baltimore, Maryland
May 3, 1821

"Mister Wright, I have a thought." Jane put her breakfast plate down on the table. With access to the fresh food markets in Baltimore, Cookie had been outdoing himself, and the morning repast of coddled eggs with local pork sausage and biscuits had tempted Jane to a second helping. She couldn't resist the urge to lick her finger and slick up every last crumb from the dish.

"Yes, Captain?"

"Mister Dawkins will be handling the sale of our mahogany in lots. We hope to entice the local furniture makers to purchase quantities on the promise of delivery. This will require a great deal of recordkeeping and organization. I wondered if Miss Wright might be interested in assisting him with that? She seems an intelligent girl and surely has inherited some of her father's skill with numbers."

"I think that is a capital idea. It would keep her occupied for a few days. Perhaps we could find other tasks for her as we conduct business here on the Bay? It would do her good to be less idle." Mister Wright positively beamed at the suggestion of gainful employment for his daughter.

"Exactly my thought." Jane stood and dropped her napkin onto the table. "Mister Dawkins, please send Baldwin to my quarters as soon as possible. I should like to speak to him on a personal matter."

Dawkins sensed the urgency in the captain's command and had the young man knocking at the cabin door within the quarter hour.

"Come in, Silas." Jane waved him toward her trunk where he perched uncomfortably, crossing and then uncrossing his arms as she gazed at him.

"As a member of the *Destiny's* crew you are clear where your duties and attention lie, I take it?"

"Aye, ma'am." Jane's stern tone made it clear that she would brook no other answer.

"Your free time is yours of course, but I expect you to conduct yourself with decorum and an eye to the good name of everyone aboard. Do I make myself clear?"

"Aye, ma'am."

Jane smiled at the eagerness in his voice. "Very well, Silas. Please bear that in mind. You may return to your duties."

Silas leaped up from the chest with a grin toward his aunt and grabbed for the door handle. As he wrenched it open, Jane couldn't help but ask, "Does it make you happy to have her aboard?"

"Aye ma'am, most happy," and he was gone with a slam of the door.

Miss Wright proved indeed to be handy with the slate and Dawkins found himself entrusting an increasing number of tasks to her steady direction over the next few days. She caught several errors in the printed sale bills and insisted they be corrected before she would accept them from the printer for distribution to the cabinetmakers. During Dawkins' negotiation with the buyers, she was adept at recording the terms and dates they agreed on and he was soon allowing her to keep the log under his supervision. Together, they managed to arrange for the sale of nearly all of the mahogany beyond the amount reserved for the New York buyer, and Jane was well pleased with their efforts.

In turn, Jane met with the Finleys to look over their stock of furniture. While it was not to her taste, she was impressed with the quality of the work and could see why it was so popular among the rising gentry. She arranged to purchase a large number of tables and Baltimore chairs from their workshop and smaller quantities of occasional tables and desks from other cabinet factories. She ordered everything to be delivered to the wharf at the end of June, when the *Destiny* would return to Baltimore to pick up the remaining mahogany lumber and the furniture. In all, she was pleased with the items and thought they would sell well back in New York. She smiled with satisfaction as she drafted a description of the goods to be attached to the bill of particulars Dawkins would send to Josias before they departed for Norfolk and other points south the following week.

The *Destiny* was brought into the wharf on Friday, where she was offloaded to a warehouse, leaving the hold empty for the onward trading cargo. She then returned to the mooring to wait while Jane, Endeavor, and Dawkins sought out goods for their summer voyage on the Bay.

Baltimore, Maryland
May 5, 1821

"We thought to seek your advice on goods to carry south." Jane and Endeavor were once again seated at the Husseys' long table with cider and biscuits in front of them. "We will fill some of the lockers with your Swaim's shipment and expect to sell it during our Bay travels this summer. But we would like to load with other goods that might be in high demand in the shore settlements."

"Aye, Jane, thee would do well to carry tea and coffee. A clipper has newly arrived from Canton and will have a goodly amount of tea, and I know a trader who is disposing of a coffee shipment from Brazil at a good price if thee will take the entire amount."

Jane nodded as she looked to Endeavor for his thoughts. "We could bring some of the furniture pieces we ordered for New York perhaps, if they are already built," Endeavor suggested.

"A good thought. Did the Canton ship also bring silk?" Jane turned to Ashael. "We could perhaps specialize in exotic goods this trip, such as silks or porcelains in smaller quantities. They would attract the same sort of buyers."

"And lace." Hepzebeth jumped up and began pulling boxes

off a high shelf. "I ordered these collars and yards of ribbon lace from a lady and her daughter here in Baltimore. They knot them in the Belgian style and the work is exquisite."

She opened a long grey box to display rolls of fine white lace nested in tissue paper. The quality was indeed wonderful and Jane couldn't resist lifting out one of the rolls and spreading it out on the table.

"What will you have for it?"

"Will thee carry it for us?" Ashael asked. "Under the same terms as the Swaim's?"

"Indeed." Jane thought they might store the lace in her own cabin to keep it safe and clean. "I would be delighted to carry such fine goods. I am sure Silas will make short work of selling it to the ladies we meet along the way."

An idea was beginning to grow in Jane's mind for a traveling storefront that could be set up on the docks at each port they visited and stocked with the finest in goods from the Orient and South America. She would speak to Koopmans about building a collapsible shop they could easily set up and take down. By selling directly to the good citizens of the towns they would visit, she could charge a premium price without the fees and levies of the middlemen and warehouse owners. Profit would accrue more quickly from a smaller number of sales, and it would give her an excuse to visit many different towns in her search for the elusive Captain Albright.

Within short order, Jane had drawn up the agreement for the lace while Endeavor arranged for a cart to take them back to the port with the boxes. "Thank thee Friend Ashael, for the assistance," Endeavor said as he placed his hat on his head and followed Jane out the door. "We shall call again when we return to Baltimore next month."

Baltimore, Maryland
May 10, 1821

By Tuesday, Dawkins and Endeavor had purchased a sufficient quantity of China goods and coffee for the *Destiny* to be brought to the wharf again. They were unable to locate a significant number of furniture pieces, to Jane's disappointment, but loaded what they had been able to obtain into the hold over the next two days. Cookie had been busy at the provisioners' shops and the *Destiny's* galley and stores were now replenished. He was particularly pleased to have come upon a small barrel of pickles from New York and a pair of laying hens to occupy the coop at the front of the aftercabin.

In the meantime, Koopmans had been busy at his workbench and was ready to show Jane what he had fashioned from the materials he had on hand.

"I thought to use some of those planks and such from the cabin walls," he explained as he gestured to what looked like a simple pile of boards lying on the dock. "Double-duty like, if you see what I mean, ma'am. Now watch."

With a flourish, Koopmans waved his arms at Silas, who was standing by to help demonstrate the contraption. Silas leaped forward and in a trice the two had pulled the boards erect to create a large display table with a sturdy backboard. A series of shelves in different sizes could be easily mounted onto the backboard by hanging them from a row of cleats at the top. Other planks slid together to become pedestals for displaying goods to their best advantage and the whole impressive construction was surmounted by a canvas awning with the words "Thorn Mercantile – The Finest Goods from Afar" stencilled across the front.

"Remarkable," Jane laughed and clapped her hands, then turned to the chief mate. "Mister Dawkins, what say you?"

"Aye ma'am," he replied, grinning as he bent to inspect the details of the clever joinery, "it will suit just fine. You are to be commended master carpenter." Dawkins reached out to shake Koopman's horny palm. "People will come just to see your wonderful invention and stay to buy something to take home if Mister Baldwin has anything to say about the matter."

"Then we shall be successful indeed." Jane looked at Silas and asked, "What do you think, nephew? Could you make a go of it as a storekeeper?"

"Aye, ma'am," Silas replied eagerly. "I have given some thought to how to show our wares already. Look here."

Silas opened a chest sitting at the dockside and began to pull out bolts of the simple muslin that was used to create hangings in the passenger cabins. Deftly, he swathed the bare wood of the storefront in soft folds of fabric that soon transformed it into a cloudlike backdrop for the boxes of tea, bags of coffee, bolts of silk, tins of ointments and elixirs, and other trade goods he then placed on the various shelves and pedestals. Finally, he stacked several boxes of the beautiful lace down the center of the table and draped one of the finer pieces in a soft waterfall that cascaded down over the stack. Standing back to admire his handiwork, he squared his shoulders and looked at Jane.

"We can leave the goods in the hold with this arrangement when we are at a dock and just replenish as we need to. It will make it faster to put up and take down, Captain. Two or three of us could do it in an hour. And look, there is a place under here for the money box."

"Aye, ma'am, that was Baldwin's idea," Koopmans said. "That young man has a head for business, sure enough."

"And when we are not at a dock Mister Koopmans? How shall we take it ashore?" Dawkins knew that most of the Tidewater settlements had shallow harbors etched in sand by the many rivers that emptied into the Bay. The *Destiny* would have to stay offshore and bring her cargo in with the skiff.

"Hoisting handles, sir." Koopmans pointed to several eye bolts that were mounted along the edges of the larger planks. "You just strap it together and throw it into the boat."

"Well, I am most impressed Mister Koopmans, Mister Baldwin." Jane stepped back to view the storefront from a few feet away, then looked up and down the dock. "Let us add some pennants at the top so that we may be seen," she suggested, "and I believe we have the makings of a successful enterprise. Did you have something more to add, Silas?"

Blushing, Silas pulled his sketchbook from inside his shirt and held it out to Jane. "I took the liberty of asking Miss Wright to try her hand at an advertisement for the shop. For the local papers to print. And for handbills. She's, well, she's awfully good at that sort of thing. Ma'am."

Jane smiled to herself as she reached out to take the book from her nephew. There was no doubt the young man was deeply afflicted. Well, that was a state of affairs she could understand, she thought as she began leafing through the pages.

There was no question but that the girl was a gifted artist, and her designs were eye-catchingly clever. "This will do very nicely," Jane said when she handed the book back to Silas. "I wonder if she might also like to help with the store? With her father's permission of course."

"Oh aye, Auntie Jinks... ma'am." Silas grinned.

And so the arrangements for the trading trip were complete. Jane sat down with Dawkins and Endeavor that evening to plot a course that would take them around the Bay to as many towns as possible in their search for good markets and the missing *Osprey*. But as she blew out the lantern before heading to her cabin, Jane was still puzzling over how to abide by her uncle's orders and yet fulfill her promise to help the Calloway family to freedom.

"I shall have to pay a call in the morning," she decided.

XXI
The New Venture Begins

Baltimore, MD
May 11, 1821

Friday dawned bright and clear with a strong land breeze out of the north. Along with her coffee that morning, Cookie presented her with a special treat of plump raisin cakes that she refused to share with Endeavor until he figured out why.

"But of course. It is thy birthday."

"It is indeed, dear husband, and without my mother to remind you, I fear you will always forget," she said with a smile.

As a plain Quaker, Endeavor did not celebrate the many holidays and milestones that marked the cycle of each year. Jane was content for the most part to let them pass unremarked, or honored only in the company of her own family. She was not by nature sentimental but always enjoyed an opportunity to tease her husband, who could be rather stiff at times.

"Well, it seems I must wish the captain many happy returns of the day then," he smiled back and made to reach for her. Just as Jane closed her eyes for the kiss, he instead snaked his arm around behind her, snagged a bun, and promptly stuffed it in his mouth. Her laughter could be heard all the way on deck.

Jane and Endeavor brought their breakfast up on deck to enjoy a few minutes of peace and quiet before preparations for leave-taking got into full swing. They sat side-by-side on the cabin roof with their faces turned to the sun and talked of their plans for the coming weeks. Eventually, Jane mentioned something that had been weighing on her mind.

"The Calloway family. I simply must bring them away with us or at least see to their safety. Will you come with me this morning to visit the Evans sisters? I would seek their guidance."

"Of course..."

Endeavor got no further, as Jane jumped up, snatched the spyglass from her pocket and pelted forward to the bow shouting, "Damn him. There he is!"

On all sides, vessels were busy hauling anchor, setting sails, and hastening to get underway with the outgoing tide. They were making good use of the stiff morning breeze, crowding toward the southern end of the harbor and jockeying for position as the fleet moved downriver. In the midst of them, Jane had seen a familiar hull.

"Here. Can you make out the name? That white two-master there?" Jane shouted as she lowered the spyglass from her eye and slapped it into Endeavor's hand.

"Aye Jane, it is the *Osprey.*"

Jane stood fuming in impotent fury as she watched the schooner fly down the river and out of sight. With no crew aboard, and the anchor still sitting on the bottom, it would be hours before the *Destiny* could take up the chase. How bitter it was to let Albright get away once more. Endeavor and Dawkins had scoured the waterfront the last two days, questioning the harbormaster and the lightermen for news of the *Osprey*, but had not caught even a whiff of Albright's trail. Yet there he was, bound for open water as he slipped out of her grasp again.

"He'll have half a day on us but we will find him, I promise you that." Jane said between gritted teeth. She slammed the spyglass closed and shoved it in her pocket. Wiping her hair back where the wind had blown it free, she stared out over the bow. "I promise," she repeated under her breath.

By late morning, the crew had begun to return from their night ashore and Galsworthy was roaring about the deck spurring the men into action. Leaving them to prepare the *Destiny* for departure on the afternoon tide, Endeavor and Jane went ashore in the skiff to pay a final call on the Evans household.

"Can you find them?" Jane looked around at the three sisters where they stood assembled in the drawing room. "Can you send word to someone in Norfolk and find them?"

Miss Eliza nodded. "Yes Captain Jane, we have contacts that will be able to ferret them out if they are there. It may take us some time to get a response. When do you return to Baltimore?"

"At the end of the month, or sooner if we do well on our trading mission." *Or if we find that scoundrel Albright*, Jane thought to herself.

"We shall also ask Mister Singleton to write to his friends. They may know more than they would be willing to share with strangers such as us," Miss Polly suggested.

"Thank you friends. I shall be eager to hear any news. And Mister Singleton – how fares he?"

"He is well," Anne replied. "Would you like to see him? He is working in the kitchen and has made himself quite useful about the place. We will be sorry to see him go when he decides he is tired of Baltimore."

"No, but I am glad to hear that he is well." Jane could not allow the man to think he had been forgiven, but she was genuinely pleased that he had landed on his feet for the time being.

As she and Endeavor were leaving, she thanked the sisters again for taking Singleton under their roof and for their assistance in locating the unfortunate Calloway family.

"I am sure I will call on you for help again," she observed. Miss Polly grasped Jane's hand.

"And we will gladly give it, dear Captain. Godspeed, and we will look for you in a few weeks."

Back aboard the *Destiny*, Endeavor and the chief set off to check the cargo hold and review the bills of lading while Jane pored over her charts one more time. Their first port of call was a scant fifty miles to the south, and the pilot would accompany them much of the way. She hated the thought of the extra expense but knew they had a good chance of running aground in the shallow waters of the Bay without a knowledgeable guide. As usual, she would pay up, but she did not have to like it.

The Wrights had been accommodated in two of the temporary passenger cabins while in port, and Jane directed Koopmans to look the berths over for soundness before they set to sea again. Father and daughter had already proven to be a real asset to the vessel, Jane thought, and was pleased to have them travel with the *Destiny* over the following month. *If only Silas can keep his mind on his work*, she reflected.

$$\Psi$$

Friday, May 11, 1821   Passed the Fort at Baltimore on the outgoing tide at 4 o'clock in the afternoon. Osprey sighted leaving harbor several hours prior. Pilot aboard. Winds brisk NNW with choppy seas.

By four o'clock, the *Destiny* and her cargo had been cleared by the Collector and the pilot had come aboard. Galsworthy had prepared the sails for raising swiftly and was stationed at the bow ready to call for "up anchor" as soon as the tide turned.

"Heave short." Dawkins bellowed from his place on the quarterdeck. "Set the jib."

"Anchors aweigh," came Galsworthy's cry from the bow and the hands rushed to raise the sails. With the wind at her back, the schooner kicked up her heels and raced for the harbor mouth and the open Bay beyond.

Jane stood next to the pilot on the quarterdeck and watched the land slip by as they sped south. To her right, she could see the gun embankments of Fort Henry bristling with cannons.

"Have they cleared all the sunken vessels, then?" she asked the pilot.

"Aye, ma'am, that they have," he nodded. As the British bombardment fleet approached Baltimore in the fall of 1814, Jane knew the Chesapeake Flotilla had been commanded to tow any ballasted merchant vessels at the docks out into the harbor and sink them.

"I myself was part of the Blue Flotilla. We took three vessels, towed them down and sunk them agreeable to orders; we were in such haste that we made no attempt to save any articles that might have been on board. Just careened 'em and cut 'em open with axes as the British bombs flew about our ears."

"Goodness gracious, how brave of you," Jane exclaimed.

"And have the owners of those vessels been compensated?" Jane was ever the businesswoman.

"No, ma'am, they are all still in court over the matter. It may be years before they see a penny of what they are owed."

"Well," she reflected, "since we were at war over the freedom of trade and the seas, I suppose the sacrifice of a few merchant ships was worth the defense of the city."

"Aye ma'am, it was most effective too. But getting the government to turn loose of the funds in reparations is going to be a tough nut to crack." The pilot shook his head with a wry smile. "Best make sure your own vessel is well hidden should we go to war again."

Once they had cleared the inner harbor, Jane ordered the chief to call the men aft for a brief talk.

"Good work, men, we are well on our way. We will be doing a little sailing and a lot of selling in the coming weeks and you should all have plenty of time ashore. We aim to clear the hold before we return to Baltimore to pick up our load for home, and our success will depend on our salesmanship." She looked at Silas with a smile. "I know we will do well."

Jane paused, then continued in a stern voice, "We are also looking for the *Osprey*. An extra half day's pay to the man who spots her first." She looked around to see the men nodding and smiling at this news. "All right Mister Dawkins, let us set the watch."

By the time the first watch went to dinner, the *Destiny* had reached the open Bay and Jane sent the pilot back to his little schooner with a bottle of port in his pocket.

"Take your time and keep a sharp lookout on the bow," were his final words as he climbed over the rail. "The shoals are everywhere and the bottom goes to ground quickly along the shore. Wait for low tide to come in so you know you can float off if you get in trouble."

Jane thought this to be excellent advice and vowed to double the watch as they approached a harbor. Indeed, they would make it a practice to wait for full daylight before attempting any landfall.

Their first port of call was in Herring Bay on the western shore, an area marked on the chart as bordered by shallow waters along the shore but with deeper water flowing through the river channel as it passed between the headlands. They would heave to offshore on the following day and send the skiff in to sound the bottom before attempting the channel, she thought. Caution would slow them down, but better to keep her keel off the sand than run herself aground and risk damage to the hull.

Upper Chesapeake Bay
May 12, 1821

Saturday, May 12, 1821   Anchored at Annapolis. Mid morning departure for Herring Bay in squally conditions. No sighting of the Osprey.

Awake at first light, Jane could feel the waves slapping against the schooner's sides as the wind picked up. She could hear the watch as they moved swiftly about the deck, then heard the call for "All hands" from Dawkins directing the crew in setting sail.

They had anchored off Annapolis the night before, and if they hoped to make Herring Bay by noon, they would have to be underway as soon as the mist lifted. Jane had been up late with the watch and decided to give herself another few minutes sleep. She knew her mates would have things well in hand up top and was enjoying the warm cocoon of her berth. Endeavor, who always slept closest to the bulkhead so that Jane could jump up quickly if needed, was snoring softly. She kissed him gently and turned away to pull the covers back over her head.

"Good heavens." Jane recoiled in surprise. Perched on her desk and staring at her with large blue eyes was a very large, very fat, orange cat. "Who are you? And how did you get in here?" she whispered.

In response, the visitor blinked at her then jumped down onto the cabin sole. By the time Jane extricated herself from the

142

quilts and tried to catch him, the cat had bounded up the companionway ladder and squeezed himself through the narrow crack she left in the hatch at night to bring fresh air below.

Wide awake now, she quietly pulled on her clothes before climbing the ladder and pushing open the slatted door at the top. As she stepped onto the foredeck, she saw the cat, settled on the cabin roof taking his morning bath.

"Where in tarnation did that come from?" Jane asked Griggs, who was manning the helm.

"It's the girl's, ma'am. She brought it aboard yesterday when she came back from town."

"Well she can jolly well keep it with her then. Mister Dawkins."

"Aye, ma'am?" Dawkins was standing at the rail, looking up at the sails to check that they were drawing well in the stiff breeze.

"Have one of the men catch that beast and deliver it to Miss Wright. I will not have it loose about the deck."

In the end, it took three of the crew more than a quarter of an hour to corral the animal and haul it away. Jane could not help but laugh at the way it would allow someone to get so close they could nearly touch it, only to duck nonchalantly away and saunter off into some inaccessible hidey-hole. She had to admire its air of self-possession but had no use for a cat aboard. She would see the thing put ashore as soon as possible.

The *Destiny* made good time down the Bay and was standing off the harbor entrance at Tracy's Landing shortly before noon. Jane ordered the skiff put out with the sounding lead aboard and directed Galsworthy to test the depth of the channel at hundred-yard lengths.

"We've plenty of water, ma'am, and the tide looks to be at slack on the ebb. We should go in now, I think, Captain, but take it slow like," the second mate reported back.

With sails ready to back at the first sign of shoaling, the schooner cautiously made its way between the flat promontories that formed the channel and came to rest in the wide harbor that marked the river mouth beyond. Through her spyglass,

Jane could see a modest pier with several oyster boats tied up at the western end.

"All right, Mister Dawkins, let us go ashore and see the lay of the land. And bring the sounding lead!"

The appearance of a large schooner in the harbor brought a fair number of the townspeople to the dock so that there were many willing hands to catch the skiff's painter line. Within short order, Jane located the town leaders and obtained their permission to set up shop on the waterfront the following day. She wanted to be prepared to open the store bright and early on Monday. Then they passed around copies of the handbills printed in Baltimore. It looked to be a promising first visit.

Jane sat at her desk later that evening as she and Endeavor, along with the chief and the Wrights, waited for dinner to be served in the saloon. She pulled out her charts and tried to plot where Albright might be with the *Osprey*, but soon threw down her pencil in frustration. Without knowing what the man was up to, she had no way to guess what direction he might be headed. They would just have to trust to luck and any information they might pick up around the Bay to locate the vessel.

A few minutes later, the main cabin door opened and Cookie entered with the dinner trays balanced in his arms. Jane rose and walked to the table, drawing a deep and appreciative sniff of the mouth-watering smell rising from the dishes.

"Beef stew, or my name is not Jane!" She was always pleased when her favorite dish appeared on the menu.

Cookie gave her a wide grin and set the dishes on the table. "Aye, ma'am, and *bon appetit* as the Frenchies say."

Dawkins lifted the lid on the terrine as Cookie opened the door to return to the galley. In a flash, an orange ball of fur launched itself through the opening, landed on the table and reached a large paw into the dish. The diners were too astonished to do more than gape at the intruder as Cookie threw himself at the cat. True to form, the animal made itself hard to capture and it took all of them to corner him. Once he had been dispatched with the cook to be returned to Miss

Wright's cabin, Jane spoke most forcefully to the pet's chagrined owner.

"Much as I appreciate your desire to rescue that animal," she began, "I cannot countenance his running loose on my vessel, inviting himself where he is not wanted and causing mayhem. He must go ashore on the morrow, and not return. I am sorry for it, but I do wish you had asked me before bringing him aboard."

"As I pointed out myself," the young lady's father added. Looking sternly at his daughter where she sat to his right, the embarrassed Mister Wright made it clear he was no fan of the cat.

Through tears, Miss Wright apologized. "I found him wandering the dock, and he looked so hungry I took pity on him. I did mean to ask, but we left so quickly, and then I just forgot. I am sorry ma'am. I will put him ashore tomorrow, I promise."

"Very well, and I do understand your kind intentions. Although he hardly looks as if has missed many meals," Jane observed wryly. "However, we will see the last of him tomorrow, so that is an end to the matter," thereby demonstrating just how little the captain knew about cats.

XXII
A New Member of the Crew

Tracy's Landing, Maryland
May 14, 1821

Jane stood back and crossed her arms as she looked over her handiwork. Dressed in neat linen trousers and a cotton shirt with a blue bow tie and striped waistcoat, Silas looked every inch the young shop clerk he would play today. She reached forward to tweak the angle of the tie again and declared herself satisfied.

"It is a fine suit of clothes, nephew. Thanks to you and your father, Miss Wright," she said, looking over Silas' shoulder at the young lady standing by the saloon stove.

"My pleasure, ma'am." The Wrights had been happy to take on the task of outfitting Silas for his new role as Thorn Mercantile's representative. Their visits to a tailor and haberdashery in Baltimore had turned the rather scruffy young seaman into the handsome man of affairs who now stood before her. Jane could see the gleam in Miss Wright's eye as she surveyed the dashing Silas.

"And you as well, Miss Wright. You look the part. I am sure the good people of Herring Bay will be quite charmed by the pair of you," Jane nodded approvingly.

Miss Wright was dressed in a neat lawn dress with a stiff collar covered by a pleated pinafore; with her hair pulled back in a tidy bun, she looked most business-like.

"All set, then." Jane clapped her hands. "Let us get ashore and open for trade."

The crew had spent the prior afternoon arranging the storefront on the dock after their half day of liberty. Many of them had taken the opportunity to attend service at St. James church, while Jane had spent the morning quietly reading as Endeavor sat in silent witness. Silas joined the Wrights for a walk in the lanes after the morning worship, and Jane could see the young couple becoming closer each day. Well, she thought, as long as the girl's father had no concerns, she would let things take their course. She knew that her sister counted on her to watch out for her nephew, but Jane thought the boy had a good head on his shoulders and needed little guidance from her beyond the occasional reminder of his duties.

On deck now, the skiff was being loaded with the final goods for the storefront, including the lace Jane brought out from her cabin. She had decided that she would take the first shift with Silas and Endeavor, but Miss Wright insisted on coming along in the boat.

"It will be good for me to see how things go," she explained. "And I can help with the more delicate items. The ladies won't want to talk to men about that sort of thing. Or, begging your pardon, the captain, I shouldn't think."

The Husseys had put Dawkins onto a shipment of lacy undergarments and corsets that arrived in Baltimore on a ship from France. Part of the shipment had been damaged in transit, and the remaining items were being sold as salvage. With a little attention, he thought they might be cleaned up and offered at a good price to the ladies of the Tidewater, who would not see goods like these in the local establishments. Jane acknowledged that Miss Wright would be a better salesperson for such personal garments and agreed to have her join them in the boat.

"Just a moment," Jane said as she laid her hand on the girl's arm. "Where is that blasted cat? He is to go ashore with you, and I do not wish to see him back aboard."

"Oh, I had forgotten. Please, wait for me." In short order, Miss Wright had returned with the enormous cat clutched in her arms. He appeared content to be manhandled and purred loudly as Miss Wright made her way to the rail. However, as she leaned down to hand him to Hitchens, who had been delegated to row them to land, the cat twisted in the air and leaped back aboard, dashing between Jane's legs as he made an attempt to escape.

"No you jolly well don't." Jane grabbed his back legs as he ran under her, scooped up a bucket that was standing outside the galley door, and dumped the protesting animal into it. She held him in while shouting for someone to bring her the lid, then used her scarf to tie it on and secure the howling cat within.

"There, no more nonsense from you, Mister Cat." Swiftly, he was loaded into the boat, where he kept up a litany of yowls and protests all the way to shore.

As the skiff nudged the dock, Silas jumped quickly up to tie off the painter. He reached for Miss Wright to help her navigate the treacherous step between the rocking boat and the splintered pier, but she ignored the outstretched hand, gathered her skirts, and leaped up on her own. With a grin in Jane's direction, she reached down for the cat in his pail and marched down the dock.

"Well, my friend, I believe you have met your match. I like that girl," Jane said laughing as she took Silas' hand and pulled herself onto the dock.

"Me too, Auntie Jinks," he smiled back.

By the time their relief arrived to give them a respite for the midday meal, Jane was beginning to wonder if her plan was as sound as she had thought in Baltimore. A few customers had found their way to the shore, but most had not purchased anything, preferring to poke at the goods and ask questions rather than open their wallets.

In addition to the lack of trade that put her out of sorts, Jane found herself having to fend off the attentions of the cat. Once released from his pail, he refused to wander off, but instead wound himself around everyone's ankles all morning. He seemed to take a particular liking to the captain, the pail incident apparently forgotten.

"You won't get rid of him that way," she observed as she saw Silas bend down to drop part of his lunch in front of the cat.

"Aye, but he looks mighty hungry and I have to give him something, ma'am."

"What you are giving him is expectations. And he is *not*

148

coming back aboard." Jane was quite clear on the matter in her own mind.

To her relief, word of the *Destiny's* arrival seemed to have spread by the afternoon, and trade picked up. By the time they closed up shop at dusk, Hitchens had made two more trips to the cargo hold to replenish the tea supply. The profits were not enough to cover her expenses yet, but Jane thought another day might help them break even. Dawkins and Endeavor agreed.

"It takes time to let folks know we are here," the chief observed. "We will see more custom tomorrow, mark my word, ma'am."

They left Griggs ashore to guard the store overnight, and half of the rest of the crew were given shore leave for the evening. Galsworthy cautioned them about creating a disturbance in the local taverns, as their actions would reflect on the *Destiny*.

"We are here to do business, so have fun, but remember that the state of your pockets depends on people coming to buy. Take care not to scare them off."

Tracy's Landing, Maryland
May 15, 1821

Jane was pleased to see a line of customers waiting for them as they rowed into shore the following morning. Dawkins was right. It had taken time for word to spread and people to make their way to town. They had scarcely pulled back the curtains on the store before they had folks crowding the stall, eager to make their purchases. Jane wondered if they had loaded sufficient quantities of tea and coffee as she watched their stores dwindle. By late afternoon, they had made another two trips to replenish the supply and Dawkins reported that they were down to the last case of tea.

Leaving Hitchens to work the shop with Silas and Miss Wright, Jane and Endeavor took a break to climb among the sand dunes that lined the shore. As they crested the top of grassy slope, Jane dropped onto the ground and pulled off her hat to let the breeze lift her hair and cool the sweat that had collected under her collar. She was not used to the southern humidity and any breath of air was a huge relief. After staring out at the horizon for a while lost in thought, Jane turned to look at her husband as he lay next to her in the sand

"I believe I have underestimated the demand, Endeavor. We might have loaded fewer silks and more tea, I am thinking."

"Aye, but the silks will bring more once we find a buyer. We shall just have to talk up the merits of coffee in the meantime."

"Have you had any word of the *Osprey*?"

Endeavor drew himself up onto his elbows as he replied, "Nay Jane, she does not appear to be known here. But I have put out the word that we are looking for her in case anyone knows something."

It would have been too much to expect that they would hear news of Albright at their very first stop, but Jane had to keep her hopes up. In the meantime, Mister Wright would continue working his way through the shipping records, logs, and the records of vessel arrivals and departures provided by Sykes in Norfolk. Somewhere in there, she was sure, was not only proof of wrongdoing, but also a clue to where she might find the *Osprey* now.

The day drew to a close, and Jane returned to the *Destiny* while the crew broke down the shop and stored the goods back in the cargo hold. Exhausted, she had to keep shaking herself awake as she sat at her desk and made her final calculations for the passage south in the morning. Wearily, she changed into her nightclothes and crawled into her berth long before Endeavor was finished overseeing the accounting of the contents of the hold.

"If you're good for nothing else, at least you can keep me warm," she murmured to the cat curled up on her pillow.

After hanging around the shop for two days, the animal had made it plain that he considered himself part of the crew. Galsworthy didn't have the heart to leave him behind after they loaded the skiff for the last time; when the cat jumped aboard as they untied the painter, the second mate let him stay.

"The captain will probably just throw you overboard," he said to the purring bundle on his lap, "but you'll have to take your chances."

In the end, Jane knew when she was beaten and arranged for water and food to be provided for him in the saloon along with a box of sand on the foredeck.

"I shall have to think of a name for you in the morning," she said as she wrapped her arm around the cat and fell asleep.

XXIII
On the Hunt

Tappahannock, Virginia
June 7, 1821

The next few weeks revealed the strengths and weaknesses of the captain's plans. Accustomed as she was to running trade goods up and down the Hudson River of New York, and along the coast to Maine and back, Jane was not prepared for the sparse settlements, and long distances, of the Chesapeake Bay. Having to skirt the many shoals and islands meant beating across the wind into narrow channels, and frequently sending the small boat out ahead to sound the depths. Passages she reckoned would take a day sometimes took two, and harbors that looked accessible on the chart turned out to be silted in from the spring runoff. Navigation was a challenge. The low dunes covered in waving marsh grasses and the dense forest behind them, obscured the landmarks and made it difficult to match the sailing charts to what could be seen ashore.

Fortunately, trading stops up and down the Potomac and Rappahannock Rivers and into the communities that nestled on the shores of the Tangier Sound had proven successful for the *Destiny*. In addition to the shopfront, which was turning a tidy profit under the increasingly skilled watch of Silas and Miss Wright, Dawkins and Jane had been successful at selling cases of the Swaim's elixirs and ointments to mercantile establishments in the larger towns. They had quickly run out of tea and then coffee, but were doing well with the silks and laces, and the undergarments that were fetching a higher price than Dawkins had expected. There was no question that Miss Wright had the knack of making a sale.

More frustrating was that they were making no progress on locating the missing schooner. The Bay was a busy waterway with many white two-masted schooners plying the channel, but the best efforts of the lookouts had not been able to identify the *Osprey* among the busy shipping traffic. While the promise of a half-day's pay had sharpened the crew's attention, so far they had come up empty.

One evening in early June, after the meal was done and Miss Wright had returned to her cabin, Jane called everyone together in the saloon to consider their plans. In the fading light of the summer evening coming in through the open ports above her head, she looked around at her officers, Mister Wright, and Endeavor, who had stripped down to his shirtsleeves in the oppressive heat.

"We have done tolerably well in trade this summer," she began. "But time is passing and we are no closer to finding the *Osprey*." She turned to Endeavor. "Is there really no news to be had of her?"

"I do not know if people really have no knowledge, or if they just do not wish to share it with me." Endeavor scratched his head in frustration and leaned back in his chair. "Folks are beginning to talk, I fear. They already know what I am going to ask as soon as we get to a new place. I reckon that Albright has gotten word that we are on the hunt for him."

"Mister Wright, are you any closer to making a guess as to his whereabouts?" Jane looked at her uncle's accounting clerk with a frown. He had been spending many hours with charts and the logs in an attempt to identify patterns in the *Osprey's* movements on the Bay as he put together a case of particulars against the captain that would stand up in court.

"Yes, ma'am, I think I am though I am not so sure that I am ready to present my thoughts."

"Come now, Mister Wright. Any thought is better than none and I confess to being at the end of mine."

"Very well, have a look here." Wright stood and opened one of the cupboards that lined the saloon walls. The mahogany front dropped forward to form a desk, revealing rows of cubbyholes filled with neatly rolled charts. Wright took one from the bottom row, closed the desk, and unrolled it on the saloon table.

"This is Norfolk." Wright adjusted the lantern that hung over the table as he pointed to the lower end of the chart. Jane and the others gathered to peer over his shoulder. "These lines I have drawn," he traced one of several pencil marks that originated in Norfolk and connected with many locations around the Bay, "show where he traveled last year after leaving Norfolk, as far as I can tell."

Wright reached into his pocket to extract a short pencil stub and began circling dates he had written on the chart next to the various lines.

"If we follow the dates, we can see that he is going back and forth between small towns along the western shore of the lower Bay and Norfolk, arriving back at the Roads every two weeks, as you discovered, Mister Coffin." He drew a circle around Norfolk as he spoke.

"But every fourth time, Mr. Sykes' notes show that he is gone for almost three weeks, like clockwork." Wright looked expectantly up at the faces surrounding him. "Where do you reckon he goes during that time?"

"What do the logs say?" Dawkins asked.

"That is the mystery of it," Wright explained. "They do not say anything at all."

Jane straightened in surprise. "At all? How can that be? Surely Captain Josias would have noticed the lack?"

"Yes, Captain, he did. It was one of the things that caused him to set you on Albright's trail. There are large gaps in the log entries that are unexplained."

"Well," Jane looked around, "what do you surmise? Where does he go?"

Wright cleared his throat and looked like he wanted to say something, then changed his mind.

"Come man, out with it." Jane had no patience for his reticence. "What are you thinking?"

"Baltimore, Captain Thorn. I suspect he goes to Baltimore." Wright drew a circle around the city as he continued. "If he were to call in to the city on those passages, it would add almost a week to his trip, would it not?"

Jane slapped her hand on the chart. "And we saw him there." She stepped away from the table and straightened her back. "When do you reckon he will be in Baltimore again, Mister Wright?"

"If he holds to the pattern, in two weeks' time."

"Very well, I suggest then, that we beard the lion in his den. I am tired of hoping we will cross paths with him as we pursue our trading efforts. Tomorrow we set sail for Annapolis where we will look to sell off the rest of the cargo and provision for two weeks at sea."

Jane stepped back to the chart and squinted at the area to the south of Baltimore where the Patapsco River widened into the Bay. "Then we shall take up a position off Gibson Island, here," she pointed to a spot south of the river junction. "And we will wait. He will not get past me again," she said firmly as she rolled up the chart and handed it back to Wright.

As she lay in her berth next to her husband later that evening, Jane could hear the port watch return aboard from their night on the town. She hoped they had gotten their fill of fun because the future promised to be nothing but long hours of sitting lookout and watching the horizon for many days at a time.

"What do thee intend to do when thee find him?" Endeavor asked.

Jane stopped petting the cat, whom she had dubbed Edwin in honor of her grandfather, and twisted her head to look at Endeavor.

"Follow him ashore and give him notice that his contract is forfeit. Then dismiss the crew and prepare the *Osprey* for the trip home."

"He is not likely to go quietly," Endeavor warned.

"Nay, that he is not. It is also possible he may seek to destroy his logs if he knows we are tightening the noose. What do you suggest?"

"I do not know how the thing might be done, but it would be best to catch him unawares I should think."

"Aye, you are right…" Jane began pondering ways to get herself and her men aboard the *Osprey* without a fight and before Albright could destroy the records.

"Do you think he has the loyalty of his men?" She asked a few minutes later, only to realize that Endeavor was snoring softly in her ear.

"Oh well," she said to the cat, "I shall think of something."

Gibson Island, Maryland
June 20, 1821

Wednesday, June 20, 1821   Continue at position at Lat. 39° 04' N Long. 76° 25' W.   hove to on watch for Osprey. Weather varied with light winds, people employed variously. Osprey sighted and pursued.

Jane was sure that if she spent one more minute staring out over the water, she would go mad. Though her straw hat shaded her eyes, she was drenched in sweat that made her trousers cling to the back of her legs and her linen shirt chafe at the neck. She could tell that the three other lookouts were faring no better, so she just wiped the sweat away and held her place.

The *Destiny* was hove-to off the east shore of Gibson Island, drifting slowly on the tides as the crew kept watch. They had been on station for over a week, watching the many dozens of vessels, large and small, that traversed the upper Bay each day. Jane knew how wearying such duty could be, and had Galsworthy put the men on half-hour lookout stints. She took her own place in the rotation, as did the Wrights and Endeavor, for which she was grateful. Even with the extra hands, it was tedious work to stand at the rail dawn to dusk and scan the horizon for a white hull with two masts.

As she came off lookout duty, Jane went in search of the ship's carpenter.

"Mister Koopmans, I think the crew needs a bath." She smiled at his raised eyebrows. "Aye, we have all sat cooking in this heat for too many days."

Under her direction, Koopmans rigged a sling off the main boom that could be raised and lowered over the side. Soon, boisterous laughter could be heard as the crew stripped down and climbed one-by-one into the sling to be dunked in the Bay. Jane had banned swimming as she wanted the *Destiny* to be ready to sail at a moment's notice, so the chance to cool off in the fresh water of the upper Bay was most welcome. For herself and Miss Wright, she arranged for an area of the deck to be curtained off and pails of water to be hoisted aboard. When it was her turn, she stripped off her sweaty garments and blissfully poured the water over her head, sighing in pleasure. No sooner had she wiped herself dry, however, than she heard the lookout's cry.

"*Osprey* ho!"

"Where away?" Jane called out as she struggled into her fresh clothing. She could hear pandemonium on the other side of the curtain as everyone rushed to the port rail to verify the sighting.

It was Hitchens who sighted the *Osprey* as she beat north two miles offshore. Under full press of sail, she was heeled to starboard making good time against the northwesterly winds. Through the spyglass, Jane could clearly see the name picked out in black lettering on the bow.

"Well done, Mister Hitchens. The reward is yours. Now, Mister Dawkins, let us pick up the trail."

"All hands to the sails!" Galsworthy's voice boomed out and sent the crew scrambling to hoist the yards and set the jib.

Within a few minutes, the *Destiny* picked up speed and swung around to port to head up the Bay in pursuit of her prey.

"Not too close, Griggs," Jane cautioned the helmsman. "Let us not alarm him. Keep well back and do not make it seem as if we are following him."

Griggs screwed up his face and glanced at her questioningly.

"Just sail, well, casually." She tried again.

"Aye, ma'am. Casual it is."

XXIV
Run to Ground

Upper Chesapeake Bay, Maryland
June 20, 1821

"Put out the sounding lead, Mister Dawkins."

Jane hung over the starboard rail watching the shore as it crept closer. For the last three hours, they had trailed two or more miles astern of the *Osprey* as she made her way north through the deeper water along the eastern shore. With plenty of steamboat traffic and ships making their way into Baltimore, she felt confident that Albright had not cottoned on to their presence on his tail.

Then, to Jane's surprise, Albright did not make the tack that would have brought him up the Patapsco River to Baltimore. He was now well beyond the river mouth and showed no signs of altering course. The charts warned of shoals in these reaches and Jane thought it wise to take their own depth soundings. Albright, however, appeared to have no such concerns and drove the *Osprey* hard ahead. As the gap between them widened, Jane stood at the bow with Dawkins at her shoulder and squinted into the late afternoon sun.

"We shall run out of daylight soon, Dawkins. If he does not put into port in the next hour we shall have to heave to for the night."

"Look ma'am," Dawkins pointed ahead. "She is coming around."

"Loose the sheets," Jane called out. The schooner came upright and slowed to a crawl as her booms swung out to starboard and spilled the wind. Off the larboard bow, they could see the *Osprey* tack to port and then catch the breeze again on a westbound course.

"Keep headway on but let us wait until we see where she goes."

158

Jane stood at the bow with the spyglass clapped firmly to her eye as she watched the *Osprey* sail to the west until it disappeared beyond a low-lying set of islands off the end of a spit of land. Snapping the spyglass shut, she strode aft and climbed the ladder to the quarterdeck with her chief on her heels.

"All right, Dawkins, let us pick up speed but keep a good watch ahead for shoals. Hold your course Mister Griggs, and we will make the turn as we come even with that inlet there." Jane pointed to a break in the shore a scant half mile ahead.

Dusk was settling in as the *Destiny* approached the islands to the west. As they drew closer, Jane could see masts that stuck up above the low-lying trees on the far side of the marshy spit.

"He's dropped his sails, ma'am," Dawkins said.

"Aye, and we shall do the same. Let go the anchor."

"Aye, aye, ma'am."

With a shudder, the schooner came to a halt as the halyards were released to allow the heavy gaffs at the top of the sails to drop down onto the booms below while the foresail sheets were loosed. With a clang, Galsworthy hammered loose the pin that secured the anchor to the bow, and it plunged into the water with a loud splash.

"Anchor set and holding," he passed the word to the quarterdeck a few minutes later.

"Mister Dawkins, please join me below as soon as you are able," Jane ordered. "Griggs, you are relieved at the helm. Please locate Mister Wright and Mister Coffin and ask them to come below."

With a final glance at the *Osprey's* masts, she jumped down the companionway ladder and made her way to the saloon. "I really must stop doing that," she thought to herself yet again. "It sets a bad example for the boys."

"We have run him to ground gentlemen." Jane paused and looked at the party assembled around the table.

"My guess is that we have discovered his hiding place," Wright said. "It would explain why no one had seen the *Osprey* in Baltimore. She is safely hidden here and it is but a few miles' walk over the dunes to Baltimore if one were to row up the river a ways."

Jane nodded in agreement. "He may very well be on his way to the city even now. But whether he is still aboard or no, I mean to take command of the *Osprey* tonight."

Endeavor half rose from his chair as if to protest then sat back down at a sharp glance from the captain.

"Mister Dawkins, how many crew does he have aboard?"

"Four, ma'am. And a mate, the bo'sun, and the cook." Although the *Osprey* was a smaller schooner than her own vessel, Jane was surprised but relieved at how few men Albright employed.

"Very well, a small boarding party should do it, especially as I doubt the crew will take Albright's side in a dispute with the owners. Mister Coffin, please fetch Captain Josias' instruction letter and be ready to leave after dark. Mister Wright, I will take Albright's orders as well. Mister Dawkins, I leave you in charge of the *Destiny*. Have Galsworthy lower the boat after the evening meal is cleared. I will take him and Mister Baldwin to round out the group."

Before going on deck later that evening, Jane ducked quickly into her cabin to pull a dark dress over her trousers and shirt. Endeavor followed and pulled the door firmly shut behind him then stood with his arms crossed and waited for Jane to look up from where she crouched on the floor rummaging in her clothes chest.

"I must protest, Jane."

With a sigh, she sat back on her heels and asked, "Why?"

"He may be a desperate man and use the excuse of darkness to claim innocence should he choose to defend himself."

Jane knew that Endeavor was wont to hold his peace, even when he disagreed with her choices, unless he was seriously concerned.

She rose and came to him, wrapping her arms around his waist.

"We will be cautious, I promise. We will leave at the first

sign of trouble, but I think we will take him by surprise and no harm will come to anyone."

"Thy crew and vessel are thine to command, of course. It is the thought of *thee* in danger Jane, that frightens me."

She stood on her toes and kissed him. "Aye, I can understand your feelings, dear man. And I promise you I will not take any risks that are not necessary to our mission. But we are going, and that is my decision."

She could feel him trembling as he held her tight and rested his chin on the top of her head. His non-violent principles might be tested this evening, Jane knew, but she was glad to have him along. With a final squeeze she stepped away and continued hunting for her navy-blue shirtwaist.

Jane took Galsworthy aside as the boarding party prepared to descend the ladder into the skiff.

"Are you armed?" she asked in a low voice.

The second mate pulled back his coat slightly to show her the two pistol handles protruding from his belt. With a nod she stepped back to let him climb over the rail then followed behind with her skirts clutched in one hand. She dropped quietly into the boat and seated herself at the starboard oar. As Galsworthy reached for the painter to pull it aboard, Jane heard a whispered "*Hoy!*" from the deck and looked up.

Mister Wright hung over the side. "Wait for me," he whispered and threw his leg over the rail. Jane had no time to protest before he had slithered down the ladder and jumped into the boat, setting it rocking so that they were nearly tipped out.

She grabbed the back of his coat and shoved him onto the stern bench. "Sit down." Jane glared at him in the faint moonlight, then decided it was not the time to argue. Let the man come. He might prove useful.

"All right, men, silence from here on out," she murmured as she nodded to Silas, who was manning the larboard oar. Together, they began to pull for shore.

It took nearly an hour of steady rowing to bring the skiff to the shore and then around the south end of the island through a shallow cut. As they rounded the eastern side of the sandy point, Jane saw the *Osprey* floating two cables offshore. A small lantern hung from her stern but she was otherwise shrouded in darkness save where the moonlight shone off her pale hull.

She reached her hand out to stop Silas from taking his next stroke and peered ahead.

"Turn around," she hissed urgently and Silas pushed the oar away to force the skiff to turn. With a few strong strokes, they soon had the skiff hidden back around the point and tucked against the shore. "Everyone down," she whispered and slid onto the floor beside Silas.

In the quiet they could all hear what Jane had noticed. The *Osprey* was lowering her boat.

"I am going ashore. Wait here." Jane tied her skirts around her waist and ducked overboard. She waded through the few feet of shallow water to the beach then struck out over the dunes to the far side. Lying down behind a stand of marsh grass she could see the shadowy shapes of the crew as they moved about the schooner's deck.

"Put the ladder over." Albright's stern voice carried clearly across the water to where Jane was hidden. The captain obviously had no fear of being discovered.

Jane watched as two men clambered down the side and into the boat then began pulling away. They were headed south, making good time in the calm water. As the sound of the oars faded, she scrambled back to the far shore and splashed quietly out to the waiting skiff.

"I think Albright has gone ashore and taken the mate with him," she reported in a hushed tone. "This is our chance." In a few words, she explained her plan then seated herself in the center of the rowing bench. "Stay down and covered," she reminded them as she took up the oars once more.

Wanting to draw attention to herself, Jane pulled out the muffling from the oarlocks and made a great deal of noise as she allowed the oars to splash on each backward pull. Within a few minutes, they were approaching the *Osprey* and she called up to the deck.

"Ahoy! You there! Anyone on watch?"

"Evening miss. What are you about there?" The man on watch lifted a lantern and uncovered it to shine on her face as he looked down at her. From his vantage point, all he could see was a young woman in a small boat with tarps covering several large objects.

Jane reached under the closest tarp and pulled out a bottle of port. Holding it up, she called back, "We thought this might be of interest. I have three cases and I can promise you a good price." She waved her hand over the tarps as if they covered a trove of the finest wine from Portugal.

The man laughed. "Nay miss, we are well supplied with all the hooch we need. But we would welcome a visit from a pretty lass like yourself. Come aboard."

Jane pretended to hesitate then reached forward and grabbed the painter to tie the boat snugly to the schooner's side. The seaman on deck held the lantern overboard to light her way up the ladder and stretched out a hand to help her over the rail.

"Welcome to the *Osprey* miss. My name's Jack," he said with bow. As much as she could see of him in the dim light, Jack looked to be a dark-haired young man of twenty or so, dressed in Thorn colors with a whistle on a lanyard around his neck. The bo'sun, she thought.

"And this here's Dog." Jack jerked his thumb over his shoulder at the man who appeared out of the dark into the halo of light cast by the lantern. Where Jack was a sturdy seaman with a handsome face and a wide grin, Dog looked as if he had some hard years behind him and, though still young, had a lifetime of scars to prove it. He scowled at Jane then threw a sneer in the direction of the bo'sun before continuing to pace the deck on his quarterly rounds.

"Just the two of you here?" She asked as she looked around.

"Oh no, miss, just us two on deck. But don't bother none about Dog. He's just ornery all the time and won't care that you're here. Come, let me show you around. The captain's ashore with the mate and won't be back for hours so we have time for a chat, if you please."

Jane had been careful to stand at the rail as she conducted this conversation so that those in the boat below could hear.

"But won't we disturb the others?"

"You mean the rest of the crew? Nah, they're sound asleep in their bunks by now. Come, follow me." Jack reached out and put his arm around Jane's waist and began to pull her toward the companionway.

"Oh, my shoe." Jane yanked away from him, bent over, and lifted her skirt to find the knife she kept tucked in the top of her boot. Palming it, she straightened up and smiled at the eager young man. "Lead the way, sir."

Jack jumped down the companionway ladder and pulled open the door to the tiny saloon. He stepped over the threshold, then lurched forward and fell onto the table as Jane shoved him hard from behind.

"What in tarnation..." he shouted, but quickly closed his mouth when he saw the knife in Jane's hand.

"My deepest apologies, Bo'sun Jack. Allow me to introduce myself. I am Captain Jane Thorn, master of the *Destiny* and representative of your employer. Please stay where you are."

Keeping her eye on Jack, Jane backed out into the landing at the bottom of the ladder and called up through the hatch, "Dog! Jack needs you!"

In a trice, a shaggy head appeared in the opening and the seaman slid to the bottom of the ladder as Jane waved frantically in the direction of the saloon door. Dog peered into the room then turned back to Jane with a frown.

"Hey." The sight of the knife in Jane's hand brought him up short at first, but then he made to lunge at her.

"No Friend, thee would be wise to stay thy hand."

Endeavor's voice stopped the man in his tracks and he backed up against the bulkhead as the rest of Jane's party trooped down the ladder.

"Please, join us in the saloon," Jane waved to Dog then followed him back into the cramped room, leaving her husband

and the others outside to listen at the open door.

"I am Captain Jane Thorn," she said again. "When is Captain Albright expected to return?"

It transpired that the captain and his mate were expected back aboard around midnight. They would have to work quickly as the clock was already gone ten. She ordered Dog, with the assistance of Galsworthy and Silas, to roust the crew out of the fo'c'sle and bring them on deck and sent Endeavor and Mister Wright with Jack to knock on the cook's door.

Once the crew was assembled on the foredeck under the light of the lantern Jane had hung from the shrouds, she looked them over. The crew was young, with none appearing much older than the bo'sun. The cook though, was an old hand of fifty or more and seemed more weary than surprised at being turned out of his bed by the intruders.

"Men, I am going to give it to you straight." Jane stood on the hatch cover so they could see her clearly in the lamplight. "We are here on behalf of Thorn Shipping and Cargo to relieve Captain Albright of his command."

A murmur greeted this news, though none of the men spoke up. There was a distinct tension in the air, Jane saw as she scanned their faces. None of them wanted to look her in the eye and a couple seemed to be inching backward out of the light.

"We have cause to believe the *Osprey* is being used for purposes both contrary to orders and possibly against the law." She paused and looked around to see if anyone had something to say. When the silence had stretched out, Jane continued.

"Mister Baldwin here," she pointed to her nephew, "will be assuming command. The *Osprey* will return to New York. Any of you that wish to stay aboard are welcome. Any who wish to go ashore now, you may do so with my blessing. We will pay your wages and put you off tomorrow. Mister Galsworthy, dismiss the men except for the watch."

Jane stood as the crew returned to their bunks and Dog and the Bo'sun were ordered back to their posts under the watchful eye of Mister Galsworthy.

"No question about it," she thought. "Something is amiss."

Leaving the second mate on deck with Silas, Jane returned to the saloon to find Endeavor and Mister Wright pulling logs and ship's papers from the captain's writing desk. She could see that they had broken the lock to open it, and was slightly shocked to see such behavior on the part of her principled husband.

Endeavor looked up as she entered and saw what had drawn her eye. "I did suggest we wait to obtain the key from the rightful owner but was overruled," he said with a smile.

Wright flipped the pages of the log book he had found in the desk. "It appears to be the same tale being told here, as in the earlier logs, Captain. A right mess they are, and no mention of this trip north."

"Let us see what the bo'sun can tell us. Endeavor, please fetch him."

Jane leaned back against the table and eyed the young seaman as he stood at attention by the door.

"Dereliction of duty, Mister Johnson. Or what would you call it when you invite a strange young woman aboard and leave the deck with her?"

"Begging your pardon ma'am, I meant no harm." Johnson was suitably contrite.

"And yet here you are, having allowed others to take over your vessel. Hardly 'no harm' there, Mister Johnson."

Johnson grew pale and swallowed loudly.

"All right, stand down Bo'sun. I am willing to overlook the offense if you help us with information about this vessel and her activities over the past two months. You can begin by telling me what is in your hold."

He swallowed again, pausing to think, then lifted his chin. "I had better show you."

XXV
Soap and Shoes

Back River, Maryland
June 20, 1821

"Lavender soap?" Jane lifted the lantern higher to look back along the rows of crates that filled the *Osprey's* cargo hold. "And shoes?" She read from the label on another crate further back. "What are you doing with soap and shoes and whatever else you have in here?"

"It is not soap ma'am." The bo'sun untied the ropes holding the first stack of crates against the main mast where it penetrated the lower deck. He lifted the top crate, one marked "Sweeney's Lavender Soap," off the pile and set it on the floor of the hold. He reached to the back of his belt and yanked out a large iron spike to pry off the top of the wooden box, then stepped aside so Jane could see what it held.

"Ah. I see you are indeed well supplied with *hooch*, as you called it. And the rest of the crates?"

"The same, ma'am."

Behind her, Wright cleared his throat. "Would we be correct in assuming that the revenue service has not issued tax stamps for this load?"

"No sir, I don't believe they have." Johnson was fighting to keep a smirk off his face.

"There are over two hundred crates here, Captain. The penalty should they catch us with it is staggering to contemplate. They could impound the *Osprey*, you know." Wright was nearly gasping in horror at this point as he shuffled along the rows holding the lantern over his head and counting under his breath.

"Where are you taking it?" Jane couldn't help but be impressed by the sheer scale of the smuggling. Albright was not making any attempt to hide the contraband moonshine under a load of goods. He was clearly counting on not being stopped or questioned when he landed the load.

"Norfolk ma'am. I don't know who Cap'n pays to turn his back but we bring it in all summer long. Man there named Weston sees to it that the load gets taken ashore. I think he and the captain are partners ma'am."

Jane could barely hide her disgust. "That, Bo'sun Jack, does not surprise me at all. And the corn you load in Norfolk? Provender for the stills?" It was a neat arrangement. By bringing the raw input to the moonshiners, Albright guaranteed he would have ample supply. Jane guessed he had people all around the lower Bay producing for him. Albright might be many things, she reflected, but he was no fool.

"Aye ma'am. We have a regular route, so the bootleggers know when to be at the shore with their goods," Johnson explained. "We send word..."

"Wait! Shh." Endeavor put his hand on Jane's shoulder and tilted his head to hear better. "There."

He shoved Johnson aside and quickly climbed to the top of the crates, then shimmied into the narrow space between the cargo and the ceiling of the hold. Jane watched as his shoes disappeared into the dark.

A moment later they heard a faint, "*my God*" and soon Endeavor's head reappeared at the top of the pile.

"They have slaves aboard, Jane. Slaves!" His voice shook with shock and anger.

"No! Not slaves!" Johnson threw up his hands as if to hold back the fury he saw on the captain's face. "Runaways!"

"Get the crew," she ordered through gritted teeth. "Get them out of bed *now!*"

It took the four seamen and the bo'sun, with the help of Silas and Galsworthy, a good quarter of an hour to shift enough crates that a small passage was opened along the port side and the fugitives could be brought out into the light. They came staggering forth, blinking in the lantern glow, weak and thirsty, and dressed in tattered clothes. Three young men and a young girl, all of them shivering in fear.

"Bring food and water," Jane ordered the bo'sun.

"Quickly."

Endeavor stepped forward and placed a quiet hand on the girl's shoulder. "Come. You are safe now." Stooping to clear the lintel, he led her gently aft out of the hold, followed by what Jane guessed were her brothers.

Jane dismissed the crew back to their quarters before taking the lamp from Wright's hand. She squeezed herself into the passage through the crates and made her way forward to view the cavity where the fugitives had been secreted. What she found disgusted her beyond anything she had ever witnessed. The poor souls had been living in a space no larger than a wardrobe for many days, it appeared, and had been forced to handle all of their bodily needs in the cramped quarters. Crumbs of food and a small canteen of stale water were the only evidence of sustenance she found. Nearly shaking in fury, Jane swept out of the hold with Wright close behind.

On deck, she strode up to Galsworthy and growled, "Muster them in the fo'c'sle, every man jack of them, including the cook. Now, Mister Galsworthy." Her voice rose to a shout as she slammed her fist onto the rail to make her point.

It took but a few minutes before Galsworthy reported back that the crew were waiting for her below.

"Good. Now lock the hatch and don't open it until I give the command."

"Aye, aye, ma'am." Galsworthy ran forward and slammed home the storm bolt used to secure the opening in heavy weather.

"Captain says you're to stay put, men," he shouted through the grate. "Best to heed her orders, I find."

"Silas, hand me that lantern, then go fetch Mister Wright and Mister Coffin so that we may prepare our welcoming committee for the captain's return," Jane ordered as she began to unbutton the dress she no longer needed to play a charade. Stripping it down over her hips, she threw it in a ball on top of the cargo hatch and stretched her arms in relief. The night air had cooled after the oppressive heat of the day and she lifted her collar to catch the gentle breeze.

"All well below?'

"Aye, Jane, all is well."

Endeavor was perched on the cargo hatch next to her as they waited for Albright. Wright and Galsworthy crouched near the rail where the ladder hung, and Silas sat lookout on the main boom.

"Thank you," she whispered back and leaned over to kiss him in the dark.

They waited, holding hands and listening to the sounds of the night as the *Osprey* rocked gently at anchor and the rigging slapped over their heads. A crescent moon hung over the horizon and provided just enough light on the water for them to see the *Osprey's* skiff when it appeared from the mouth of the river to the west.

"Boat inbound, ma'am. Port quarter at half a mile," Silas whispered from his seat over Jane's head.

She slid as quietly as she could off the hatch and made her way to the rail, being careful to stay low and out of sight. She soon realized they need not keep so silent. The raucous shouting from the boat would cover any sounds they made.

"Pull hard, Markham. Pull like your life depended on it. That's the ticket. No, not that way. Over there."

It was apparent that Albright and his mate had spent time in the tavern that evening and were thoroughly awash in spirits. It was a wonder they found the boat, much less made their way back to the *Osprey* in that condition. It took them three attempts to tie the boat up at the bottom of the ladder, each time nearly tipping one or both of them into the Bay.

"Hoy. Watch on deck. Blasted man, where are you? Here, come help." When no answer came from above, Albright swore, then grabbed for the bottom rung of the ladder, hauled himself up the side, and rolled over the rail onto the deck, where he lay on his back snorting with laughter. Jane and the others stood to the side and watched as Markham followed Albright up the side and then, equally as inebriated as the captain, stumbled over Albright and collapsed in a heap.

"Is he dead or just in a swoon?" Jane took the lantern from Silas and opened the cover to shine light on Markham where he lay, limply draped over a coil of rope.

"Swooned, ma'am," Galsworthy reported after checking the man's pulse. "But he will wish he were dead when he wakes up tomorrow."

"Put them to bed and bolt the doors. We have business to finish tonight. Silas, fetch the bo'sun."

Jane was feeling marginally less angry about the mistreatment of the people crammed into the hold once she realized they were being delivered not into captivity but into freedom. Johnson related that they were known to the freemen who ran mercantile establishments in the Norfolk harbor as being willing to carry fugitives north.

"We always just put them ashore here, ma'am. I don't rightly know what happens to them after that." Johnson was looking less smug by this time as the precariousness of his position became clear. "I surely would tell you if I knew."

"Why, Mister Johnson? Albright hardly seems the type to care for his fellow man."

"Money, Captain. He makes 'em pay through the nose. Says he is taking the risk, so they should make it worth his while."

The number he named as the price of a ticket made Jane catch her breath. "They can hardly have that sort of coin in their purse."

"No, ma'am, there are people in Baltimore and Philadelphia who pay, I am told. Abolitionists and the like." The Evans sisters, Jane had no doubt.

And therein lay the solution to her current problem.

XXVI
A Change of Command

Back River, Maryland
June 21, 1821

In the *Osprey's* cramped saloon, Jane searched for pen and ink in the captain's desk, then sat down at the table to scratch out a letter of instructions to Dawkins.

Aboard the schooner Osprey
21st of June, 1821

> *Hugh Dawkins, as Chief Mate of the schooner Destiny, you are hereby directed to dispatch Able Seaman Abraham Griggs and Seaman Robert Boniface to the schooner Osprey to serve under the command of Silas Baldwin as master. Their articles will transfer to that vessel for the return passage to New York.*
>
> *You are further instructed to transit the Destiny under your command to the harbor at Baltimore with all possible speed. Mister Coffin will acquaint you with additional details as necessary. He has my full confidence with regard to all affairs, and you may rely on his word as if it were my own.*
>
> *I look to rejoin you tomorrow.*
> *Capt. Jane Thorn*

Blowing on the ink to dry it more quickly, Jane carried the letter to the deck. She found Endeavor and Mister Wright helping the fugitives down the ladder into the *Destiny's* skiff. Endeavor had rifled through the ship's stores and found a few articles of clothing to cover them. Jane was glad to see that kindness and a hot meal had brightened their spirits.

"You are among friends now," she said as she held out her hand in farewell. "We will see that you come right at the other end, and I wish you Godspeed and a successful journey."

"I have thy instructions, Jane. It will be as thee wish," Endeavor promised as he took the letter from her. "Please take care until I see thee again."

With a quick embrace, Endeavor said good-bye, climbed over the side and slid down the ladder to join Wright on the rowing seat. A few quick pulls turned the skiff smartly and it was soon lost in the night. Jane waited until the sound of the oars had died away before turning to Galsworthy and Silas.

"Mister Baldwin, you are now in temporary command of the *Osprey*." She handed him the orders signed by Captain Josias. "Mister Galsworthy will serve as your mate and I am sending you Griggs and Boniface as crew."

Although he was still only fifteen, Jane agreed with her uncle that Silas could be trusted with the task of sailing the schooner home. Her nephew hoped to be given his own vessel in due course and had been working hard to earn the family's trust. Galsworthy would steer him right, she knew, just as the mate had done for Jane during her own apprenticeship.

"And the *Osprey's* crew, Captain Jane?" Silas asked.

"You may ask them tomorrow. We have caught our big fish, and can let the minnows escape, if they so choose. If you want to allow any to stay aboard and sail home, Mister Galsworthy will keep a firm hand and a watchful eye on them."

"Very good. And my cargo? What do you suggest we do with that?"

Jane smiled. "Go get the crew and meet me in the hold."

Dawn was breaking by the time the crew had finished carrying out Jane's orders. She first had the men set aside four of the crates. Then, one by one, they hauled the rest onto the deck, opened each bottle within, poured the contents over the side, and threw the empty bottles and cases into the water. Jane could see how much it pained them to dispose of perfectly good spirits, and she watched like a hawk to make sure that no bottles disappeared into pockets. As the crew opened the last of the crates, Griggs and Boniface arrived with their seabags in the *Osprey's* boat and lent a hand to finish the job.

Meanwhile, the cook, who had agreed to stay on for the

voyage home once he had been assured of amnesty from the Thorns, was busy preparing a meal for the crew. After he sent everyone to breakfast, Silas brought his own mug of brew and joined Jane on the forward hatch. Wearily, he sank down onto the grating and leaned over his knees with his eyes closed.

Jane watched him for a moment with an indulgent smile, then said, "Welcome to your first day of command."

At the start of the forenoon watch, Silas called the vessel's company aft.

"Good work this morning, men. I know the task was not to your liking but it was done well. You now have a choice to make, each and every one of you," he said as he looked at the four seamen who made up the *Osprey's* crew along with Bo'sun Johnson.

"You can pledge to put your past behind you and sail the *Osprey* home, where I can assure you that no blame will be placed at your door." He paused to look at Jane, who nodded in agreement. "Or ask now for your pay and we will put you ashore."

Silas stood quietly and waited as the men made up their minds. Finally, only two stepped forward. Jane was not surprised to see that Dog had decided his chances were better in Baltimore than New York. It did come as a disappointment though, that the bo'sun also chose to give up his berth. She thought he had the makings of a reliable seaman under the right command but she guessed they would never know.

"Mister Galsworthy, pay them off and row them ashore," Silas ordered. The men would be taken two miles up the river and dropped at the bank near the settlement of Edgemere with their pockets full of coins, but no letter of recommendation from the captain.

"Good riddance," Galsworthy muttered under his breath as he motioned the pair to follow him below to collect their wages.

While the crew prepared the *Osprey* to weigh anchor and sail to Baltimore on the ebb tide that evening, Jane took the opportunity to rest. She and Galsworthy had checked on

Albright and Markham, but both men were still snoring loudly and could not be roused. After going without sleep all night, Jane herself could barely keep her eyes open. Unfortunately, there were no empty cabins she could commandeer, but the floor of the saloon felt just fine, and she dozed off within a few minutes of lying down on it with her wadded-up dress as a pillow.

Several hours later, she was jolted out of a sound sleep by someone pounding loudly on the door of the captain's cabin. Albright was awake.

"Markham! Get in here you, you blighter. The door is jammed. Markham!" Albright alternated between jiggling the door handle and hammering on the planks as he shouted for his mate.

Jane struggled to her feet and wiped her eyes. As she pushed her hair off her face and tucked the stray ends back into her braid, she stuck her head out the saloon door and called up the ladder for Silas. When his face appeared in the companionway, she asked if he would join her below for the interview with Albright. "And bring Galsworthy."

"Let him out," Jane ordered.

Galsworthy pulled back the bolt and swung open the captain's door just as Albright lifted his fist to pound on it again. The look of consternation on his face when he caught sight of Jane was quickly replaced with pure fury.

"What are you doing on my vessel, missy?" he raged as he staggered into the saloon.

"Sit down, Captain Albright." Jane thundered back at him, pointing to a chair. He was so shocked at her tone that he actually dropped into it.

"Now," she said in a quieter voice, "you will listen to me. In the first place, this is no longer your vessel. Captain Albright, you are hereby relieved of your command pursuant to orders from Captain Josias Thorn as a result of your illegal activities and failure to carry out the instructions you were given for the voyage."

"You can't do that." Albright half rose from his chair then

175

fell back when Galsworthy laid a hand on his shoulder from behind.

"Yes, Captain Albright, I can. Here is your notice of dismissal," she said as she laid Captain Josias' letter in front of him.

"He can't dismiss me. I shall bring suit against you all and ruin the name of Thorn."

"I fear, Captain Albright, that it is we who will be bringing suit against you. We have ample record of your activities to show that you have failed to prosecute the journey you were hired to make. When you return to New York, I would recommend that you avail yourself of the services of a good attorney." Jane watched Albright carefully as she talked. She had no desire to engage in fisticuffs with the man, much as she might enjoy the thought of knocking him flat on his back.

Sure enough, as soon as she finished speaking, Albright launched himself over the table toward her. Quick as lightning, Galsworthy grabbed him by the seat of his pants and hauled him back. He shoved the enraged captain into the chair, then pulled one of the pistols from his waistband.

"That's right, sir, stay in your seat," he cautioned as Albright's eyes widened at the sight of the barrel a foot from his nose.

All the noise in the saloon had finally roused the other sleeper. Like Albright before him, Markham began pounding on his door and rattling the handle.

"Open it," she said to Silas.

"Please join us, Mister Markham."

"What the devil…" The mate stood staring at Jane.

"No, not the devil, but you may wish it were by the time I am finished. Please, have a seat."

In a few words, Jane explained the situation. She handed Markham his own dismissal letter from Josias and then gave them a scant five minutes to gather their belongings before Galsworthy herded them onto the deck at the point of the pistol. She was grateful that Griggs had thought to keep the crew busy on the foredeck. Witnesses to the captain's humiliation might goad him to violence in retaliation. As it was, he and Markham did not resist when she directed them to the rail.

"There, gentlemen, I am not completely without mercy." Jane pointed over the side.

Albright and Markham craned their necks to peer down the ladder. Albright straightened and glared at Jane. "Where is the rest of it?" he demanded.

Jane glared right back at him. "Poured into the Bay, and good riddance to it. It is no good getting angry, Captain Albright. It is gone and that is the end of it. Now, those four cases should earn enough to get you wherever you are going, so you ought to thank me."

"The devil take me before I bow to you." Albright growled through gritted teeth. "Come, Markham."

Jane and Galsworthy stood with Silas and watched the boat pull away. The crates of moonshine weighed it down such that water lapped over the gunwales, but Albright was a good boatman. He steered the bow into the waves, keeping dry as they headed up the Back River. It was not long before they rounded the bend and disappeared from view.

Jane sighed as she watched them go.

"Do you regret setting them free, Auntie Jinks?" Silas asked.

"No," she replied. "I regret the loss of that boat. We shall have to buy a new one in Baltimore before you sail for home."

XXVII
Truth Revealed

Baltimore, Maryland
June 22, 1821

The *Osprey* arrived in Baltimore with the late morning tide on Friday, backing and filling her sails to steer through the narrow channel. She had spent the night at anchor off North Point after the wind died with nightfall. In the morning, she picked up a pilot and rode the rising waters up the river to the inner harbor, then moored just astern of the *Destiny* and signaled for a boat to be sent across.

"Morning, ma'am," Dawkins greeted the captain when she stepped onto the deck of the *Destiny*.

"And a good morning it is." Jane was relieved to have the *Osprey* found and Albright off her hands. "Is Mister Coffin below?"

"No, ma'am, he went ashore early with the guests you sent to us. We expect him back soon. Ah. Here he comes now, Captain."

Dawkins pointed to a low boat approaching from the direction of the harbor. In the stern, she could see her husband seated next to a woman wrapped in dark shawls and a large bonnet despite the warmth of the midsummer day. The waterman pulled up next to the *Destiny* and waited while Endeavor helped the woman mount the ladder, then slipped the man a few coins before following her onto the deck.

When their visitor pushed back the flap of her bonnet as she turned to face Jane, the captain was delighted to see that Miss Polly had come to call.

"Welcome back aboard, dear friend. Come, join us below and tell me all the news."

While they waited in the saloon for the coffee and biscuits Jane had requested, Endeavor handed her the day's edition of the Daily Advertiser without comment. He had folded it open to a small notice on the third page.

Smugglers Apprehended in the Night

The Revenue service has reported the taking of a boat with over twenty gallons of illegal spirits aboard just after dusk yesterday. A tip from a local source pointed the officers to the landing at Stansbury where they took two men into custody. Found in the cargo were a full set of records detailing the nefarious work of the criminals along with testing vials and other instruments of distillation. We commend the efforts of the Service in stemming the trade of dangerous 'rotgut' on the Chesapeake Bay and hope that all good citizens will play their part and report suspicious activities when seen.

Jane looked up at Endeavor. "Do you suppose they would give us the boat back?"

Endeavor just shook his head with a smile and opened the door at Cookie's knock. Taking the tray, he set it down on the saloon table and waited for Jane to indicate that they should be seated.

"My goodness, please, do not stand on ceremony. Miss Polly, let me help you with your shawls. It is mighty warm in here."

Once they had all helped themselves to coffee and cakes, Miss Polly leaned back and regarded Jane with an approving look.

"Thank you for your assistance in bringing our most recent travelers to our refuge." The corners of her mouth dropped as she continued. "We were not aware of the conditions aboard his vessel, Jane, or we never would have relied on Captain Albright. Nor were we aware that he was acting on his own without the permission, or at least the blind eye of the owners."

Jane listened in silence. She was not at all sure the Committee was as innocent of knowledge as Miss Polly was professing, but she could understand their grasping at any chance of liberation for souls escaping servitude.

179

"Has he been carrying fugitives for long?"

"Yes, a couple of years now."

"And did you know his true business? And what would happen if he were taken by the revenue men? Surely they were put into mortal danger by traveling with Albright," Jane said sternly.

Miss Evans lifted her chin and replied, "Yes, my dear, we did. But not many masters are willing to embark such passengers. At least we knew where Captain Albright's loyalties lie. As long as we paid him handsomely, he would take them on and deliver them reliably to Baltimore. Frankly dear Jane, it is all we could hope for. If he was motivated by nothing more lofty than greed, so be it. He was still a tool of deliverance. One we have now lost."

The light dawned for Jane. "You knew we had the Calloways aboard the *Destiny*."

"Yes Jane, we did. It was a happy circumstance that you decided to embark passengers on your trip to Baltimore. We had traveled to Norfolk to arrange transport for several families, among them the Calloways. Our friends in New York had alerted us that another Thorn vessel would be on the Chesapeake this summer, and we thought to approach you with the same offer we made Albright. But when our man in Norfolk met your crewman Singleton, he told us that money would not matter to you. He thought though, that you might be persuaded by principle. When my sisters and I booked passage with you, it was in the hope that we would get to know your heart. Unfortunately, events overtook us with the Calloways, whose master had sent his best trackers to find them. You saw them, on the cutter that day."

"And so you smuggled them aboard and consigned them to the misery of the cargo hold. Children. How could you?" Jane rose from her chair in consternation. "And you deliberately put my crew and my vessel in danger. How could you?" Jane repeated as her voice rose in anger at the way in which she had been duped.

Miss Polly sat still and watched the captain as she began to pace the saloon. After a minute, Jane turned to Endeavor.

"What have you to say about all this?"

"It would have been better had they asked, Jane. But they did not know thee. It seems they could not take the chance that thee would say no."

"It was foolish." Jane glared at Miss Polly. "Had I known, I would have ensured that we made the passage as swiftly as possible, and I would never have surrendered to the cutter. Never!"

"Yes, dear Jane, I see that now. And that is why I have come. To beg your pardon. We did not know you. We just knew we had the work to do. People to bring out of bondage by whatever means were at hand."

Jane sat back down as Miss Polly continued.

"We were greatly relieved when Endeavor came to us yesterday to let us know that the travelers on the *Osprey* were safe. We received them this morning and will ensure they are taken care of and sent on their way."

"I am glad to hear that, anyway. And tell me of the Calloways. Have you located them?"

"Yes, we know where they are, and the situation is dire I am afraid. We sent Singleton to Norfolk with the steamboat, and he returned with news that they were sent south to the plantation but tried to escape again. They were brought back to Norfolk and are to be sold at auction next week. A man is putting together one of those dreadful drives to walk slaves to Louisiana, and any that have tried to run away will surely be sent with him. The children won't survive the trail, I fear."

She paused for a moment and contemplated the captain. "What would…"

"No. Absolutely, unequivocally, no. I will not do it, Miss Polly. Not with a vessel that I do not own, and not with a crew who is in the dark about our activities. If you wish to involve us in your work, then you must gain the agreement of my family. I cannot make that decision on my own. I just cannot, I am sorry."

"There are captains who make a different choice." Miss Polly thought to argue the point. Endeavor knew it was a fool's errand.

"As the supercargo, I must stand behind the captain on this matter, Polly Evans. Regardless of her personal feelings, she has been explicitly instructed by the firm not to risk the voyage or the vessel on such ventures," he explained.

Miss Polly rose and held out her hand to Jane. "Very well, I hope that you will still see us as friends, Captain Jane. My sisters and I would welcome you to our home at any time should you find yourself in Baltimore." She stooped to gather her shawls and wrap them tightly around her shoulders before pulling on her bonnet.

"The perils of growing older," she observed with a wry smile. "I am always chilled even on the warmest days. Good-bye, dear girl. Our fondest blessings go with you."

Jane remained behind as Endeavor accompanied Miss Evans to the deck and arranged for her to be rowed ashore in the skiff. When he returned, Jane was stirring her now-cold coffee, lost in thought. He seated himself opposite her and waited.

Finally, she looked up. "Dawkins got word to the authorities, then? About Albright?"

"Aye, he did. They had enough time to round up men to meet him and Markham when they came ashore."

"Will they want to pursue the matter of his activities with the *Osprey*, do you think? Are we likely to have trouble from them?"

"I think not. They know there is no further evidence to find, and I gave them our assurances that we were unaware of the business he had been doing here. I confess I felt a right fool explaining how ignorant we were. I must speak to thy uncle about our oversight of the fleet when we return to New York." Endeavor sounded frustrated.

"And no chance of the boat, you think?" It gnawed at Jane that they had to leave behind a perfectly good vessel that would cost a pretty penny to replace.

"No Jane, no chance of the boat." She could tell that Endeavor was doing his level best not to roll his eyes. "Thee must put it out of thy mind as we would do well not to stir that hornet's nest any further."

"Very good." She slapped the table and stood up. "Let us send for Silas and Dawkins. It is time we make our plans."

XXVIII
Ready for Departure

Baltimore
June 23, 1821

It had been a busy two days for the Thorn crews. Silas and Galsworthy had undertaken the task of loading the mahogany lumber from the warehouse aboard the *Osprey*. There was no room left for the furniture Jane had ordered, so that would have to travel north on the *Destiny*. Bo'sun Jack and Dog had been replaced with two new men from the hiring halls who would help take the schooner home to New York. By Saturday morning, a new skiff was purchased and the *Osprey* was being prepared for departure. Jane sent for Silas to have a final word before he sailed on the afternoon tide.

"Are you satisfied that all is in order?" Jane was seated at her desk reviewing her charts when Silas arrived and she waved him onto her berth.

Dressed in a smart pair of navy trousers with the Thorn colors of red and white at his waist and on the piping of his tailored coat, Silas looked every inch the young captain. He would not keep the uniform for long but Jane knew it would not be too many years before he assumed the role of master aboard his own vessel. It was good for him to get this taste of command.

Her nephew settled himself gingerly on the edge of the berth so as not to create any creases, and ran a hand around the inside of the stiff collar before answering.

"Aye, Aunty Jinks, as well as can be. He may be a scoundrel, but Albright ran a tight ship. Koopmans could find no fault with her, and Galsworthy says the men know their stuff. With fair winds we will be safely home in a week or so."

"I imagine you will be happy to arrive," Jane said with a teasing glint in her eye. To Silas' dismay, Mister Wright had chosen to take the steamboat north to the stagecoach line, taking his daughter with him. Jane knew that Silas had hoped to bring her aboard his vessel so he could peacock around in front of her, not that he would admit it. He was quite put out when his hopes were dashed but his spirits bucked up soon enough when Mister Wright extended an invitation to him for dinner at the Wright household on his return.

Silas nodded and quickly changed the subject. "We are almost provisioned and we will call for the pilot to join us at the afternoon watch change. The wind looks to be swinging to the north, so we should make good time down the Bay."

"Good news, and I think you are right. We will not be far behind you as we anticipate weighing anchor first thing in the morning. If I pass you on the way down the Bay you will never live it down, you know."

Silas' eyes lit up at the challenge. "Never! Galsworthy is the best sailing master I know and we will fairly fly, mark my words."

"Very well, when you have left the harbor this afternoon, tie a pennant to your bowsprit. If I can tell you what color it was when I get back to New York, you shall owe me a new song." Silas had been trying his hand at making up work ditties to teach the *Destiny's* crew as they sailed that summer. Jane had to admit he had a knack for it.

"Done."

"In my honor."

"Fine."

"In which you admit that I am the better sailor." She grinned.

"Now you go too far Aunty Jinks," he protested.

"Very well, you may skip that part. But you must sing it for me at the next family dinner. Agreed?"

"Agreed."

"Good. Now, one final piece of business. I have a note here from Miss Evans." Jane leaned over and handed it to Silas, who quickly scanned it and handed it back.

"Do you think I should take him?" he asked.

"It is up to you as master of the *Osprey*, if you wish him to join your crew. He may never again serve on the *Destiny*, I have made that clear. But it was me he betrayed, not you, so you must make up your own mind."

"Singleton is a good seaman," Silas observed.

"Aye, he is that. And I would welcome the return of Hitchens to my crew. Both he and Griggs will be sorely missed."

"Very well, I will send for him and see what he has to say for himself. If I am satisfied, I will return Hitchens to you with his papers."

Jane rose and pulled Silas off the berth, then wrapped her arms around him in a warm hug. "Take care, and I will see you in New York," she whispered in his ear.

In the late afternoon, Jane stood with Dawkins and Endeavor at the stern rail and watched the *Osprey* slip out of the harbor past the fort. The heavy rains of the past week had swollen the creeks that poured into the waters of the Bay and the current was so swift that the schooner was out of sight within minutes.

Letting go of the rail, Jane straightened and quickly wiped away a few small tears. She wondered if her own father had felt the same way when he watched her leave the dock on the deck of her first command.

"Mister Dawkins, please check the anchor. The waters are boisterous this afternoon and we may need a second one to hold us here. And alert the watch to keep careful note of our position. I do not wish to drag onto the shore."

Dawkins acknowledged the order and made his way forward while Jane and Endeavor returned to their cabin to prepare for a trip into town. They planned to pay a call on the Husseys to settle their accounts and make an outright purchase of the remaining cases of Swain's ointments and the other items they had carried for the couple. The *Destiny* had done well with the lace and elixirs they carried for them on consignment, and there was relatively little remaining in the hold. Jane thought she could sell the rest at auction for a profit in Norfolk and was willing to buy the goods on Thorn Shipping's behalf.

Finally, Jane wished to visit the Evans sisters. She had sent a message earlier in the day that she would call on them this afternoon. In it, she laid out a plan for their consideration and hoped they would agree, as no other ideas for solving the problem had occurred to her over the past twenty-four hours.

"I doubt we have that much money to hand," Anne said with a frown. "All four of them would cost a prodigious amount, especially for a man like John Calloway. He will fetch a price of five hundred dollars or more, I should think."

"Nevertheless, that is my proposal. Buy them all and bring them away to New York as your property until we leave Virginia waters. Then set them free."

"I will do it." Eliza stepped forward and thrust her hand out to Jane. "If the Committee does not have the funds, I will use my own money. My inheritance. It is not much, but should suffice."

Jane shook her hand. "We leave with the morning tide. Best you come aboard tonight. You may take the stage home from New York, but you will be gone for two weeks or more."

As they took their leave of the sisters, Miss Polly took Jane aside for a moment. "Thank you, Jane. It is a costly solution, but fair to you."

"Aye, I will not traffic in runaways if I can help it, but we must save them, Miss Polly. We must."

Miss Polly gave her a quick hug and stepped back to allow Jane to pass through the door.

"Godspeed," she called as Jane and Endeavor made their way down the walk and turned at the gate to wave good-bye.

The *Destiny* was still being loaded at the wharf when Eliza Evans arrived at dinnertime, so she came aboard straightaway. Koopmans had rebuilt the passenger cabins and Eliza was soon comfortably installed in one. The others would be given to the Calloways for the trip to New York, should their plan succeed.

Ashore, Cookie was scavenging the grocers for last minute supplies to feed the additional people aboard. In particular, he wanted to find treats that would tempt the children. He thought they might be frightened after all that happened to them and hoped something sweet would help soothe their feelings.

It was dark before the final load of furniture was delivered and stowed in the hold. Jane stood on the quarterdeck and watched as Dawkins supervised the closing and securing of the hatches and sent the second watch to dinner. He joined her to report that all was well and the schooner was ready for departure.

"We shall stay on the dock tonight," Jane informed him. "I arranged it with the harbormaster. You can clear us out in the morning and bring the pilot in good time to get underway at slackwater."

"Aye, aye, ma'am." Dawkins stared out over the town, where the lamps were being lit as the city settled into the drowsy summer evening, and rocked back and forth for a moment.

"Out with it, Mister Dawkins. What is on your mind?"

Dawkins cleared his throat and said, "It is not my place to say anything, ma'am, but I think what you and Miss Evans are doing is admirable."

"Thank you Dawkins." Jane was surprised that Dawkins' approval meant so much to her. "We will see what comes of it. But I am glad to hear you are behind me." Her chief mate had not expressed an opinion when she sat down with him and Endeavor that afternoon to discuss their plans for the trip home. He simply looked thoughtful and asked if the accommodations should be prepared for the family that was to come aboard in Norfolk as well as for Miss Eliza.

"May I suggest that I escort Miss Eliza to the sale, ma'am? When the time comes? I think she will be in want of a steady arm at the auction yard."

"Indeed, Mister Dawkins, I think that is a capital idea, if she is agreeable. I leave it to you to discuss with her," Jane suggested. "Now, let us join her and Endeavor for dinner and I will look over my charts one more time."

It was a lively company at the table in the saloon that

evening. There was a shiver of tension in the air that expressed itself in laughter and loud voices. Miss Eliza, in particular, seemed in high spirits and kept them entertained with the exploits of the three Evans sisters as they grew up in a motherless household on a farm in Lancaster County.

"We were hellions, there is no question about it," she exclaimed after relating a story that made it clear that the three girls ran circles around their poor father.

Jane found herself liking the youngest Evans sister a great deal. In her mid-forties, she was a tall, elegant woman with masses of dark blond hair swept up in a neat pile on the back of her head. Her green eyes were matched by a simple gown in a rich fabric that hugged her trim figure. As the night wore on, Jane watched Mister Dawkins taking care to make sure that their guest's water glass was filled, and that she was offered the best pieces of roast from the platter. Jane and Endeavor traded glances when Dawkins rushed to pull back Eliza's chair at the end of the meal. *Interesting*, Jane thought.

As the second bell of the first watch rang, Endeavor turned down the lantern that hung over the table in the saloon. In their cabin, Jane propped open the hatch to allow the night breeze to waft down the ladder, and for the cat to come and go as he pleased. Jane had become attached to the animal in spite of herself, and would go in search of him if he did not join them at bedtime.

"Perhaps we could let him stay outside for a while longer this evening," her husband suggested, as he reached an arm around Jane and pulled her close.

XXIX
Passage to Norfolk

Upper Chesapeake Bay, Maryland
June 24, 1821

*Sunday, June 24, 1821   Departure Baltimore 9 o'clock. Passed Bodkin Point at noon
Lat. 39° 08' N Long. 76° 25' W. Winds fair NW*

With no anchor to weigh, it was a simple process to get underway in the morning.

"Bring three. Bring two." Jane called out to the hands as they pulled the docklines aboard one by one. The tide had begun to turn, so by the time the number one line was hauled in, the nose of the schooner started to swing into the stream.

"Bring four." The last line that tethered them to the dock came aboard and the harbor tugs could begin the long pull out into the channel. The pilot stood by the helm with his spyglass glued to his eye as he watched for movement among the many ships anchored in the inner harbor. At the start of the tide run, there were still many vessels that might swing on their moorings, and a clear path could become blocked quickly. Jane breathed a sigh of relief as they rode the outgoing current past the fort and released the towlines.

"Raise the mainsail," she directed, and the crew ran to the halyards to pull the heavy gaff up the mast, filling the sail with the morning breeze.

As the schooner picked up speed, Jane threw back her head and drew a deep breath. Here at the top of the Bay, the water was still fresh and the air had no tang of salt, but she could smell the dank scent of the swamps that lined the shore. As she stretched her arms over her head, her sleeves fell back to reveal the angry welt of the fresh tattoo on her forearm. On the way back to the *Destiny* from their visit to the Evans family, she had convinced Endeavor to accompany her into an inking den near the port.

"It looks clean enough, and I shall insist that he hold the needle in the flame first. It is but a small drawing and will not take long."

In the end he agreed, as long as she did not force him to watch. Endeavor had never been one to seek dangerous pursuits as the sight of injury and blood tended to cause him to swoon. Jane pulled a scrap of paper from her pocket and handed it to the artist As in previous visits to new ports, Jane had designed a flower tattoo that represented the local landscape. This time, she would add a small yellow-petaled flower with a deep brown center. She had seen them growing in enormous stands along the edges of the low forests that dotted the shores. The proud gardeners of Baltimore frequently featured them in their colorful beds, and Jane had asked Miss Polly what they were called.

"Oh, all sorts of things, but mostly black-eyed susans," she said.

"They are so cheerful," Jane exclaimed. "We have something like them in New York, but not so grand. They must like the warmer climate."

Now, she would have one with her all the time as a reminder of her first trip to the Tidewater.

The wind held fair out of the north and the *Destiny* made good time down the Bay, dropping the pilot off near Annapolis in the late afternoon. Jane gifted him her customary bottle of port once Dawkins had paid him off, then ordered the sails sheeted in on a course for Norfolk.

Her uncle had been quite clear in his instructions that Jane was not to divert her vessel to assist the Calloways with escape. She was to make trade and profit her priority, but had permission to do what she could for the family within those boundaries. With goods aboard that could be sold in Norfolk, and a passenger who was paying for transport there, she felt justified in making the stop for commercial purposes, especially as it was barely out of her way. In addition, if all went as planned, they would pick up four more paying passengers for the trip to New York, so Uncle Josias could hardly complain that she was neglecting her duty to the firm.

Chesapeake Bay, Virginia
June 25, 1821

Monday, June 25, 1821   Ded. r. Lat. 39° 06' N Long. 76° 15' W. Heavy squalls, ship taking on water. Seams started lar. bow. Will put in for repair Norfolk.

The wind died back in the early evening but then picked up again at midnight. By morning there was a steady blow with squalls visible on the horizon. Jane ordered the *Destiny* secured for heavy weather and pulled out her charts to check the surrounding depths. She wanted to be well out in deeper water when the weather hit to avoid being driven onto the shoals that lurked in so many places on the Bay.

Over the next few hours, the schooner made excellent time with speeds up to ten knots. Rough seas from the south meant they had to alter course to keep from being pounded by the waves, but Jane was optimistic they would make landfall in the Hampton Roads by late afternoon.

The heavy cloud cover meant there would be no noon sighting that day, so Jane spent an hour figuring her course and position from the speed logs and compass headings of the last twenty-four hours. Leaving her calculations on the chart table for Dawkins to verify, she picked Edwin up from the chair next to her and carried the cat into her cabin. As was often the case when they first left port, Endeavor was struck down with nausea and ennui and had stayed in bed that morning.

"How goes it, my intrepid sailor?" she asked as she set Edwin down next to Endeavor on the berth.

In reply, the poor man leaned over and retched into the bucket he kept on the floor by his head.

"Oh dear, no better is it? Come, let's get you out of bed and onto the deck." She handed him his clothes and climbed the ladder to the quarterdeck.

"Dawkins, please send a couple of the crew to assist my husband up the ladder. I'll have Koopmans hang the hammock."

Once Endeavor had been tucked in and covered with an oilcloth to keep off the rain, the cat hopped up and burrowed under the quilt. There, he spent the afternoon happily purring as the hammock swung from side to side with the movement of the schooner through the mounting waves.

Jane was pleased they had made no sighting of the *Osprey* by the time they turned west to make for Norfolk. Silas would be well on his way north by now, safely away from the revenue officers that patrolled the Bay. Bo'sun Jack did not know for sure but had told her that he thought many of them were in the pay of Captain Albright, as the *Osprey* was frequently stopped and boarded but no fines were ever levied. Jane hoped Silas had made it to the open ocean without attracting a visit from any of them in the mistaken assumption that their friend Albright was in command.

In the late afternoon, the *Destiny* left behind the high waves of the Bay and hove to in the calmer waters of Hampton Roads an hour or two earlier than Jane had dared hope. They would anchor there overnight, then see about selling their cargo and locating the Calloway family in the morning. Jane would also send Koopmans ashore for caulking supplies. To keep the men busy while on patrol for the *Osprey*, Dawkins had the crew jump over the side and scrape away the growth of barnacles and weeds that were slowing the schooner. While working near the bow, they had discovered several open seams leaking into the hold and filling the bilge. Koopmans thought they could manage until the *Destiny* could be hauled in New York, but they were having to pump more often than her small crew could sustain for days at a time. They would take advantage of the short stay in Norfolk to pound tarred cotton into the worst of the seams and hope to make it home before any new leaks appeared.

They had not been anchored long before one of the many boat-borne sellers of water and provisions drew alongside.

"Ahoy th' *Destiny*. Ahoy th' watch," came the call, and Dawkins stepped to the side to answer. Below, he saw a long, flat-bottomed boat with a smiling man at the oars. Dressed only in ragged trousers and a large straw hat, the waterman was surrounded by casks and bales of goods, including an open basket of oysters.

Jane joined Dawkins at the rail and waved to the man below.

"Ahoy, there!" Dawkins called back. "Belay while we get the cook."

Dawkins sent Hitchens at a run to fetch Cookie out of the galley, then stepped to the mast at Jane's beckoning hand.

"Do you think he is a slave, or a freeman?" she asked in a low voice.

"Freeman, I should think. Why?"

"Can we send a message with him to Miss Evans' friend?"

"Yes, I expect we could. I will delay him while you consult Miss Eliza."

While Cookie dickered with the waterman over the price of a bag of onions and a bushel of oysters, Jane hurried below to knock at Miss Eliza's cabin.

"We have means of sending a message to your friends," Jane said when Eliza pulled open the door.

"Very good, I will be with you shortly," she said and closed the door firmly. Jane was pleased at how quickly Miss Eliza seemed to grasp the situation. She was a woman of strong resolution and Jane knew she could count on her good sense in the coming days.

As the first watch rang seven bells that night, the waterman returned, this time with a passenger aboard. Quietly, the visitor was helped up the ladder and the waterman was asked to wait. Dawkins ushered him swiftly down the ladder and closed the companionway hatch before opening the lantern cover. He knocked on the saloon door, then showed the visitor in.

"Good evening, Mister Jones, it is good to see you again." Eliza proffered her hand for a warm shake.

Jane recognized Jones immediately as the man she had seen in discourse with Singleton on their last visit to Norfolk.

"This is Captain Thorn, Mister Jones, and Chief Mate Dawkins. Mister Coffin is the Captain's husband." Eliza waved her hand at each of them as she said their names.

"Pleased to make your acquaintance," Jane said as she shook his hand. Now that she saw him at close range, she was struck by the determined look of the man. Neatly dressed in a dark suit of clothes with a black felt hat perched on his head, Benjamin Jones exuded an air of confidence.

"Likewise," he said as he shook hands with everyone. "I have news, if you would care to hear it. I am sorry to be so abrupt, but I must return quickly."

"Yes, yes, sit down." Eliza pulled out a chair and sat down. The others followed suit and Jones began to speak.

"Here is the notice." He drew a paper out of his pocket and handed it to Eliza. She opened it and read aloud.

"Slaves at sale, Hiram Calhoun, auctioneer. Will be sold at auction Wednesday, June 27, 1821. At Hughes Arcade at 12 o'clock, the following described negroes..." Eliza stopped speaking as she ran her eye down the page. "Yes, here they are, John and Bess, and the two children. I aim to bid for them, Ben."

"Yes, I thought you might. You will perhaps be successful with Bess and the girls, but John may be more difficult. He is still young and trained to work hard, and he will have a reputation as a runaway, a hard case. You may find the seller won't let you have him, especially if they think you may set him free."

"Surely that is not their concern," Jane said.

"No, perhaps not," Jones replied. "But people won't like it, and I can't say what may happen."

"Well, we shall just have to do our best. Can you get word to them, Ben? That we are here and seeking to bring them away?" Eliza asked as she reached into her reticule and handed

Jones a small purse.

"Aye, I will do my best, miss. Thank you." He shoved the purse into a pocket and took his leave.

After Dawkins returned from seeing the visitor back into his boat, Jane voiced her concerns for Miss Eliza's safety at the auction.

"It sounds as if things might become heated. Are you quite sure you wish to attend, Eliza? Perhaps there is another way. Endeavor, what say you? Perhaps you might go in her place?"

"No, ma'am, begging your pardon Mister Coffin, but I will be accompanying Miss Eliza," Dawkins said as he stepped to her side. "She will come to no harm."

"It is settled then." Jane looked around the room and continued, "We will go ashore in the morning to see if we can find buyers for the small goods. Endeavor, you and I will pay a call on Mister Sykes as I owe him information. He may also know something to our advantage about the auction. Eliza, I suggest that you remain aboard and out of sight. There is no point in making yourself conspicuous before the day."

Jane bent down and picked up the cat rubbing himself on her ankles. "Good night, all."

XXX
The Auction

Norfolk, Virginia
June 26, 1821

The ride into Norfolk in the skiff was a wet affair. The winds out on the Bay were gusting mightily, kicking up waves that sloshed water over the stern as Dawkins and Endeavor leaned into the oars. Jane was glad that her husband had recovered from the latest round of seasickness and admired his pluck. No matter how bad he felt, the man never complained. She was deeply appreciative of his willing spirit but wondered if he would ever consent to go to sea again once they returned home. Well, that was a worry for another time. For now, they had to get their goods sold. Cookie also wanted to reprovision the fresh produce and meat before they set sail for home, and was sitting at the bow of the boat, where he looked as if he were enjoying the tumultuous ride.

"Return here at noon," Jane ordered as she checked the securing of the skiff's painter.

"Aye, aye, ma'am," Cookie and Dawkins acknowledged as they each set off in their own direction.

Jane and Endeavor walked up the hill to Sykes' newspaper office, clutching at their hats to keep them from blowing away in the stiff breeze. This time, Jane was prepared for the sound of the loud bell that announced visitors, but she forgot to warn Endeavor, who jumped mightily when it rang out right over his head.

Sykes appeared in the doorway of his inner office, then came forward with an outstretched hand and a wide smile.

"Captain Thorn. And Mister Coffin, it is good to see you." Sykes shook Jane's hand heartily as he waved them into his office. He hurriedly gathered up the stacks of paper that cluttered the chairs in the dimly lit room, turning about with them in his arms as he searched for a spot to put them down.

Eventually, he gave up, and dropped the stacks onto his desk, where they threatened to tip over and bury him.

"As you can see, I have been busy. Do excuse the mess. Now, tell me about your travels, Captain. I saw that the *Osprey* had loaded in Baltimore last week. The master was someone named Baldwin. Albright has been relieved, then?"

Jane knew Sykes kept abreast of events around the Bay. She could see the latest weeklies from Baltimore and Annapolis on the piles on his desk, and suspected many other towns were represented there as well. The daily shipping columns would have told him of the *Osprey's* arrivals and departures.

"Aye, we put him ashore after we discovered he had been running moonshine around the Bay. The revenue men caught him with enough in hand to put him in jail for a while."

"Ah, your doing, Captain?" It seemed Sykes had a good understanding of Jane's sense of justice.

"Perhaps... in any case, I wanted to acquaint you with the facts, as I promised last I was here. Now, we have another matter to discuss with you. The slave auction tomorrow; what can you tell us about it?"

Sykes raised his eyebrows and looked questioningly from Jane to Endeavor.

"Are you thinking of participating?"

"Yes, Friend William, a family with two children. We hope to purchase their bondage papers and thought thee might have some advice for us," Endeavor explained.

The newspaperman frowned. "Are you thinking of taking up slaveholding, then?"

Endeavor merely looked at Sykes with a gentle smile on his face in reply. Sykes brow cleared as he understood what they intended, then shook his head in warning.

"It won't go down well with people if they know what you are about. These new Acts have everyone on the defensive as they know people like you are trying to choke off their livelihood and end the practice of slavery. If they have a hint that you are abolitionists, things could become dangerous."

"What do you suggest we might do, then?" Jane asked.

"Keep *him* well away from the bidding to start." Sykes pointed his thumb at Endeavor. "Meaning no offense, Mister Coffin, but everyone knows how you Quakers feel about slavery and they will suspect what you are up to the moment you open your mouth."

"Aye," Jane agreed, "we have other parties who will be bidding. The family will come aboard the *Destiny* for passage to New York, however."

"Well, you might put the word about that you are sailing for Wilmington, then. Everyone is moving their slaves further south, and it will seem natural if you were carrying them to the Carolinas."

"Can thou tell us how much we are likely to pay? The children are both girls, very young."

"I should think you will find your pockets considerably lightened if you are successful. Perhaps a thousand dollars or so, all told."

Jane flinched and hoped that the Evans sisters' purse was that deep.

From the deck of the *Destiny* that afternoon, Jane watched as a familiar hull made its appearance in the Roads and anchored off the breakwater. As soon as her hands had furled the sails and secured the deck, Jane ordered the skiff put out and had O'Reilly row her across.

"Ahoy the *Sophie Jones*. Captain Thorn of the *Destiny*. Permission to come aboard?"

From the high deck of the frigate came a booming voice. "Permission granted."

A jovial Captain McKnight met Jane at the top of the ladder and helped her over the rail. Behind him, she could see dozens of men busy coiling lines, opening hatches, wrapping sails, and conducting all of the other tasks to be completed at the end of a voyage. Jane admired the sharp way the crew moved about and the uncluttered cleanliness of the deck with its gleaming brasswork. It is how things can look if you have a hundred men aboard, Jane thought.

"Captain Thorn. Welcome aboard, lass." McKnight held out

his hand in greeting.

"It is good to see you, Captain McKnight. How goes the hunting?" Jane asked after they had settled themselves with a glass of whiskey in the frigate's sumptuous saloon.

"Very well, ma'am. We have been sailing with the African Squadron and managed to snag a slaver or two."

"And the *El Almirante*? Any news of her captain or crew?"

"No luck there, the devil take him. But we have made it hot for those who seek to flout the Act and bring in slaves, so I doubt he will be back to try it again. We can't catch 'em all, but we catch enough that captains and crews think twice before taking on the smuggling of Africans. Especially since they know the penalty is death by hanging."

The captains passed an agreeable hour talking about the *Destiny's* travels and McKnight's plans for the future as a privateer and trader. As the slaving blockades had reduced the number of vessels subject to capture by the privateers, he thought they might try for a commission to Manila.

"We have the guns to scare off the pirates and it has been many years since I rounded the Cape. Think o' the adventure," he exclaimed.

By her third glass of whiskey, Jane thought it prudent to wrap up her visit and return to her own vessel before they would need to carry her down the ladder.

As she stood at the rail with McKnight and waited for O'Reilly to bring the boat around, he asked, "When do you depart Norfolk, Captain?"

"Thursday, on the morning tide."

"Then we will make company down the Bay since we sail for Philadelphia that day."

"Very good, Captain." Jane shook his hand. She did her best not to stumble as she mounted the rail and slid down the ladder but landed in the skiff with a thump and tumbled backward onto the seat.

She glared at O'Reilly, "That will not be talked of aboard the *Destiny*."

"Aye, aye, ma'am," he said with a solemn face and reached for the oars.

Norfolk, Virginia
June 27, 1821

The auction was set to begin as Jane and Endeavor took up places under the spreading branches of a flowering magnolia tree. In front of them, waves of heat rose from the cobbled surface of the plaza, and Jane fanned herself vigorously with her hat to keep from fainting. Her heart broke as she watched dozens of people, their necks in iron collars chained in a line, stumble into the square and sink to the open ground with no shade from the broiling sun. When they had all been herded into place, the auctioneer's assistant stepped forward, and Jane once again recognized him. It was Mister Weston.

Over the next hour, she watched in horror as Weston pulled people onto their feet, singly and in family groups, and made them climb onto a rough wooden platform to be poked at, prodded, and sold to the highest bidder. More than once, she turned to Endeavor to share her indignation at the treatment and each time he stopped her with a small shake of the head. He knew they were not among friends here and the wrong word could land them in jeopardy.

Across the square, Jane could see Eliza Evans with Dawkins by her side. She seemed entirely at ease, and chatted cheerfully with the mate as they waited for the Calloway family to be brought to the block. Finally, Bess Calloway and the girls were dragged forward.

Bidding was swift, and Jane had trouble following the numbers and who was ahead. It wasn't until the gavel hit the auctioneer's table and she saw Miss Eliza step forward that Jane was sure they had been successful. She and Endeavor edged closer to the sale table as the clerk stated the total.

"That will be seven hundred dollars, ma'am."

Jane drew in her breath. She knew there was only another four hundred dollars in Miss Eliza's purse beyond that amount, and John Calloway was sure to attract higher bids than that.

With a serene countenance, Miss Eliza counted out the bills and signed for the release of Bess and the girls into her keeping. For the time being, however, she left them among the other women and children and returned to her spot at the edge of the crowd to wait for John Calloway to be brought forward. When it was his turn to take his place on the block, Jane could wait no longer.

"We have to help," Jane said, and pulled Endeavor with her across the square to stand with Miss Eliza and Dawkins.

"I will pledge two hundred dollars to the cause, Eliza," she whispered urgently. Miss Eliza kept her face pointed forward but nodded slightly to show she had heard. They stood together and watched as Weston yanked the chain fastened to Calloway's collar so that the man stumbled and pitched forward. Jane could not help but cry out and start forward to help him back onto his feet. Endeavor made to pull her back before her outburst drew the attention of the crowd, but it was too late.

"Stay back, ma'am," Weston growled, and pointed at Jane. The light of recognition dawned in his eyes. "Captain Thorn, is it? Back to meddle in our affairs again, I see. Control your wife Mister Coffin, and keep back." There was no mistaking the lethal hate in his eyes, and Jane allowed Endeavor to pull her away to stand next to Dawkins.

"Opening bid, then, is one hundred dollars. One hundred, I say. Who will give me one hundred?" The auctioneer started the bidding even as Weston was still prodding Calloway to show him to best advantage.

Miss Eliza stuck her hand in the air, and the auctioneer acknowledged the bid. As he began to call out for an advance, Jane saw Weston step to his side and whisper in the auctioneer's ear. When he moved away, he looked straight at Jane with a sneer and a nod, then marched over to the chain of remaining men to be sold.

"Hold up." The auctioneer called out to the crowd. "That was a mistake."

Jane felt Miss Eliza go rigid as four more men were released from the chain and brought forward.

"This group will be sold together, all or none. Opening bid, all five, a thousand dollars for the lot."

From the pen where the women and children were being held, she heard Bess cry out in despair, "No! John!" and then collapse in tears on the ground.

An inconsolable Bess Calloway was brought aboard after the close of the auction and settled into one of the cabins with her sobbing children. Miss Eliza spent considerable time with her, promising to do her best to track where her husband ended up and bring him back, but everyone knew the chances of finding him once he was sent south were exceedingly small.

"I will see Mistress Calloway and the girls settled with friends in New York while they wait," Miss Eliza said as she sat in the saloon after dinner. Jane noticed that Dawkins held her hand under the table and looked at her with deep concern as she spoke. "I sent word to Jones and he will do his best to keep track of where John Calloway goes. We can only hope he does not die on the way," she said in despair.

It was a solemn company in the saloon that evening, with little conversation and much silent contemplation. Eventually, Jane suggested everyone go to bed as they would be leaving on the early morning tide. Dawkins agreed, and walked Miss Eliza to her cabin before going above to check on the watch.

XXXI
Breaking for Freedom

Norfolk, Virginia
June 28, 1821

Jane mustered on deck with the mid watch. It had just gone midnight but she could not sleep for thinking about John Calloway. Turning to close the hatch behind her, she heard Dawkins approach and clear his throat.

"No rest for you either, ma'am?" he asked in a low voice.

"Nay, Chief, I cannot help but feel there was something we could have done. It pains me to leave here without him."

"Aye, Captain, but I doubt there was aught to be done, or Miss Eliza would have done it."

"You admire her, Mister Dawkins," Jane stated the obvious fact.

"I do, ma'am. She has given me to understand the feeling is shared on her side." Although she could not discern his face in the darkness, Jane heard the warmth in his voice and was glad of it.

"I have come to be quite fond of her myself, Mister Dawkins," she smiled at him, though he could not see it. "My best wishes to you both, Chief. It does me good to see you content."

"Aye, ma'am, after the death of my dear wife, I had not thought to find such happiness again."

"Well, life is most assuredly full of surprises," she observed. "It is wonderful when they turn out to be good ones."

Within the hour, Dawkins had the watch working to prepare the *Destiny* to get underway. At four bells, he called for all hands to man the capstan and begin the laborious process of hoisting the anchor. The tide slacked as the crew worked to bring the schooner over the anchor chain and raised the jib in preparation for heading out into the Bay as soon as it turned.

To starboard, Jane could see activity on the deck of the *Sophie Jones* as McKnight's crew likewise readied the frigate for sailing. It seemed that McKnight was also looking to catch the front of the tide. They would have to keep a sharp lookout not to get in his way.

A faint light on the horizon heralded the coming dawn. After two days of quiet, the wind had picked up again overnight and veered around to the south. It was now blowing ten knots with gusts strong enough to pull the hat from Jane's head. There had been no hurricanes on the coast this year, and she sincerely hoped this was not the leading edge of one. She said a quick prayer for good weather to get them all safely home as the *Sophie Jones* weighed anchor and raised her sails.

"All well, Mister Dawkins?" Jane turned to the chief as he came onto the quarterdeck.

"All is well, Captain."

Jane was about to give the command to hoist the anchor and get underway when she heard a hail from the water off the larboard beam.

"*Destiny*, ahoy. Ahoy there!"

With Dawkins at her heels, she jumped down the ladder and ran to the rail. Peering into the darkness where the schooner's side blocked the faint morning light, she could make out one of the low-sided harbor boats with three men aboard.

"Captain Thorn here. What is your business with us?"

"It's Jones, ma'am. I have Calloway here and he is sore hurt."

"Bring him up," Jane ordered, and sent Hitchens running to rouse Miss Eliza.

It took three of the crew to hoist the injured man aboard. They laid him down on the deck at Jane's feet as she demanded an explanation from Jones.

"He broke away, ma'am, from the pens where they were holding them. A group of them tried to make a run for freedom, and he thinks some of the guards may have been killed. I found him on my doorstep when he threw a rock through my window. Can you take him? They'll kill him if they find him, sure as I was born, ma'am."

Jane did not hesitate. "Get back in your boat, man, and go home. And thank you."

"Dawkins, set sail. Now!" Jane ran for the quarterdeck and threw open the hatch that led to her cabin. "Endeavor! Endeavor! On deck!"

When the sleepy man appeared a minute later, she sent him forward to assist Miss Eliza in bringing Calloway below. Directing Dawkins to pile on all sail they could safely carry, she ordered the helmsman to follow McKnight in the *Sophie Jones* as he skirted the point and made for open water. Jane looked over her shoulder every few minutes to check for pursuers, but the harbor was quiet behind them. She did not imagine that happy state of affairs would last and meant to put as many miles behind them as the *Destiny* could deliver.

As soon as they had entered the Bay, Jane went below to check on her passengers. She found them huddled in the saloon, where Miss Eliza had brought Calloway and had him laid on the table. In the swinging light from the lantern hung above, Jane saw that he was unconscious, which she figured was a good thing given that Bess was probing a deep wound in his shoulder with a knife.

She looked up when she saw Jane. "Bullet wound, ma'am."

Jane nodded. "Do you need anything?"

Bess grimly shook her head as she pointed at Eliza and Endeavor standing at either side of the table. "They are enough for now and thank God the girls are still asleep. Just pray that he makes it, ma'am."

"That I will surely do."

On deck, Jane waited until the crew had the sails sheeted in and the *Destiny* sailing smartly before asking Dawkins to call them aft.

"Thank you, men, that was handily done. You know we are bound for New York, and we must make the best time we can." She paused and looked around at the dozen faces staring up at her.

"We have a fugitive aboard, and this time it is my doing. I do not intend to be caught, but it is my business and mine alone. Should we be boarded, you are all blameless, and I shall make that clear, but I do *not* intend to be boarded. Mister Dawkins, find every scrap of speed you can. Dismissed."

Shading her eyes against the morning sun as it rose ahead of them, Jane peered over the bow to see the stern of the *Sophie Jones* a mile ahead and drawing slowly away. She turned to look behind them, then snatched her spyglass from her pocket and snapped it open.

"We have company." She handed the glass to Dawkins, who scanned the water behind them before lowering it and handing it back to Jane.

"It's a cutter, ma'am. They won't catch us as long as the wind holds."

"I am not certain of that. They can traverse the shoals and know we must keep to the channel. We are still miles from open water and still in Virginia waters until we leave the Bay."

The next hour tested Jane's nerve as she paced the quarterdeck and willed the *Destiny* to go faster. Dawkins hounded the men to adjust the sheets at the slightest shift in the wind and refused to reef even as a squall appeared out of the south. As the boat heeled further to leeward, Jane was forced to wedge herself between the aft cabin roof and the forward rail to keep herself from sliding down the deck. The on-deck watch was having as much trouble holding on as she was, and she gave Dawkins a questioning glance.

"We can drop the main at the last minute if we need to," he yelled over the humming of the rigging and howling of the wind. "But that little cutter will have to abandon the chase if the wind picks up much more. We just need to outlast them."

To Jane's dismay, the wind soon began to die back and swing to the west, driving the squall out to sea. The *Destiny* settled back onto her feet, making for an easier time on deck but no longer outpacing the boat hunting them off the starboard beam. The *Destiny* and the *Sophie Jones* had been forced to cut north for six miles as they left the Hampton Roads to avoid the shoals before turning to the east. The little cutter sailed straight across the shallows, however, and was soon gaining on the *Destiny*. Within another hour, it had drawn close enough that Jane could see the cutter's crew clearly as the vessel charged across the Bay in pursuit. Unless they could make the mouth of the Bay and pick up the Gulf Stream soon, they would have to deal with the cutter's guns.

No sooner did she have the thought than she heard the sharp report of the pursuer's foredeck cannon.

"They are shooting at us. Everyone down below the rail." she ordered. Although they were still a long way off, Jane was taking no chances. A second shot from the cutter's cannon was visible as the ball fell into the Bay no more than half a mile off the *Destiny's* bow.

"Hitchens," she called to the young seaman as he emerged from the fo'c'sle at the sound of the firing, "Go below and warn the others that we may be boarded shortly. And tell Endeavor he must look to concealing Mister Calloway. Go."

Keeping her head low, Jane ran along the larboard side deck and crawled up the ladder onto the quarterdeck. She crouched down next to Dawkins, who was helping hold the helm.

"Bear away." she ordered O'Reilly. The seaman was clutching the wheel and ducking his head behind the cabin, sticking it up from time to time only long enough to catch his bearing.

"Ten points to port."

"Aye, aye, ma'am. Ten points to port."

Jane watched over the rail as the *Destiny* turned her tail to the cutter and picked up speed.

"Hold your heading, Mister O'Reilly. We shall outrun them yet."

"She's turning ma'am." The lookout yelled from the bow and pointed frantically to the *Sophie Jones*.

Indeed she was. McKnight swung the frigate sharply to starboard and was soon on a course back along the channel heading straight for the *Destiny*. Within minutes, she passed narrowly to starboard and they could see that her gun ports were open with the cannons run out.

"Holy hell! He means to fire on them!"

Jane grinned. "That hardly seems sporting, Mister Dawkins. But I welcome the assistance."

The *Destiny's* crew ran to the starboard rail to watch as the *Sophie Jones* bore down across the cutter's stern so that her beam was facing the smaller vessel. At less than a mile, any ball that landed on the cutter's deck would slice it in half, sending the entire crew to the bottom.

"I will be surprised if they think it worth the chance of being sunk just to catch one runaway slave," Jane remarked as, through her spyglass, she watched the first officer of the frigate give the signal to load the guns.

In the end, a single booming shot from the *Sophie Jones'* forward gun was enough to send the cutter scurrying back in the direction of Norfolk. The *Sophie Jones* tracked it for some minutes, then turned away as the cutter slunk in along the shore. It took another hour for the frigate's crew to wear ship but she caught up with the *Destiny* soon enough, sailing just off her beam as the two vessels rounded Cape Henry.

At the rail of the *Destiny*, the crew lined up waving their hats and cheering the frigate as it passed them to starboard on a northbound course with her signal flags flying in the breeze.

"Good journey," Dawkins interpreted.

"Hoist a thank you," Jane directed. "I shall have to send him a whole case of port when I get home."

XXXII
Home

New York, New York
June 30, 1821

The voyage home up the Atlantic coast passed without further incident, although not as quickly as Jane wished. Despite Bess' efforts, John Calloway's wound looked no better after two days, and Jane thought he needed the attention of a skilled medic. She had turned over the medicine chest to Miss Evans, who had some small skill with doctoring it turned out, but Jane could not see that anything proved efficacious beyond the laudanum they were dosing him with day and night.

Finally, three days out of Norfolk they picked up the Sandy Hook pilot late on Saturday afternoon and began the final trek north through the busy harbor. As they were towed the final mile to the Thorn docks on the East River, Jane searched the waterfront eagerly for signs of the *Osprey*.

"There she is, Endeavor. Well done, Silas." Jane was beaming with pride. "I knew he would do it."

"Aye, he has the makings of a Thorn captain," her husband agreed.

Jane put the spyglass to her eye. "And look, he has forgotten to take off the pennant. It looks to be blue. Remember that, Endeavor."

The two of them stood side by side at the stern as the pilot brought the schooner to the dock and the lines were run ashore. Jane thanked him in her usual way after Dawkins paid the pilotage bill. She was becoming known among the pilots for her generous hand with the port and there was much competition to reach her vessel first when it appeared in New York Bay.

At the top of the pier, Captain Josias waited with his clerk for the Collector and the harbormaster to clear the *Destiny* for landing the crew and cargo. The health inspector came aboard and insisted on seeing the crew and passengers.

"Bring everyone on deck, Captain, if you please."

"We have an injured man, below, sir. He will need to be taken ashore on a stretcher."

"Let me see him."

Jane led the inspector to the cabin where Calloway was lying in a sweat. He jerked back as he saw the patient and looked at the captain.

"What ails him, ma'am?"

"A wound to the shoulder. He needs a doctor but we have done our best to keep him alive until our arrival."

The inspector took in the scene in the crowded cabin where Bess was perched on the edge of the sickbed with a damp towel to wipe John's forehead and the two girls played quietly on the floor.

"I see you picked them up in Norfolk three days ago," he said as he paged through the passenger manifest. He glanced up at Jane with a knowing look before rummaging in his case and pulling out a newspaper. He handed it to Jane while he bent over the patient and pulled back the bandage enough to see the suppurating wound.

Jane unfolded the broadsheet and read the headline at the top.

Slaves Break Out of Norfolk Jail

She read quickly through the article and was relieved to see that none of the guards had, in fact, been killed in the breakout. The writer said eight men had waited for the door of the cell where they were being held overnight after the auction to be opened for the delivery of the evening meal. They then jumped the guard, who nevertheless managed to fire his gun in the melee, and ran. The article indicated that all except three of the fugitives had been caught, and included a promise of a reward for the capture of the rest.

Jane finished reading and refolded the paper. She handed it back to the inspector as he straightened up and looked at him steadily.

"That is a grave injury, but there does not appear to be any fever. I will just have a look at the others." He turned away and climbed back to the deck. His review of the remaining passengers and crew was quickly completed, and he saluted Jane as he walked down the gangplank.

"Take care, Captain. The sooner that family is on their way, the better."

Jane could not agree more.

As soon as the health inspector stepped off the gangplank, Captain Josias and the clerk came aboard.

"Welcome back Captain Thorn," Josias exclaimed as he embraced his niece and nodded to Endeavor. "Mister Dawkins, Vaugine has the payroll."

Josias waved his clerk forward and watched as he and Dawkins made their way to the foredeck where the crew had mustered with their seabags. When they were out of earshot he turned to Jane.

"Silas has related the events pertaining to the *Osprey*. Well done Captain. He also gave me to understand that you were going to call into Norfolk on your passage home." He paused and waited for Jane to speak.

"Follow me, uncle."

Swiftly, Jane led Endeavor and Josias down the main companionway ladder and forward into the hold where Josias looked around appreciatively at the temporary cabins built along the centerline.

"These are nicely done. My compliments to Mister Koopmans. Your design?"

"Aye, but his execution. We might look at doing something like it for the *Osprey* and the other vessels, Uncle," Jane said as she knocked on the door of the first cabin.

Eliza Evans pulled open the door and stepped out into the passageway followed by Bess Calloway. With a few words Jane introduced them to Josias.

"Eliza has been the means of purchasing freedom for Mistress Calloway and the children. She granted their manumission as soon as we left Virginia."

"And is that Mister Calloway then? He looks to be ill." Josias stuck his head in the cabin and ran his eye over the still form of the man on the berth.

"It is, and we must get him ashore as quickly as possible as he is injured. May we bring him to Beekman Street?"

Josias quickly assented and Endeavor was sent to fetch the Thorn coachman who was waiting at the top of the pier. Meanwhile, Jane led Josias into the saloon and closed the door.

"You said Miss Evans purchased the freedom of Mistress Calloway and the girls," Josias said with a frown. "What of Mister Calloway?"

"He is a fugitive," Jane began.

Her uncle stood silently and listened as Jane related the events of the auction and the jail break. His eyes opened wide as she told of their being chased out of Virginia by the cutter then burst into laughter when he heard of the gallant action taken by Captain McKnight.

"Do you think there will be consequences, Uncle? Not for us, as the authorities do not know for sure that Calloway was aboard the *Destiny*. We did nothing worse than evade being boarded. But for Captain McKnight?"

"Aye, McKnight may find that the magistrate is somewhat less inclined to look favorably on his activities in the future. He can hardly approve of armed frigates firing on Virginia officials, but I doubt McKnight much cares as he has the power of Washington behind him. For now. He will seek his fortune where he can."

Josias paused and gave his niece a searching look. "You did the right thing, Jinks. You are lucky that all went well but you knew the risk. I would like to think that I would make the same choice in your shoes, Captain."

Josias extended a handshake to Jane, then pulled her close for a warm hug. As she let the tension of the last few days melt away and relaxed into his embrace, she heard him ask, "And what in tarnation are you wearing?"

Night had fallen by the time the crew had been paid off and

released and Dawkins had delivered his records and the log to the shipping office. Cookie and Koopmans would stay aboard until Monday, when Dawkins would return with Galsworthy to supervise the offloading of the cargo. In the meantime, Jane and Endeavor arranged for their seabags and chests to be delivered to her uncle's house and followed soon after with Edwin, the cat.

It was a weary party that gathered around the table for a late dinner at the house on Beekman Street where Aunt Meg had the servants busy preparing rooms and cooking for the tired travelers. The Calloways had been settled in a room at the back of the house and the doctor called. His report was not as grim as Jane feared but he was adamant that the patient not be moved for several weeks if he were to have a chance at a full recovery. Eliza Evans had been invited to stay and personally see to his care so the house was rather full.

"But not too full for one more," Meg said as she stood in the entryway eyeing Dawkins and Eliza, who sat on the bench by the door with their heads together in quiet conversation. The mate had accompanied Miss Eliza in the carriage and seemed loathe now to relinquish her hand and make his way to a hotel for the night. Meg promised they would find a bed for him, "even if it is with the horses."

Newburgh, New York
July 1, 1821

Jane rousted Endeavor out of bed early on Sunday morning. She hoped to be aboard the Newburgh steamboat at ten o'clock and knew her husband would want at least an hour for his First Day quiet contemplations. As it was, they nearly missed the boat as they discovered that Edwin had escaped from the closet they had locked him in the night before. It took everyone in the house over an hour to locate and capture him.

Jane held the purring animal up to her face and stared him sternly in the eye. "If you get loose again, Mister Cat, I am leaving you to your own devices. No more chasing around after you. You will just have to make your own way," she declared, thus demonstrating again that she still had much to learn about cats.

By the time the luggage had been loaded into the carriage along with the yowling cat, who protested at being asked to travel in a satchel, nine o'clock had come and gone. Fortunately, traffic on the streets of New York was light on Sunday morning and they made the gangplank just in time.

The steamer pulled up to the wharf in Newburgh in the afternoon, and Jane could see her father and sister waving from beyond the fence that separated the docks from the passenger terminal. As she waited for their luggage to be brought ashore, Jane looked up the hill that loomed over the riverbank. Near the top, she could see the pillared front of the Thorn house with its expansive view of the Hudson River and the busy dockyard where the family's fleet of sloops were moored. It was good to be home.

The family gathered for dinner at her parents' home that evening to welcome them back. Jane was eager to hear from Silas how the passage home aboard the *Osprey* had gone and was relieved to know that there had been no interference from the revenue cutters.

"Of course, your blue pennant may have been seen by them as some sort of warning signal..." she remarked.

Silas' mouth dropped open. "What? But how? I did not see the *Destiny*... how did you pass us?"

"Ah, not only are you slow, but you have lazy lookouts," she said with a reproving tone.

Silas looked fit to explode, so Jane confessed, "You forgot to remove the flag from the bowsprit. It hangs there still."

A long round of laughter followed, and her nephew joined in good-naturedly. "I was worried for a moment as I have not written you a song, Aunty Jinks."

"Well, perhaps you might write one for me anyway as a Christmas present?"

With a devilish grin, he replied, "Oh yes, Aunty Jinks, I

think I very well might."

After a cheerful evening in front of the fire, Jane and Endeavor made their way up the stairs to Jane's cramped childhood bedroom.

Surveying the small chamber with the large bed her mother had installed for them, Jane observed, "I think we shall have to look for a house of our own, my dear husband."

She wandered around the room for a moment, touching the mementos she had gathered over years of travel aboard her family's boats. She had just lifted a piece of scrimshaw off the mantelpiece when she heard a booming explosion outside the window that rattled the panes and caused her to drop the carving. In a trice, Endeavor was throwing back the curtains and peering into the night.

"It is the steamboat, Jane! She looks to have blown her boiler!"

Down at the waterfront, Jane could see the boat drifting in the tide, its entire superstructure engulfed in flame as people jumped into the water to escape a sure death aboard the burning vessel. To the north, she could see that some of the wreckage had been ejected with such force that it landed aboard two of the sloops at the wharf, and they were now alight as well.

Jane grabbed her coat and pelted down the stairs, calling back to Endeavor, "Wake my father!"

Shrugging into her coat as she ran, Jane made her way down the steep hill to the riverfront. The noise had brought out what seemed to be half the population of Newburgh, and she had to push through a crowd to reach the gate to the Thorn Shipping boatyard. As she hurried through the courtyard and rounded the corner to catch sight of the burning vessels, Endeavor caught up with her.

"Quick, throw off the lines!" he yelled to Jane as he raced past.

By the time they reached the wharf, several men from the crowd had joined them, and they all worked to cast the sloops loose before the fire spread to the neighboring vessels. The ebb tide pulled them slowly away as flames licked at the sails and decks began to give off oily smoke. Within minutes, both vessels were fully engulfed, and the crowd watched silently as they burned to the waterline and sank.

Jane turned away from the horrible sight and saw her father, wrapped in his housecoat with only slippers on his feet, moving among the men who had acted so selflessly to save the rest of the Thorn fleet. Shaking their hands, he was thanking them even as they slapped his back in commiseration for his loss. Eventually, he made his way to where Jane stood and put his arm around her shoulder as he stared out over the water.

"Well," he said in a quiet voice, "perhaps it is not quite time to purchase a steamboat yet."

Author's Note

History is a tricky thing. Once we write it down, a story becomes the truth that is told to future generations. When it comes to pivotal events of the early years of the American republic, those stories were overwhelmingly written down by members of the dominant culture of the day, leaving today's reader with the impression that those storytellers were at the center of the events they describe. Nowhere is this more evident than in the tales told of the exodus of enslaved people from the southern colonies and states to the north and west. Ask most Americans to describe the Underground Railroad, and they will tell of good-hearted white folks in the north, many of them Quakers, who helped slaves escape along "stops" that included the farms and urban dwellings of white abolitionists. While that is certainly part of the story, it is hardly the central truth. Escaping slavery was something black folks did for themselves, calling on free black people to aid in their passage, and help them on their way to Canada and points west outside the boundaries of the United States. Black seamen were an important part of the informal "railroad", and were eventually banned from going ashore in Virginia as they were a known link to the escape routes. Mister Singleton, accomplished black sailor and conduit to freedom, would have been a familiar figure in the maritime world of the early 19th century.

Thanks for purchasing and reading *Destiny's Freedom*, I hope you enjoyed it.

A lot of people don't realize that the best way to help an author is to leave a review. So, if you had fun accompanying Jane and her crew on their voyage, please return to the site you purchased this book from and say a few words. It doesn't have to be long, just saying what you thought is fine and much appreciated. It also helps other readers make an informed decision about their purchases.

I love hearing from readers and authors alike, so if you'd like to stay in touch and be the first to know about forthcoming books and what I am up to, please visit me at:

www.pamelagrimmauthor.com

www.facebook.com/pamelagrimmauthor

Printed in Great Britain
by Amazon

29664714R00128